L

MW00831171

FORESTLANDERS

Book One

The Harp Thief

Written By

James Kelton
And
Dennis Harold

(Created by James Kelton)
Map of the Forestlands by Dennis Harold
U.S. Copyrighted@2014 #1-1373401441

To Jane Trauernicht

~JK

To my creative light, Paramahansa Yogananda. To my Gabrielle, Sean and Genevieve. To James.

~DH

Follow Thru Productions
PO Box 2171
Overton, NV 89040
general@followthrupros.com
www.Followthrupros.com

© *2014 James Kelton. All rights reserved.* KELTON *&* HAROLD

No part of this book may be reproduced, stored in a retrieval system, or transmitted by any means without the written permission of the author.

Published by Follow Thru Productions 10/01/2020

Third Edition

ISBN: 978-1-7359084-0-3
*Library of Congress Control Number:*2020919354

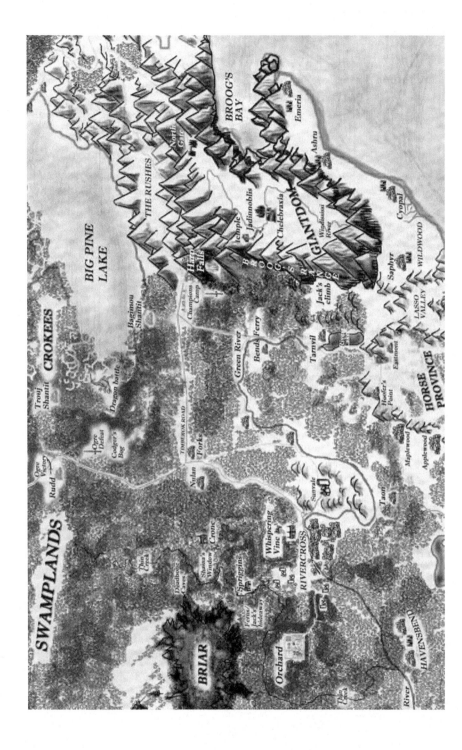

Chapter 1

JACK

Jack Spriggins was always being chased and never caught, often with someone else's belongings stashed under his arm. A streak of thief's luck usually ran with him but on this day, it must have turned tail, because Jack found himself lying bruised and alone on a mountain ledge. There was a taste of blood in his mouth and his ribs felt broken. The Gogmagogg harp could still be heard clanging as it fell, slamming against the cliffs below. Worse was the flash of Roidaroy's terrified face as the young giant plummeted by with a final look that burned Jack's conscience like a branding iron.

~ 1 ~

"Is this what yeh brung me too?" said Jack, groaning to the silence behind the wind. "Thirteen years of me stealing and dodging, keeping Ma and myself fed with no hand-outs just so I can die up here?"

The spirit-voice, not as loud as a whisper yet clear as a plucked harp string, spoke in Jack's ear. "*Where else would you wish to be?*"

The pain stabbed as Jack tried to roll to his side, crying out. "Home, I reckon."

Above him were the cities of Giantdom and below, the sprawling wilds of the Great Forest. Both had been "home" at different times but now, dangling between them, Jack was sure neither would welcome him back.

"Reckon I'll keep running."

The spirit spoke on, "*Then you might as well stay here until the end.*"

"This ain't what I wanted."

"*How did you get here then?*"

Odd warmth crept up Jack's spine and the pain moved away. He let his mind drift back, remembering. "Well it sure weren't Beirboor's fault. Or even Roidaroy's. It started long before I climbed up these giants' mountains."

"*Did it begin with the Champions?*"

"Naw. It weren't them neither. Or the beans for Ma. It weren't even Allwise, that shifty old meddler. Not Ella and the wolves. It's hard to pin."

"*Imagine your journey and tell me where it starts.*"

"It was the woods." Jack drew a breath. "With that harp."

"*The giant's harp?*"

"Naw," Jack said, feeling warmer by the second. "I mean the little elf harp—the one I got from the cutthroats' bag—and my crossbow. That's where all this started."

The Silent One had always been words without a face, yet Jack could swear the spirit was now smiling at him.

"*Take me there, Jack Spriggins. We'll find the answers together.*"

Like a parting mist, the cold mountain seemed to draw aside. The memory of his journey grew clearer and the ache in his ribs went away.

"I see Thin Creek," he said. "Like it's yesterday."

The wilds of the Great Forest were Jack's first home. Its twisted half-paths and black-water brooks often led to nothing but trouble for outsiders. Not even locals knew the woods like Jack and none had his streak of luck on their side, so if ever strangers ventured by Thin Creek, near where he lived, Jack kept an eye on them until they met with inevitable misfortune.

"It started with those three loud fellas who trudged away from Rivercross," he said to the Silent One. "They was toting a full bag, so I followed 'em. Figured maybe they had real treasure. Whatever their bag held was going to be mine."

"*That's true,*" said the spirit.

"It weren't easy pickins," Jack recalled. "The men were no hunters, but they was armed and didn't know where they was headed."

In fact, all three men looked odd. Their helmets, high boots, and plumes set them apart from the folks of Rivercross, the village where he picked pockets. When the strangers stopped in a glade where sunlight landed between the trees, one of them dropped the bulging leather bag on top of a log.

"I stayed low in the grass," Jack went on, "Shimmied beneath a stretch of ferns until I got in real close."

"*The strangers began to argue,*" said the Silent One. "*What did you do then?*"

"I hunkered down and waited."

* * * *

"Are you certain this is the way, sirs?" said the round man, who had been toting the bag.

"It sure don't look right to me," grumbled a more dangerous fellow. He was armed with a longbow.

"I rely on ingrates and fools," bellowed their leader. He was loud-mouthed, wearing an armor chest plate that was too small for his plump frame and a bronze, crescent helmet that slipped forward whenever he looked at his map. "It's no wonder we always get lost," he said, pushing it back. "Must I do everything myself?"

"It's yer map that got us here," said the bowman, tightening the string of his weapon. He was a wiry, slouched man with an ugly scar that curved across his face from his right cheek, over his lips, and down the left side of his neck.

"Nonsense, Mister Hatch," said the leader. "My maps are very accurate, I assure you. There is a king's treasure buried in this forest. It is my quest to uncover and claim it, and your job to secure the way."

Hatch, the scar-faced one, was the most threatening, so Jack watched him closely.

The fatter man looked like an idiot. He was short and greasy, wiping his sweaty neck with a rag. "Master Thane, s-s-sir, did you hear the noises?" he stammered nervously. "Something bloodthirsty is following us."

"Never mind that," said the leader, shaking a compass. "There, you see? The needle is pointing at my family crest. Northeast is yonder, through those yew trees." He pointed away from where Jack was hiding, which was wrong because he was pointing west.

"Dimwits deserve to get stolen from," said Jack. He pushed up on his elbows to reach for the sack but the wide sweaty man placed his foot on the log by it.

"Ooh, my poor feet," moaned the idiot, unlacing his boot to jiggle out some pebbles. "They hurt too much."

Jack froze.

"Werrius!" yelled the leader. "You two-legged cheese, bring me the map."

Werrius fumbled with obedience, hopping away on one foot with the boot and map in his hands. "Master Thane, s-s-sir," he wheezed in a voice that was part donkey bray, part groan, "I think we turned west when we should've gone north."

"Shut up, slack-jaw. When I want the opinion of my lackey, I will ask for it." Master Thane grabbed the crinkled map and rapped Werrius in the face. "Consider yourself lucky I haven't abandoned you to fill the bellies of a wolf pack."

"I hear them, s-s-sir," said Werrius, trembling. "There be low growls and hungry eyes around us."

Jack could also smell the jerky the strangers were carrying. It had drawn wolves, at least two or three, lurking nearby.

"I've heard little but your wheezing since we departed Rivercross," said Master Thane. "Do not think, Werrius. Just lug. There is no creature in these woods that cannot be fended off by Hatch's arrows or this musket from my family's armory."

Thane brandished a weapon that looked like a shiny horn with a wooden handle and trigger. Such firearms were uncommon in the Great Forest and would have fetched a good price if Jack could get his hands on it. "Maybe there's another in their bag?" he wondered.

Hatch took several paces towards the lurking shadows in the trees. "It might be a good thing to put an arrow or two into them wolves," he said.

Thane tiptoed along behind the bowman; musket ready. "Do so then, and rid us of the nuisance."

Werrius flopped onto the grass to get his boot back on.

This was Jack's chance. He reached over and got a firm grip on the sack, which was heavy, but he lifted it away without any noise. He backed under the ferns for several yards before rolling to his feet. Running for the trees, he slung the loot over his shoulder with a backward glance. The strangers were unaware of being robbed.

"Ha-ha! Free and clear," Jack snickered. Then, he ran into a flock of quail nesting in the long grass. They chirruped and thrashed as noisily as if crying out, "Thief! Thief!"

The strangers turned and Master Thane let fly with his musket, unleashing a blast that rattled the air. A puff of gunpowder rose when it discharged but no sound of a lead ball whizzed by.

"Drats! A misfire. Stop that boy," said Thane.

For not the first time in his life, Jack was being chased. Hatch came fast with his longbow aimed. Jack charged into the cover of the woods, which shielded him from the arrow. It struck a redwood and sent chips of bark zinging through the air as he ran past.

"Dare not let the boy escape!" ordered Thane.

Beyond range of the musket, Jack was grateful to see the blast had scattered the wolves. The bowman was the immediate threat now.

"Let's see how good a tracker this Hatch is," said Jack.

He hustled over gnarled roots and slippery moss towards a wide oak stump that stood beside Thin Creek. It was a landmark he used often. Only a few strides upstream there would be a field of giant ferns where he could lose the strangers. Vaulting the oak into knee-deep water, Jack pulled himself along by the exposed tree roots that jutted over the embankment. Hatch splashed into the creek several strides back.

"He's fast," said Jack, ducking into a nook beneath the overhanging limbs, his pulse throbbing in his eardrums.

Hatch glared up and down the brook with a hateful scowl. Luckily, he moved away downstream but then stopped, staring at the water. The silt in the creek bed, stirred by Jack's steps had created a murky trail.

"Aw bunk! It's giving me away," Jack realized.

Sure enough, Hatch spun round and lifted his bow.

Jack took off, splashing across the creek. He raised the stolen satchel to shield himself as Hatch released an arrow. It struck the bag with a clank followed by a shivering sound that was somewhat musical. Jack was knocked forward from the hit but managed to stay on his feet and not lose stride. The ringing sound that had protected him was a mystery he would break open soon enough.

"Next one's going to stick yeh clean-through," said Hatch.

"Bet yeh thought that 'bout the first one," Jack taunted. He had not survived for thirteen years by surrendering his spoils at the first bit of trouble. As good a shot as this bowman was, Jack could lose anybody in these woods. "Yer bag's mine now."

On the opposite embankment was a ridge that jutted out above the fern field. Jack ran up it until he came to a chute of mud and clay. Clutching the bag to his chest, he leapt, sliding on his butt down the hill with his feet lifted. Usually, this was for fun, but today it was an escape. He dug his heels in at the bottom and took off again.

Hatch's next arrow went whizzing by, barely missing Jack's ear. "Whoa, that's trouble," said Jack. The shot had been fired as the man came skidding down the chute behind. "This Hatch is a devil-good tracker."

Switching course, Jack headed for the one place in the woods where no one went willingly, no matter how brave or foolish.

The Briar.

He could not count the times Ma had scolded him about this stretch, or how often he overheard Rivercross woodsmen tell travelers to steer clear:

"Don't go near the Briar," they would say.

"The thorns be cursed, take the long way around."

"Cross the Briar and it will cross you!"

The warnings had rambled on for as long as Jack could remember. Naturally, he spent as much time there as possible.

"Old Claw Nose better not be waiting round to pounce me," Jack said. *Claw Nose* was the nickname of a giant brown owl that hunted critters in the Briar. Jack had escaped it once by hiding in the hollow of a dead oak.

"If Hatch and the others see me go into the thorns, they'll give up."

Jack stopped at the edge of the Briar and searched for a way in. The hedge was barricaded with vines fifteen-feet high. Thick black limbs spiked with thorns snaked around each other in a bramble that stretched for miles. The stench of dead vermin drew the constant buzz of flies.

A voice in the distance shouted, "Ahoy!" It was Thane.

"Ahoy-hoy! I see him!" said Hatch, who was closing in.

There was little time. Jack pushed through a small gap and crawled through. It was a struggle dragging the bag in the tight, thorny crawlspace but he yanked it inside fast enough that Hatch could not grab it. Only elves could have been quicker. Jack hated elves.

"Ah, blood and spit!" cursed the bowman, who got caught on the barbs. "Curse yeh, boy. Yeh ain't getting away with our bag. Yer dead meat."

Thorns scraped the back of Jack's neck as he scooted on hands and knees further into the burrow. Trickles of blood ran down his cheek. "These gaps are tighter than they used to be," he frowned.

The Briar paths (if they could be called that) were narrow game trails that wove through the thorns, used by badgers, raccoons, and sometimes Jack Spriggins. The tunnels were tricky to spot and if he chose wrong, he might never get out.

Hatch could be heard kicking at the Briar limbs, trying to find his own way into the bramble. More footsteps approached.

"Did you kill the thief?" said Master Thane, out of breath.

"Yeh don't see him twitching in the mud, do yeh?" said Hatch.

"Where is he?"

"He crawled into them thorn branches like a burrowing hound."

"In the Briar? Why did you let him get in there?"

Jack could not help jeering, "Because he ain't fox-quick like me," he said.

"Listen to him laughing at us," said Thane. "Kill him."

"Can't shoot worth spit in those thorns," said Hatch.

"I don't pay you for excuses," said Thane. "You were hired for your marksmanship and you missed. Unsheathe your hatchet and go after him."

There was no reply. It seemed that Hatch might be considering the best way to use the ax, on the Briar or Master Thane's skull.

"What are you waiting for?"

"There better be plenty o' gold at the end of all this trouble," grumbled Hatch.

"You'll get your promised share," said Thane.

The ax crashed into the brambles.

"Jits! They're coming," said Jack, who scrambled to the dead oak, crawling into a narrow split at its base. The outside sounds went dead. Inside, the dingy hollow was thick with cobwebs and a smell of mushroom rot. Beetles and worms crawled over Jack's hands as he groped in the dark, trying to make the tricky climb up.

"Oof," said Jack, gagging. "This rot smells worse than anything ever." He clambered up towards a sliver of light and poked his head out the top.

Jack was met by the contorted skeleton of a man impaled on the thorns. Its mouth stretched in a permanent shriek of silence. Bits of rusty armor still clung to the ribcage, and the hilt of a broadsword was clasped in the finger bones.

"Yeh stuck around here too long, mister," Jack said to the bones. Squeamish, he craned his neck, peeking over the rim of the oak. Thane and Werrius could scarcely be seen through the thorny web.

"Worthless is too decent to describe you, Werrius," said Thane. "I left you in charge of the supplies and you let that backwoods scalawag steal them."

"He were no scaly-wag, sir, just a boy. Skinny – all arms and legs with black hair and yellow eyes. Eleven or twelve at most."

"Thirteen, Saggy," said Jack, feeling his chin for whiskers he was sure would grow in any day.

Thane chuckled. "Are you telling me that Hatch, the most cutting of cutthroats, has been outrun by a mere boy?"

"With yellow eyes."

Jack puffed up with pride. "Hear that, Bonehead?" he said to the skeleton. "I outsmarted the best cutthroat."

He lifted his legs and stood on the hollow treetop. There was an overhang of reachable sycamore boughs above. Latching on, Jack climbed towards safety out of the Briar, over the heads of Thane and Werrius who were jabbering too much to notice him.

"You morons have been outdone by a common urchin," said Master Thane.

"We be lost, sir," said Werrius.

"Use the maps! The scrolls."

"The boy took them, except this one I gave you."

Jack secured a foothold on the tree trunk and watched the men at the briar's edge, waiting for his chance to drop down.

"Hatch! Did you find him yet?"

"No," grumbled the axman, still chopping his way further in.

"I'll strangle that wretched brat myself," said Thane, who flung the map to the ground.

"But, sir," said Werrius. "Maybe the kid knows about the fortune we're hunting for?"

"The local bumpkins know nothing of the riches on my map - they know only the lore," said Thane. "They cling to the faith that there is still a forsaken princess sleeping in these woods and she's been waiting to be awakened for hundreds, if not thousands, of years."

"She must be very old," said Werrius.

"She's fiction, you mushwit. The Sleeping Beauty is lore. '*She sleeps in peace, protected by thorns*,'" he recited.

"Nice poem, sir."

Thane pushed back his helmet, looking at the Briar. "*Thorns*, Werrius. The legend said *thorns*."

"I see them, sir. Were they on the map?"

"You drooling dolt, the yellow-eyed thief led us right to it. The Beauty's lost kingdom is within this prickly mesh. Grab your sickle and give Hatch a hand."

"Into the Briar?" Werrius frantically picked up the map, looking at it. "Oh nooo. My poor feet have followed you off pirate planks, through mummy tombs, and across burning bridges, sir, but are never going in there."

"Ah, Werrius," said Thane, "Stay behind if you like but the time of great explorers is coming to an end. We live in an age between ages, when swordplay, moon dances, and horse-drawn carriages are giving way to steam, gunpowder, and wind-up music. This Great Forest is the last frontier where one can reap a treasure of the past. I intend to seize it, with or without you."

"But s-s-sir, the thorns!" begged the servant.

With a dismissive wave, Thane squeezed through the breach made by Hatch's ax. "Of course," he added, "You'll forfeit any part of the bounty we find inside."

A look of piggy greed overcame Werrius. "No, I go!" he cried, hustling in after Thane.

"They're as cracked as bad eggs," said Jack. "Make all that noise in the Briar and yer done for."

He shimmied to the ground. The ax chops in the Briar stopped and a man screamed. Vicious growls followed, like wolves tearing into their prey. Thane's musket went off. *BOOM!* A huge shadow passed overhead, accompanied by the ear-splitting screech of an owl.

"Claw Nose!" said Jack, covering his ears. He drew back against the tree, watching the sky. The giant owl plunged into the brambles. There was a terrible thrashing of branches followed by an even scarier silence. Claw Nose then took to the sky carrying a crescent helmet in her claws, the same one that had been worn by Master Thane. The owl flew too quick to tell if the explorer's head was still inside it.

Jack took off, still lugging the leather bag, and did not stop running until he reached Thin Creek where he could finally tally up his loot.

The haul was disappointing.

Jack dumped it out beside the creek. There was no treasure, money, or food, just a bundle of rusted spikes, some arrowheads, a tin cup, and a frying pan all crammed together with some worthless papers.

"They chased me into the thorns for this junk?"

The busted shaft of Hatch's arrow stuck out from the frame of a small, round wood harp no bigger than a dinner plate. Jack liked music well enough but one pluck of the strings was enough to know he had no knack for playing it. "I was hoping for a shield of some kind, not some blarn song-strummer," he shrugged. "But maybe it'll fetch a price."

He unraveled some old scrolls, watching bits of the parchment flake off and flutter into the creek. The pages were scrawled with loopy writing (Jack could not read). A smudged drawing did grab his attention. It was of a woman asleep on a bed of roses.

"I bet that's the Sleeping Beauty."

It was not enough to hold his interest - her story seemed so made-up and did not matter to him much. The townsfolk were swayed by it, though. They held yearly flower festivals in the Beauty's honor in Rivercross Square. "Chee! Singing and praying to a snoozing girl they ain't ever seen."

Even his Ma chanted part of an old rhyme of the lost princess:

In times before the times we know,
A beauty sleeps within the thorns,
She dreams of heroes yet to come,
Who'll waken her from days of lore.

Ma always hummed the rest. She also talked about the Eight Great Spirits folks prayed to. Jack recalled as many as he could, "One for water, one for fire, and the Green Ma." The rest he did not know. "Why bother? I ain't gonna ask eight ghosts for things I can do myself."

He wadded up the paper and chucked it aside. The metal items – the pan, cup, and rusted spikes – he stuffed back into the bag. Tinner, the tinker in Rivercross, could melt those down.

"This bag ain't much, but Tinner pays for stolen metal. Might hold enough to get decent food for a few days and shoelaces for Ma."

A glint inside the tin cup caught his eye. He took and turned it over, and a ring-shaped pin dropped into his hands. "It's a brooch." The circle was inlaid with blue stones, molded in the shape of a snake that swallowed its own tail. "Evil-looking thing. Still, the stones might be worth some good," he said, sliding the pin into his pocket. There was one last item, but he could not make sense of it. "What the blarn is this?" At best, it was a set of folded sticks connected by wooden joints and screws, all wrapped with bowstring.

Jack unwound the bowstring and flicked a lever, which caused the arms to pop open. "A bow!" It was not like the large, heavy longbows that deer hunters used, which had wide, bendable arcs and required strong forearms to wield. This was lightweight, with a groove that ran down its middle for an arrow. "Crossbow!"

He notched one of the spikes from the sack into the weapon. "Fits right. Only, how come the arrow ain't got a pointy tip?" This one was crowned with three prongs, pried shut. The shaft-end had a hoop, which looked like it could be used for threading rope. "How the heck-spit do it shoot?"

A twig cracked. Jack crouched low by the stolen bag. A lone stag stepped into view. Jack lined up the crossbow sights and tried to fire the weapon but the trigger stuck.

* * * *

"*When you aimed the crossbow,*" said the Silent One, "*Something strange happened.*"

Jack's ribs shot with pain in the cold mountain air, reminding him that he was still laying on a mountain ledge conversing with the Silent One.

"The crossbow didn't shoot," said Jack, "But all the noises of the woods – the bird's songs, the creek-babble, and rustle of leaves – sorta got lost."

"*What did you see?*"

"I saw myself as a hunter with a string of adventures that folks would talk about."

"*It was the first step of your journey.*"

"Weren't much but daydreaming."

"*Where did it lead you?*"

"I stuffed the weapon in the bag and waded along the shallow side of Thin Creek, toward town."

"*Did you wonder what happened to the three explorers?*"

"More skeletons for the Briar, I reckon. That weren't what I wanted. Can't say fer sure, maybe they picked up my trail again. I glanced back aplenty."

"*Only nobody followed.*"

"I bet they went back to a tavern and made up lies over a mug."

"*Their fates would not become lore.*"

"Reckon not."

"*So, where did you go next?*"

"I went to the last place I should've gone, and 'cause I did, I'm lying here now."

"*Was it a den of thieves? A dark corner of the Rivercross docks?*"

"Naw. I went home to my ma."

Chapter 2

MA

Ma was not feeling well. Jack sat on the windowsill listening to her complain. As always, he kept one leg dangling outside the shack so he could run off if she got too weepy.

He had heard it all. If there was no ache in Ma's knees, then there was a cold in her head, or hunger was making her see spots and the end was near. "Some folks is meant to live in the forest, others is meant to only know it's there," she cried. "I ain't meant fer it but here I am. That's the life for poor me."

~ 18 ~

Jack wondered why he had bothered to come home. A short time back, he would have just made his way to town without stopping but lately a tiny voice had begun to nag him to check on Ma more. She needed looking after.

"Twas love that put me here," said Ma. "Love of a brute. Good lass from Arborville, I was. Oh, not too bright for book learning but fine enough at cow milking. Then I come to Rivercross and yer pa, Jodd Spriggins, swaggered into town. All shoulders and musky from his hunt, he were." (She always sighed here.)

Jack started counting the strands of cobweb clinging to the cold clay oven in the center of the room.

"Wed and fled, that Jodd," Ma went on. "Left me in this dirty den with nothing but yeh, wee Jacky, and my spirit-blessed wits."

"Kind of stingy, them spirits," said Jack.

Their one-room hovel stood in a glen next to Thin Creek, miles from what Ma called "civil life." It had ramshackle walls and a thatch roof. A rickety outhouse stood twenty paces away in the blackberry shrubs, gathering flies. Their only furniture was a wobbly, three-legged stool and pair of empty grain barrels. Woven straw mats covered the dirt floor. Two hammocks were strung in the corners for sleeping but Jack seldom used his. He liked the rooftop better when it was warm and clear, to see the stars.

"Twelve years Jodd Spriggins be gone, next fall," said Ma. "Wish he could see how tall yeh got."

Jack had no memory of his pa but had pieced together in his head the image of a brooding hunter who would lick anyone that glanced at him the wrong way. "He was real tough, only not tough enough to stay put."

"Look what I snagged today, Ma," said Jack to change the subject. He dumped the stolen contents on the floor. "This could buy us a sack of cornmeal and some bacon."

"It'd be nice if yeh helped me do chores round here instead of playing with rangers in the woods."

"Weren't rangers, Ma. Just three blockheads trying to find the Beauty."

"Oh." Ma groaned. "But it's new faces with new voices. Son, if yeh only knew the pang I feel to be a part of bigger things. Makes me so tired, the pang. My heart begs for a change."

"Come to Rivercross Square with me. That'd be a change."

"To the village? Oh, son! I just couldn't." Ma stumbled over an empty wooden bucket. Filling it with creek water was supposed to be Jack's chore.

"Why not?"

She drooped down on the stool. "I was a real looker once. Everyone said so. I could've been crowned Light's Maiden at the Festival of Hearts. If they saw Ludi Spriggins now, think what they'd say."

"They'd say nothin, Ma," Jack thought to himself that she may have had a curvy shape but he doubted she was ever a looker.

"I know the ways of folks, Jacky. Babbling tongues. Judging looks. Saying things they ought'nt, like, 'I told yeh so.' Oh, I hate that one most of all."

"Me too, Ma."

"I just need a small change".

Her ragged bodice was barely laced and her shoes were on the wrong feet. A thick curl of hair drooped out of her kerchief. Yet, in her pale green eyes, Jack saw a glimmer of the hopeful girl who once believed she could have been the Light's Maiden.

"What do yeh need?" he asked.

"Fruits," she blurted out, "Gold ones with juicy red insides. Oh, I've been dreaming about them as long as I can remember. My poor soul needs a different taste than stale bread and lard-fried squirrel. Gold fruits with red insides be just the things!"

"I don't know what kind you're talking about. Want me to pinch a few apples from the square?"

"Apples is apples!" Ma began heaving violent sobs. "N-n-no. I'm talking about the big gold fruits from Allwise's Orchard."

"The Orchard?" Jack could not have been more surprised if lightning had struck the floor. "The old magician's place? Are yeh crazy, Ma?"

She smiled dreamily. "Ah, I saw them in his garden when I was a dairy girl, lugging jugs o' milk to his place. Yer pa said he'd get me them fruits but he run off instead."

"Ma, nobody goes near that Orchard if they can help it. Folks would rather brave the Briars. Yeh told me that yerself once."

"But yeh could do it, son, yeh've got skill. All the stuff yeh fetch keeps us alive, it does."

She gently stroked the scar that split his left eyebrow. It happened when Jack ran into a blacksmith's anvil when he was six, stealing nails to fix her shoes. He pulled away from her hand. It was time to dodge out but Ma caught his arm before Jack slid off the windowsill. She was the only person with a faster grab than his own.

"I'm sorry, Jacky," she said. "I know I'm up and down all the time."

"Yeh think these gold fruits'll help yeh, Ma?"

"I do, son."

The thought of creeping around the magician's place made the hairs on Jack's neck stand. He fished the snake-brooch out of his pocket and handed it to Ma. "Some jewelry for yeh. It ain't gold fruit but it's shiny."

She glanced at the pin. "That's the ugliest thing I ever saw!" She dropped it to the floor. "Get rid of it."

Jack pocketed the pin and decided not to show her the little harp, which also bore the symbol of the snake. He repacked everything and decided to sell it all. "A'right. I'll get the fruits for yeh."

"Oh, yer a good boy, Jacky." Ma, patted him fondly on the cheek. "Nearly a man by the way yeh take care of me."

It was nearing sunset, which was the best hour for making shady deals with Tinner in Rivercross. Then, he would go to Allwise's Orchard and poach the fruits after dark. "That magician catches me, Ma, ain't no telling what he'll do. Turn me into a possum."

"Jack, Jack, Jack," she cooed. "Yeh've turned my heart right and rosy, like yeh always do, son."

"Alright," Jack scowled, folding the crossbow in his belt. He toted the satchel down the footpath toward the village.

Ma started singing, "Goldy, goldy, goldy fruits, all my long-gone dreamy fruits." He heard her singing, even after he had rounded a bend and the shack was out of view.

Chapter **3**

RIVERCROSS

Jack could deal with a deadly briar, but people were a different story. As he neared the frontier village of Rivercross clutching the stolen leather bag, a knot tightened in his belly.

"Ma calls it 'civil life'. It's a rat's nest."

Jack tramped out of the woods along the dusty road that led into town.

Rivercross was situated beyond the bridge on the south side of the Green River. It had a port, a marketplace, inns, smithies, a butcher, and fish sellers. Farmers and traders rolled their wagons daily over the sturdy stone bridge for which Rivercross got its name.

On his way there, Jack grimaced as he passed by a wooden parishioner house. The building served as the village school, where proper book learning had ended badly for him. The schoolmaster, Parcey Piper, who smelled like medicine tonic, had hated Jack from the start.

"Long-legged, spidery coot," muttered Jack. "Rapped my knuckles raw with his hickory switch while that hayseed brat, Peter Crosspatch, said things he shouldn't about Ma." After Jack had pounded Peter into the floor, Parcey ordered him to leave and not come back.

Jack never did.

Next to the Parishioner House stood stables and the blacksmith's forge, where Jack heard the clang-clang of a horse being shod in the stall. Smoke spurted from rock chimneys of stone-and-plaster houses along the way and the dim haze that lingered stung Jack's eyes. Folks came out on their porches to beat dusty rugs and chuck wash-water into the road. None ever gave him a kind look or word.

"Real civil," said Jack.

A hay cart pulled by an ox nearly ran him down as he stepped onto the bridge. "Watch yourself," called the farmer. Jack leapt aside with a scowl, falling in behind the dusty cart.

Halfway across, Jack peered over the side at the river port (as he often did). The topmast of a barge went by below, close enough that he tried to swat it. The vessel was loaded with livestock and guided by an oarsman to the docks.

"Ha!" shouted herdsmen as it docked, driving cattle up the landing's ramps.

There were canoes tied off at cleats around the port. "I'll steal one someday. Ride the river," Jack decided, "Paddle off and see Majesty Bay. Make folks wonder where I'm off to for once."

Rowdy jeers echoed up from under the bridge. Peter Crosspatch, Magath Turlson, and Nelson Dowler were whooping and splashing in a water fight. When the boys saw Jack, their game stopped.

"It's Yellow Eyes!" said Peter loudly.

"Out of the woods like a dirty skunk," taunted Nelson, who had once got his eye blackened for making cracks about Jack's smell but now, with his pals nearby, was trying to play tough. Jack shot them a cold look and moved on. He had more important business with Tinner and gold fruits to steal.

Across the bridge was the market square where the road entered, split, and went in opposite directions. The hard-packed gravel lanes were framed with planked lumber and formed footpaths around the square. Rows of shops, inns, and eateries surrounded the center of the marketplace, where a cluster of makeshift stands was mobbed with folks who had wares to sell and coins to spend.

The men had tanned faces with clipped beards and wore overalls and suspenders. The rich ones wore overcoats, polished boots, and carried walking sticks. The townswomen rustled by in skirts and petticoats, filling their baskets from booth to booth.

Jack shouldered his way through the ruckus of vendors who yelled, "Fresh trout!" "Ripe blueberries!" "Baked bread here!"

One distracted young mother absently dropped coins into her purse. As a coin fell to the ground Jack quickly stepped on it and leaned down to re-buckle his shoe. She eyed him curiously with a snooty lift of her nose and went on her way. Jack snatched up the coin. It was a nickel, stamped with the likeness of the Grand Count of Havensbend, the wealthiest landowner in the realm. With this, Jack could buy a pouch of oat grains.

He ambled along the merchants' booths, getting the usual cold stares from the sellers. "There's Jack Spriggins, like a bad shadow," said the butcher's wife to Polly Kettle in the next stall.

"That boy's a sneaky villain," said Polly, grasping the cameo at her neck. "Green Mother, spare his wretched soul."

While they grumbled to each other, Jack snatched jerky from the butcher block and a pair of pastries from Polly's stand into his shirt. Already several stalls away, he had pocketed two pear tarts, a slice of salted pork, a tiny flask of lamp oil, and a blue hankie for Ma.

He would have gotten more stuff if the sheriff, "Big Bill", not lumbered into view tipping his hat to passersby. "Keepin' the order, just keepin' the order," he said. Big Bill always had an itch to catch Jack in the act of stealing.

"Big, slow ox," snickered Jack, "Too narrow between the eyes to catch me." Still, he was the law in Rivercross and had the authority to run a thief out of town, so Jack ducked between the stalls to avoid questions about the sack he carried.

By now the sun was sinking behind the buildings of the square as Fulbis Regent, the town crier, stepped up on a millstone and rang the heavy iron bell. "Sun down! Market closing," he shouted over the *CLANG! CLANG!* The merchants began to scuttle their tents and fold up shop.

Jack wove back into the bustling crowd from behind a canvas flap.

A childish, familiar laugh trilled nearby in the lane. He glimpsed at the scarlet cape and hood of a girl approaching from the crowd. She was another person Jack wished to avoid, so he ducked behind a fish vendor's cart to hide. "Chitchatting, eleven-year-old pest, Whatshername," he muttered. "Loony kid. Always acting like she talks to birds and critters."

The pest's red hood was down as she drew closer but the fisherman wheeled his cart away leaving Jack out in the open. The girl looked up and giggled.

"Jits!" Like a panicked deer, Jack bolted across the lane and ran into a tall, dark man who reeked of tobacco.

"Clumsy mongrel," barked the scoundrel in a thick, unfamiliar accent. He had a mass of black, curly hair, and thick sideburns on his cheeks. A wolf-fur cloak, much too warm for summer, hung from his wide shoulders. His bloodshot eyes were shaded beneath a felt-brimmed hat. "Out of my way, scrawny rat." He knocked Jack aside and pressed on through the crowd.

His chilling scent lingered.

"He even smells like a wolf," thought Jack, rubbing his shoulder after the shove. "At least Whatshername – Riding Hood – is gone."

Tinner's shop (more like a shed) was nestled between the buildings of an alleyway, away from the main square. He was seated on a barrel beneath a lighted cresset, guzzling mugs of beer with three Rivercross tradesmen. Their faces glowed red and they did not notice Jack coming.

"That's bad news," said Mincey, the butcher, a rail-thin man with huge forearms. "Two more girls, you say, gone missing in Arborvale?"

"So the woodsman say," confirmed Tinner. The tinker was a gangling man who reminded Jack of a mud slug. He wore a set of metal teeth that gleamed and spit whenever he spoke an "s". "Just like them other girls in Sunvale."

Agitated, Parson Barns sloshed brew onto his thick beard. "The Green Mother's curse upon any villain who preys upon young girls."

"Whoever or *whatever* it is," added Mincey, "What kind of monster would do that?"

"A demon wolf, I wager," said Tinner.

"Yep," agreed the parson, "Elves sing about one that's a man by day, beast by night."

"Elves?" muttered Jack, who chose to hang back out of sight. "Chee! What'd elves know about anything?" It was the brute in the wolf-skin cloak who sprang to his mind.

"My good money would be on dragons," said Scratch, the shoemaker, who refilled the parson's mug from a barrel spigot. He was a slight, white-haired man with a goatee that was trimmed to two points. "Geetis McGorkee of the Swamplands says dragons snatch youngsters right out of their chanteys."

Tinner spit a wad of tobacco but it missed the spittoon and landed on his shoe. "No surprise," he said, shaking his foot. "Crokees live out in the open."

Jack cleared his throat to get the Tinner's attention.

With a nasty frown, the tinker motioned him to go to the side of the shed. "No tact, as usual," he grumbled. "I told yeh, Yeller Eyes, not to come around so early." He pushed the side door of his shop open to let some light spill into the alley. "Whatcha got?"

Shaking the bag, Jack emptied it on the ground.

Tinner bent over and slobbered. "That's decent." He picked up the arrow with the folded prongs. "Grappling arrow. Can prob'ly sell that as is."

"Naw," said Jack, as he snatched it back. "Arrow's mine."

"Yer a weird one." The tinker nudged the metal spikes and the pan with the toe of his boot. "I can melt them down, I reckon. Gimme the bag too."

"How about this harp?"

"For what, square dances? That ain't metal, keep it."

As Jack tucked the strummer back under his arm, he glanced over his shoulder. Scratch was leaning around the corner eyeing him with interest. The shoemaker grinned with a puff of his pipe and went back to talking with the other men.

"How 'bout this?" Jack tossed the blue snake brooch on top of the pile.

Tinner leapt back as if it were a live serpent. "Ain't gonna touch that," he said, kicking the brooch aside. "Don't yeh know an ogre piece when yeh see one? Get rid of it. Bad luck."

Jack had never seen an ogre. All he knew was that they were a tough lot who came from the deserts and hated all Forestlanders. That the pin was "ogre-made" made it interesting – a worthy keepsake for his stash in the woods. "Think I'll keep it."

"Yeh should pitch it in the river," warned Tinner. "I mean it. Folks see yeh have it and they'll hate yeh even more."

Jack shrugged.

The tinker ducked into his shop and came back with two bits of copper.

"That's it?"

"Think yer being cheated?" grinned Tinner, tobacco juice drizzling down his chin. "Well, if yeh learned to count like other boys, it wouldn't be a problem, would it?"

"I know money."

"Count yerself lucky yeh got anything for this junk."

The grimy slug was right but Jack had enough in hand for a fresh loaf of bread and grains for Ma.

The Sheriff had joined the other men for a mug of brew. As Jack was leaving, the lawman caught his arm.

"What did yeh have in the bag, Yeller Eyes?" said Big Bill.

"Half the marketplace, I'll wager," said the butcher.

"Come now, Bill, has the youngster done any wrong?" said Scratch in Jack's defense. The shoemaker filled a tankard from one of the barrels, adding, "I'm sure if we checked our pockets, we'll find them undisturbed."

"For once it's true," said the parson.

"Yeh ain't ever caught me with anything," said Jack

The sheriff pushed him away. "The less I see of yeh in Rivercross, the better."

Scratch handed the sheriff a foamy mug. "Our worthy attention might be better spent finding those poor lasses who've gone missing."

"Think I wouldn't know a killer if he were right under my nose?" said Big Bill.

"Yeh wouldn't know if a wolf were chewing on yer big butt," said Jack, heading away to the square.

"Keep yer nose clean, Yeller Eyes," shouted Big Bill over his shoulder. "You'll be bunking behind bars soon enough."

* * * *

Coldness on the mountain ledge returned with a biting rush that made Jack shiver but he dared not open his eyes; he did not wish to jinx this conversation with the Silent One.

"*There was an entertainer in Rivercross Square,*" the spirit reminded. "*Tell me about him.*"

"I already did," said Jack. "He was the big man in the wolfskin cloak." The memory sparked vividly.

"Torches were lit," Jack went on. "Villagers gathered 'round the crier's Platform. That lowdown scoundrel in the fur was standing there with a big grey wolf at his side. Folks seemed impressed so I got closer."

"*A captive audience.*"
"Yeh got that right."

"*His dazzling smile,*" said the Silent One. "*Did you find him charming as everbody else?*"

"Naw," said Jack. "Weren't a smile. It was a leer, cold and cruel."

"*You know a monster when you see one.*"
"Reckon so," said Jack. "Always have."
* * * *

"Gather closer, ladies and gentlemen," said the hairy entertainer in his deep, foreign drawl. "I am the famous Likov Fen, Master of Wolves!"

The wolf-master threw his cape back over his shoulders. He wore a fancy, ruffled shirt and crimson vest, complimented by the tight trousers and high boots. "Come meet my good friend Lobar."

~ 31 ~

A huge grey wolf, restrained by a chain, pawed the floorboards at his side. Fen passed a metal hoop through a stage-side torch, igniting it with a burst of flame. The crowd oohed.

Dominant and poised, Fen held the flame-ring away from his body. "Jump, Lobar!" he commanded. "Jump, my brother, jump!" The wolf obeyed with a fierce spring, leaping through the fiery hoop. Like the others, Jack had never seen a vicious beast so well trained. The crowd applauded.

With a suave shake of his wrist, the showman extinguished the hoop and gave a majestic bow. "Back in my homeland of Karvothia, the wolf," he said, "The wolf is like a puppy-dog. Show them, Lobar. Show the good people how you love them."

Lobar rolled on to his back and panted. A long, black tongue flapped out of the lethal jaws. Fen patted the wolf's belly. "You see?" said Fen. "Gentle as a lamb." He beckoned to several young ladies in the crowd. "Come, which of you lovely misses would like to pet the scruff of his throat?"

Many takers raised eager hands but one pushy milkmaid nudged her way ahead of the others. Giggling, she gathered up her yellow petticoats to clear the steps. "Ooh, you sure he don't bite?" she asked, batting her eyes.

Likov Fen turned to the crowd, mimicking her: *"Ooh, are you sure he don't bite?"* It was surprising how well he matched her voice and manner. The villagers clapped. The milkmaid blushed and buried her head on the showman's broad shoulder. Nudging her towards the wolf, his smile gleamed, "There-there, dumpling, Lobar will keep his teeth to himself."

The maid drew back with bubbly squeals, "Ooh! Eeh!"
Again, the entertainer mimicked her: *"Ooh! Eeh!"*

Fulbis Regent, town crier, stepped out from among the
laughing crowd. "That is not very gentlemanly of yeh, sir," he said.
"To mock a lady like that."

The wolf-master answered by skillfully imitating Regent's flat
drawl. *"No one ever accused me of being a gentleman before, sir. I
thank yeh."*

The crier's mouth fell open as the crowd laughed.

"Chee," observed Jack. "They'd let Mister Wolf get away with
murder so long as he makes 'em laugh. That's a handy trick with his
voice, though."

Lobar rolled to his paws and crooned long howling notes.
"Lobar thanks you for your kind attention," said Fen, removing his
hat. "And for your generosity, if you please." Applause and a flurry of
coins showered the stage with their approval. "Ah, thank you, thank
you," he beamed. "Lobar and I thank you."

"That wolf ain't as tame as it looks," said Jack.

As the audience scattered, he kept his eyes on Likov Fen. The
rogue had a heavy collar around Lobar's neck and he led the wolf to
the bridge, where the young girl in the red cape fell in beside them
and started tagging along, making chitchat.

"Aw bunk," said Jack. "It's the pest. That girl ain't got any
good sense. What trouble is she getting into now?"

The tall man lowered the hood of the girl's red cape and
stroked her auburn curls. Jack's blood boiled. He dropped the harp
on the road by the bridge as he yanked the crossbow from his belt.

Aiming it at Fen's back, he shouted, in the lowest voice he could summon, "Git away from her, Wolf Man!"

The showman spun round. Jack met his ferocious eyes. Lobar the wolf bared fangs, ready to lunge. The girl shrieked and nearby onlookers stopped.

"No, Lobar!" ordered Fen, holding the wolf's collar with a firm grip. He barked out a command in a dog-like tongue, "*Garakha! Rhakaaw!*"

The animal cowered.

Fen donned his charming smile, as if it were all part of an act. "You see, my Rivercross friends? Like a puppy dog."

It was enough to prompt good-natured chuckles as the onlookers went their way.

With this Fen kissed the young girls and - hand; or as Jack saw it, he tasted it.

Whatshername shyly withdrew her hand and pulled up her red hood.

Likov Fen bowed. "I set forth for Havensbend to join a troupe of wandering minstrels. But I will pass this way again."

"Don't bother," said Jack.

The man came forth and grabbed Jack's collar. "Brazen mongrel," he seethed. "You are treading towards a bloody snare." With a swash of his cloak, he let go and led Lobar into the darkness down the lane. The wolfish scent lingered.

Jack fought the urge to follow them to make sure they left town. Lowering the empty crossbow, he shook the anger out of his shoulders. He was now alone on Rivercross Bridge with the same red-hooded girl he had tried so hard to avoid.

Chapter 4

ELLA

"Hello, Jack," said Whatshername the Pest. "I was hoping you'd stop hiding from me."

"I weren't, er, hiding," stammered Jack.

"You've forgotten my name again, haven't you?" she smiled playfully. "It's Ella Vintner. Remember? Ella. You saved me from walking into that hunter's trap when I was in the woods talking to a family of foxes."

"Yeah, I remember." Jack tucked his crossbow into his belt. "It's hard to forget a kid who thinks she can talk to a fox."

"Oh, that was such a terrible day." Ella picked up the little wooden harp Jack had dropped. "I was still going to the village school then. That morning, Peter Crosspatch and the other boys threw stones at a helpless pigeon just to be mean. When I begged them to stop, they threw stones at me."

"Those farm boys are lucky I weren't there to see that."

"I ran with the bird into the woods but the poor thing didn't survive, so I buried her. I don't know how Peter could have been so heartless but Papa says there are many things I don't see. I guess that's why I got so lost, but then I met the foxes and then you."

The girl's auburn hair was pulled back from her face with a pair of green ribbons that bobbed when she spoke. She had soft gray eyes flecked with blue. Jack found himself staring at them again.

"Hello?" waved Ella, bringing him back to his senses.

"Stop talking to old letches in the square." said Jack, walking away. "Next time I'll let him haul yeh off."

Ella caught up, skipping alongside. "Thank you. But you really didn't have to rescue me, you know. I just mentioned to Mister Fen that Lobar was unhappy and he seemed very interested when I said so."

"The wolf?" said Jack.

"No, silly, *the man*. He understands growls and meows like I do."

"Yer nothing alike."

"He was a bit – how would you say it? Mysterious?"

"Ain't how I'd put it at all. Just stay clear of him."

"You sound like Papa. He scolds me all the time for talking to strangers."

"He should scold yeh cause yeh never stop talking." Jack then noticed Ella was holding his harp and snatched it back. "Gimme that and leave me be." He followed the road toward the magician's orchard.

"I am far too curious, aren't I?" said Ella, who managed to keep up with him. "I wander off at the drop of a hat. That's why Mama made this scarlet cape for me. It's easier to find me in a crowd. Of course, I get teased for wearing it. Gertie Kettle made up a skip-rope rhyme. Wanna hear it?

'Ella, Ella, don't wear yella,
Never kissed by any fella.
Always acting, good, good, good,
Call her plain Red Riding Hood.'

"I guess I'll never have friends like others do," she added. "At least ones that don't tease and call me names."

"I call yeh names too," said Jack.

"But you get called much worse things so it doesn't hurt when you do. Anyway, we're friends."

"Naw, we ain't." Jack walked faster.

Ella skipped beside him. "Oh, yes we are. You've always talked to me. That's more than you do with other folk, so you must like me."

"Chee."

"I like you," she twinkled. "Anyhow, I love my cherry-red cape and I wouldn't wear anything else. Besides, I don't go to the schoolhouse anymore. Papa pays a tutor from Havensbend to teach me now."

"Git on home." Jack did not want her at his heels all the way out of Rivercross. "I mean it, get lost."

"But I was so glad to see you in the village," she went on. "Papa didn't want me to come." She pointed a finger, mocking her father: "*You'll get lost, Ellie, or drag about with heathens.*" Breaking character, she asked, "What are heathens, exactly? Oh well, I guess he was wrong because I met up with you instead, which is good because I can help."

"Help me?"

"Why, yes. This road leads out to Allwise's place. No one goes there. He guards it too closely."

"Look," Jack clenched his teeth. "I ain't got time for yer fool-talk. Go pester someone else."

"So, you really do mean to go to the Orchard now. I was right! Are you planning to steal something?"

All Jack's excuses got gummed up in his head, so he took a shortcut across a grassy farm field, ducking between the slats of a wood fence.

"Don't be angry," said Ella, who slipped through and followed him. "I know you're a thief. I've seen you take things from the market, like that blue hankie today."

Cutthroats, lowlifes, and Big Bill had never caught Jack in the act. How could this red-hooded nitwit have seen his sleight-of-hand?

"You're not bad at it," she said. "Foxes are a bit better, of course. Maybe I could talk one into giving you a lesson."

"Shut up about talking to foxes and such." Jack glared with what he imagined to be his harshest look. "They'll lock yeh up and I'll be the one to laugh."

The giddiness went out of Ella's eyes. She leaned against a wooden totem, which stood in the field where they had stopped. It was carved in the form of the Green Mother Spirit to bless the crops.

"What's wrong with yeh?" said Jack.

"I *can* talk to animals," Ella said quietly, as if listening to the whispers of angels. "Papa and Mama tell me not to let folks know—but you've already seen me do it. It's a secret I can share with you." She pointed to the smile on the totem's face. "She's the one that gave it to me."

"The Green Ma?"

"It was her spirit gift to me when I was born. Animals may bark and bray to you, Jack, and birds may cheep, but to me, they speak. And I can speak back to them."

Ella's innocent soul tugged at Jack like a fish on a line. He wanted to protect her. She was true and warm, like a tune he had once heard played on a wooden flute. "What are you going to steal this time?" said Ella.

"Gold fruits for Ma."

"Is she ill?"

"She says so. Reckon them fruits will make her feel better."

"Maybe you won't have to steal them." Ella seemed to perk up. "Allwise might just give them to you, if you ask."

"The old wizard? Why would he? Yeh know what folks think of me. If a fool girl can tell I'm a thief, think what a wizard sees."

"Then let me ask for you." She reached for his hand, but then stopped, as if she knew it might anger him. (Later, Jack would muse it would have been all right if she did.)

"I'll do it myself," he said. "Stop following me."

"At least let me help. I know a wren who can guide you over the Orchard Wall. There are lots of snags and tricks in it. With a pair of sharp bird's eyes to spot for you, you might not be hurt."

"Bird's eyes? Why don't yeh beat it already?"

At the far end of the field he jumped the fence but Ella slipped through the rails and continued to pester him. "This could be such fun, Jack. A real adventure! Of course, Mama wouldn't want me to actually steal anything, but I could be your lookout."

"Can't yeh take a hint?" Jack snapped. Just as he was sure he would never be rid of her, a carriage harnessed to a black steed stopped at the road's turn.

The driver stood tall; one leg propped on the dash rail. He was holding a lantern, which reflected the red of Ella's cape brightly. His face twisted with anger.

"Ella!" he yelled, loud enough to startle the horse. "You were told to stay in the village square. You were told not to talk with riff-raff. I let you come along when you promised to behave like a young lady and stay in the square."

"Papa! This is my friend, Jack Spriggins."

"No, he is not your friend," said Mister Vintner. "He is that yellow-eyed thief from the woods. He'll grow into nothing but a menace if he isn't hung first."

Ella marched over to the carriage. "You mustn't say that!" she cried.

In one swift motion, the man reached down and scooped her up beside him. "No tongue from you, child. There's talk of missing girls and then you disappear from my side. It's all I'll stand from you tonight."

Jack noticed for the first time how finely Ella and her pa were dressed. Their clothes were of a cut and cloth that made the common villagers look shabby. The carriage was sleek. Its wheels were polished and the horse well groomed, bridled in an expensive harness.

"Papa," said Ella, "Jack needs our help."

"He needs to be horse-whipped," said Mister Vintner, his black, trimmed mustache quivering with rage. "And he's lucky I don't do just that. From now on, you will keep yourself at our vineyard. Rivercross is no place for you."

With a whoosh and crack of the whip, the horse and carriage were off. Ella looked back, waving both hands like a bird's wings and mouthing the words, "I'll send the wren." Her father yanked the scruff of her red hood and they rode out of sight.

"Mister Highfaluting Moneybags," shouted Jack. "I ain't no riff-raff." He turned away and marched down the road, muttering to himself. "Like he's ever scrounged a day in his fancy-smancy, shiny boots-and-carriage life." As the hoof stamps and rattling carriage faded in the distance, Jack picked a pinecone off the road and hurled it in their direction.

"If yeh knew how I saved yer dizzy daughter from trouble," he shouted, "Yeh'd shut up quick! Like Fen the wolf man tonight. He's the real bad one, not me."

Chapter 5

ALLWISE

Jack followed the Orchard Road past village farms until trees engulfed the way in darkness. No other travelers passed by. "Allwise," said Jack with a sneer, "A wizard." He recalled schoolroom gossip Gertie Kettle had spread about the Orchard: *"Allwise, the magician talks with the dead! He teaches dark arts, spell-casting, and potion-brewing."*

"Fool-talk,"said Jack." From folks too scared to find out what's real."

What captured his own interest about the so-called wizard were his many apprentices, who sold produce in Rivercross Square. These were boys about Jack's age, who held themselves apart from the other village kids. Their crisp gray uniforms had a badge resembling a tree sewn on them, and their confident manner made him curious.

"Maybe they learn how to grow apples where there ain't much sun?" he wondered. "Or how to corral big swamp-lizards? Maybe they learn to knock elves out of trees. Jits, I'd sit up straight for that." Either way, Jack had always secretly yearned for a crack at getting inside the Orchard.

As he got nearer, he grew more wary. The Orchard was enclosed on all sides by the wizard's wall. There was a high gate set back from the road but its two wooden doors were braced with iron latches. Above the gate spanned a wooden arch, carved to look like apple boughs.

"It don't look that spooky," said Jack.

The chirr of crickets stopped and the silence seemed unwelcoming. He did not muster the courage to knock. Instead, he followed the wall. "Prob'ly ten feet up. But why does it look different further along?"

The wall's surface changed from one segment to the next. The first stretch was several paces wide with a wet, slimy surface. The next had sharp metal spikes and then it was matted with rotten moss.

"Outsiders sure ain't welcome," said Jack, taking it all in. He set the wooden harp on to the grass. "I can sneak under," he figured, spotting a stretch of wall made of red bricks where he found a weakness. A dug-out gap below the wall was wide enough to crawl through. With a satisfied smirk, he got on his elbows. "Nobody here, coast is clear."

A warning-tingle went up his neck. Jack looked around. "Something don't seem right." He broke off a branch from a nearby holly bush and thrust it under the wall. The branch was forced from his hands with a powerful yank. *SNAP!* The stick dangled from a snare through the gap, broken in half.

"Yep, too easy."

His words echoed back: "Yep-too easy-too easy-too-easy-easy."

"Who's that?" whispered Jack. "Somebody there?" There was no echo this time.

He moved on to a wall section built of white rocks. With a grip and a foothold, he started to climb but it was very slippery and he fell on his backside with a thud. "Aw bunk!"

"Aw-bunk-bunk-bunk," echoed a voice under the wall again.

Jack went peered through. "Who's there?" No answer came back.

Scratching his head, he shifted over to a length of wall that looked like a common wood fence. As soon as he slid his fingers between the boards, they shut together, pinching him with ruthless snips. Wherever Jack gripped, the panels collided on his fingers. Once again, he fell to the ground, now blowing on his swollen fingertips. "Buzzards guts!"

"Buzz-awguts-awguts-awguts," This was no echo.

"Who are yeh?" said Jack at the mimicker. "Stupid elf! Show yer lousy elf-face and say that again."

"Stoobadelf-stoobadelf-lousy-face." The annoying voice spoke above the wall.

~ 45 ~

Jack took off his right shoe, ready to pitch it. A cheerful head – just a head – beamed back at him from atop the wall. "Yeh ain't an elf, that's for sure." The oval head was bald with tiny flat ears, blinking blue eyes, a pug nose, and a broad, sincere grin. There was no telling its age or even if the head had a body attached to it.

"Who are yeh?" said Jack, wobbling on his right foot.

"Wooeryeh-eryeh-eryeh," repeated the bald grinner, inching a bit more into view. Jack was relieved to see shoulders.

"Yeh sure ain't Allwise the Wizard," he said. "Yeh gonna tell folks I'm here?"

"Gonna-tell-em-bunk-bunk-bunk," beamed the head. Only babies or witless old men smiled that way.

"I hope that meant 'no'." Jack then took a stab at an easy way to finish the robbery. "Say, Baldy, yeh wanna toss me over some gold fruits? I'll trade yeh this wooden harp."

The bald head ducked behind the wall and stayed hid.

"Baldy? Reckon I'll just climb then." Jack, slipped his shoe back on.

The head popped up again. "Climb-climb-climb."

"Reckon I'll get the fruits myself," said Jack. "Ain't afraid. Except the place might be a house o 'nuts, full of others just like yeh."

"Nuts-nuts-nuts."

Jack crossed to a wall section covered with blue fungus. "Don't tussle with that. Itchy, right?"

"Itch-itchy-itch!" blurted the bald fellow.

"Yeah, I get it."

"Agid-agid-agid!"

"Shutup, will yeh? Shh!"

"Shh-shh-shh!" said the mimicker, ducking out of sight.

"And stay gone!"

A bird swooped down and landed on a patch of ivy-covered wall, chirping and chirping.

Jack hissed and waved it off. "Pipe down, stupid bird. Stop yer tweeting." He then noticed it was a wren, the same bird Ella had promised. "Naw, can't be. Beat it, bird."

The next part of the wall was knotted like a tree and pocked with holes and knobs. Easy to grip, like an ugly old oak. Jack pried his way up the crusty nodules. One of them squished in his hand and burst open with a sickly *SPLORCH!* A stream of white sap hit him in the neck and oozed down the front of his shirt.

"Jits!"

BLORP! Several spouts that were even more vile erupted on him. *PLURT! GWARP! OORP!*

Jack leapt away, covered in glop and struggling to breathe. "Aww, smells like bad cheese," he moaned, wiping his eyes with his sleeves.

He stumbled against the wall as a mass of bugs came skittering out of the cracks. Countless centipedes, beetles, cockroaches, and large ants climbed up his pants, went up his back and everywhere a person would not want them to go. Even into his mouth.

Jack threw himself on to the ground, twitching and spitting like a madman. "Git off me! Scab-picking bunk! Git off me!" Caked with sludge and squashed insects, he glared at the cursed wall. "Choke on yer stinking tricks, yeh shifty wizard."

Then Jack remembered Ma. Life had been hard on her and, like it or not, this was his chance to make it better. With a long, weary sigh, he whispered, "Still there, Baldy? Look, I just want Ma's fruits. That's all I'll take."

The bald fellow did not show his face but the wren bobbed up and down on the ivy-covered wall, chirping without stop.

"Shut yer beak," Jack swiped at it again when his sleeve cuffed a tangle of leaves. This triggered a long straight branch to swat down with a *CRACK!* against the stonework. The branch recoiled and sprang back to its origin.

"Happy, featherhead? Another wizard trick to wallop me but good!" The bird chirped on, sounding just as chatty as Ella.

It was then that Jack saw the branches in new light. "Why, I bet those could throw me over if I'm fast enough."

The wren hopped again on its perch. "*CHIRP! CHIRP!*"

"Yeah, yeah, I get yeh. Now, shut up."

Jack reached out and flicked the tangle of branches. One of them swung down hard enough to knock his head off but he dodged it, grabbed the leafy end as it recoiled, and the branch flung him over the wall like a kite soaring into the air. "Whooaa!"

He landed on a mound of raked leaves inside the Orchard.

"I flew," said Jack. It had been a short flight but he grinned, eyeing the defeated wall behind him. "Haha! I'm over."

Of course, that meant he was sealed inside the grounds now, instead of out.

"So, this is the Orchard," he muttered, brushing leaves off his shirt. He darted over to a stand of trees. Tiled trenches sparkled in the moonlight, ushering water to carefully arranged groves. A crisp breeze carried rich scents from the soil, full of wonderful spices and mint, and braided wind chimes spun on the branches with docile tings.

"Ma's fruits ain't gonna be easy to find. So many strange trees about."

A giant shadow was cast on the grounds by a spire of stone that rose higher than the trees and blocked the moonlight. It looked older than a forest redwood and much spookier. As he came to it, Jack felt with his fingers the worn etchings carved on its sides. He did not believe in ghosts but in the shadow of this pillar, he felt haunted.

"Hey, Baldy. Yeh still around?"

The smiley bald head stayed out of view.

Jack drew a breath. "I can feel it. Like I'm being watched. Jits, where's Ma's fruits?"

Broken clouds passed in front of the moon, so he waited a moment for them to clear. When the light shone through again, it revealed a grove of slender trees with the gold orbs.

"Those're the ones. They gotta be."

Jack slinked under tree cover and plucked one of the orbs. The weight of the gold fruit in his hand was impressive. It had delicate, shimmery skin and a dark red juice dripping from the split.

He was about to take a bite, when a low voice warned, "I wouldn't do that if I were you, Thief."

Jack froze in place trying to figure the best direction to run. A man stepped out from behind a glass house near the trees and approached him. His eyes were deep-set, crystal blue, and penetrating.

He folded his arms. "Trolling for fruits?"

Even without introductions, Jack knew he was face to face with Allwise, the ancient magician.

"Jits."

At second glance, *ancient* did not best describe the man. Nor did *magician*. Allwise was long past his youth but not decrepit and there was little to suggest a warlock. His beard was a peppery goatee cropped close to the chin. There were few strands of hair on his head and his belly sagged over his belt. Wearing a gray smock, he looked more like a gardener than a dreaded conjurer.

"Not talking, eh?" said Allwise. "I'll take your crossbow then if you don't mind." Before Jack knew it, the man whisked the crossbow right off his belt. "And, even if you do mind," he added, with a calm click of his cheek. He held it up for inspection. "Classic old piece. It works better loaded, of course. Stolen, I suppose?"

Jack looked at his empty belt loop. How could the old coot move so fast?

"That little maneuver is a riki-grab," stated Allwise. "They use it in the jungles of Zan. Perhaps, I'll teach you it someday."

"Bow's mine," said Jack. "Anyway, it don't even shoot."

"Interesting. You favor empty weapons and poison." Allwise pointed to the gold fruits. "Those are not to be eaten. In fact, *they eat*. Do you see?"

Jack looked closer at his prize. Tail feathers from a small bird, glazed with red ooze, were being sucked into the split of the fruit. "Yuck," he said, pitching it aside.

"I call them Gold Charmers," said Allwise. "They attract and eat insects, mostly. Sometimes birds. Their nectar makes a fine red ink. Very useful in keeping accounts. To drink it, however, is deadly."

"Chee, that figures," said Jack. "Just like Ma to crave something that'll make her drop dead."

"Stealing for your mother then, Thief?"

Jack was done with questions. He lunged for his crossbow but Allwise stepped away and whistled through his fingers. Two lion-hounds barked and came bounding towards them from just beyond the grove.

"Micca. Max. Heel!" commanded the old man.

The dogs yielded but continued to growl at Jack, who saw it was best not to move.

"You're brighter than that, aren't you, young man?" sighed Allwise. "After all, you've successfully scaled my wall. Others far more accomplished than you have failed trying to do that. Tell me your name?"

Jack kept silent.

"Well then, I shall continue to call you '*Thief*'. It's quite shrewd to keep your real name private, by the way. People call me '*Allwise*', '*Ancient Magician*', '*Wizard*'." He spoke as if he were talking to an old friend. "Elf tribes address me as '*Old Eyes*'. The dwarfs prefer '*Calculator*', blah blah blah. My birth name, I keep to myself; a luxury that someone of your profession could appreciate, I imagine."

"Blah-blah-blah," called a voice. Jack turned to find "Baldy" seated on the wall again, rocking his stubby feet back and forth like a kid. He was dressed same as Allwise in a gray smock and breeches.

"You've already met Humfrey," said Allwise. "He's keenly taken with you." "Aw-bunk-aw-bunk-aw-bunk," shouted Humfrey, waving excitedly.

"And you've added colorful new words to his vocabulary, Thief," said Allwise. "How considerate."

"He ain't exactly – *right*," said Jack, twirling a finger at his own head." Is he?"

"No, he's perfect," said Allwise. "Humfrey is my finest gardener. He chooses to grow only yellow things at the moment; hollyhocks, corn, butter squash, but it is the most splendid, pristine fare of its kind."

Humfrey continued to wave from the wall.

"How long is he gonna keep that up?" said Jack. "Until you wave back."

Jack chopped the air once with his arm.

"Well, that was pathetic on your part," said Allwise. "Humfrey, why don't you go and have Missus Linnie scramble you some eggs. I'll see to our guest."

"Scram-linlin-eggs, scram-linlin-eggs," said Humfrey, as he stood and waddled briskly atop the wall. The hounds followed below, yipping playfully.

"Use the ladder!" Allwise called out, but Humfrey jumped and landed in Jack's pile of leaves, his bald head popping up with another broad grin. "Ah me, he thrives on risk, just like you. On that subject, Thief, you're younger than your filthy appearance suggests and the crack in your voice betrays you to be thirteen or so. Your skill intrigues me."

He signaled with his hand and a pair of boys approached, armed with magnificent longbows.

"You want us to keep watching him, sir?" said the slender one with dark hair. He looked to be in his late teens.

"I'm fine, boys. And this resourceful lad here has jumped the wall."

"He did what?" said the older boy, looking at Jack with surprise.

"In under an hour," added Allwise.

"Only an hour?" said the second boy, who was shorter and stockier. He also gazed at Jack with amazement.

"Weren't hard," gloated Jack with a lift of his chin.

Allwise handed Jack's crossbow to the stout boy. "Perdur, see what you can do with this."

"Yes, sir."

"And Redvere," he said to the older student. "I'd like you to ready my telescope."

"Even with those gathering clouds?"

"Rain's coming, but I believe it will be clear by morning. We will stick to our scheduled astronomy class."

"Yes, sir," said Redvere. Both boys left.

"Stealing for your mother, you say?" continued Allwise, as if they had never been interrupted. "Not a very creative lie."

"Ain't a lie," said Jack.

Allwise drew closer. "You know, I believe you. There's not a shred of imagination in your head, is there? Just cunning. And survival. Come and walk. Tell me about your mother."

Ma was the last person Jack wanted to talk about. The footpath wound past the spire. He gazed up at the stone tower and tried to switch the subject. "Yeh build that?"

"I built everything around it," said Allwise. "I can't say who originally built it, nor do I care. I asked about your mother."

Jack fessed up. "She's sick and says yer fruits can help her."

"Sick? Or does she *think* she's sick?"

"She just thinks it." Jack was surprised at how the wizard seemed to understand.

"Did you ever consider asking for my help?"

"Chee. Nobody helps me."

"That can change. But you're young, you're from a village that is steeped in gossip and suspicion. Why should I expect more of you?"

"I ain't no Rivercross dit! Me and Ma live in the Forest."

"That must be difficult. You're a determined one, Thief. Even now, if I turned my back, you'd snatch something for your mother, wouldn't you?"

"Turn yer back and find out."

The old man laughed. "I do not doubt your skill. What I'm questioning is your character. Are you just obnoxiously stubborn or permanently damaged?"

Allwise stopped in a courtyard of evenly laid stones before three large houses.

"I need a cow," he said. "A white one."

"Yeh what?"

"A white cow. I need one."

"For magic stuff?"

The old man puffed in disgust. "Do I look like the Old Crone of the Woods? No. I'm a scholar and a teacher, an architect and builder. An artist. A scientist. Only idiots believe I'm a 'wizard.' Prove yourself better."

Thunder rolled overhead.

"I ain't no wizard neither, so why send me for a cow?"

"Farmer MacDonald has agreed to sell his to me. I need the cow to breed with my bull and I want you to make the payment at his farm. Bring the beast back here to me."

He tossed over a coin pouch. Jack caught it. The purse jangled heavily in his hand.

"Why me?" said Jack.

"Consider it an exchange for your mother's sake," said Allwise. "Gold Charmers won't help her but I do grow other things that will. Bring me the white cow and you won't return to her empty handed."

It felt to Jack like there was more to this deal than wrangling a cow. "Why not get it yerself?"

"Because I want you to do it."

"I'll get my crossbow back?"

"You'll get it back and a reward that will make your mother feel better. Look for the green barn near town. Old MacDonald keeps a light going. I'll see you and my cow back here, say, before breakfast? Goodnight then."

"Wait," fumbled Jack. "Yeh mean do it now? Rain's coming."

"You'd best hurry then."

"Farm folk don't like me."

"Yes, you'll have to work that out." Allwise strode off towards the main house, his singsong voice trailing, "And, Thief? Use the front gate. It opens and closes just fine."

"Crafty codger," muttered Jack. "Thinks he's got me cornered? He ain't so all-wise."

Rain clouds blotted out the moon and their pitter-pat began falling on the flat stones of the courtyard. Jack's first meeting with Allwise was far from over.

Chapter **6**

SONGS

The downpour caused puddles on the road. Through the mist the farmsteads west of town were impossible to see, but MacDonald had a green barn and there was no other like it in Rivercross, so Jack knew where to find it.

He slipped through the fence of a muddy field and spied on the place.

"Reckon I'll keep hid," said Jack, bouncing the soggy coin purse in his hand. "Sure is a lot of money to come by so easy."

MacDonald kept a hound on watch but the rain masked Jack's scent. The old dog lay asleep on the porch of the farmhouse. MacDonald was in the barn, milking the white cow beneath a lantern.

"It's past midnight, don't this geezer even let his cow sleep?" said Jack.

"That'll do, Blossom," said the farmer at last. He lidded the milk pail and carried it into the house. The hound rose to follow him.

Jack snuck into the barn. Blossom the white cow flicked her ears at him. He stuffed the coin purse into his pocket and started plastering loose hay to the underside of his shoes to avoid muddy tracks. Lifting a coil of rope off a hook, he leashed Blossom and led her out the back of the barn without making the acquaintance of Farmer MacDonald or paying for the cow.

Jack found his way to the riverbank Down a slippery path, and led Blossom away from the farm through dense groves. The cow mooed.

"Don't sweat it, old girl," said Jack. "The rain's gonna wash our tracks out. I got yeh, the coins, and Ma's reward." "Allwise sure ain't gonna be the wiser now."

The rain let up and a shift in the wind carried a familiar, unsettling stench.

Jack drew a deep breath. "Wolf."

Blossom began pitching her head.

"Easy, girl," cooed Jack. "I know that stench. It ain't just wolf-stink. Tobacco. Blood. It's Likov Fen, the man in the wolfskin cloak."

The enormous moon appeared low between the clouds. Two black shapes moved across the horizon. It was Likov Fen leading Lobar by a chain across a hillock at the end of the vale. The scoundrel crooned a corrupt little tune:

"Pretty, pretty, plump and witty,

Just a morsel, such a pity."

Blossom yanked on her rope with a snort.

"Easy," whispered Jack, petting her.

Fen halted with a low, intimidating chuckle as he stared down at them. Lobar's leash went tight as the wolf locked in on the cow. The master did not let go but crooned another verse:

"At such an hour before dawn wakes,

Who prowls about but thieves and snakes?

Or gents that sing an eerie ditty,

Of the pretty, plump, and witty."

With another chuckle, Fen clicked his cheek and yanked the wolf's leash. Jack was grateful to watch them saunter away.

"Yeh stay away from Ella!" he called, adding under his breath. "Liar. I knew he weren't going to Havensbend."

At first light Jack returned to the Orchard. Pushing through the front gate with Blossom in tow, he found the students were already up and about. Some of the boys carried quarterstaffs out to the yard. Others had longbows and quivers with arrows. A few led horses from the stables for a morning trot.

"They learn to ride here?" said Jack. Horses fascinated him, especially ones like the strong, groomed chestnuts and greys that these boys rode.

Allwise climbed down a ladder from the giant stone spire, still accompanied by Redvere and Perdur. The older, good-looking student toted a long segmented looking-glass, while the stocky one carried a wooden stand over his shoulder.

"Welcome back, Thief," said Allwise. "Right on time. "

"Jits," yawned Jack. "The roosters ain't even crowed yet."

Blossom mooed.

The old man petted her back and smiled. "Ah. There's my lovely lady. Milky white and not too bright. Perdur, please take her to the stable."

The stout lad led her away.

"And Redvere, get this boy bathed, clothed, and fed," said Allwise. "Then bring him to the greenhouse."

"I'll do my best, sir," said Redvere. His tone hinted this was the more difficult assignment.

Jack's temper flared. "That weren't the deal! Just gimme Ma's stuff."

"You will wash," said Allwise. "You will dress. You will eat. And you will not give Redvere trouble. Only then will you get your reward. Anything to add?"

Tired and angry, Jack sulked behind Redvere to a row of wooden stalls. "Step in there, far left," said Redvere.

"What for?"

The apprentice smirked. "To get this over with." He did not seem arrogant but carried himself with privilege, like a gentleman. Redvere was the kind of fellow that village girls swooned over but there was a trace of sadness about him.

"Bet yeh make up poems, don't yeh?" said Jack as he stepped into the stall.

Redvere ignore the remark. He cranked an iron water-pump that stood alongside the stalls. "You know your clothes are going to get wet."

"Git on with it." Jack was still damp from the rain. A deep gurgle rattled overhead and icy water streamed from a mounted spigot, dousing him. "Jits!" He tried to duck away but Redvere shoved him back in.

"You can stand it," insisted the older boy. "You and your clothes needed a good rinse."

"I'm freezing!" yelped Jack.

Redvere tossed a bar of soap at Jack's feet. "Here. I hope you know how to use that."

"Yer lucky I don't cram it down yer throat, pretty boy."

Jack quickly realized that Redvere was bigger and probably a better fighter than Peter Crosspatch, so he scrubbed without making more threats.

The dousing stopped as Redvere reached into a cedar bench and tossed Jack a cotton wrap. "Cover up with this and get out of those drenched clothes. We're going inside." He marched to the door of a large building. "C'mon, we'll get drier things for you to wear."

Cold and surly, Jack wrapped his shivering body and snatched up his wad of clothes, careful to keep Allwise's coin purse out of view.

Inside, the building smelled strongly of varnished pine. It was a large house, not fancy, but clean and ordered. Glass oil lamps hung from the ceiling along a central hallway. Jack felt envious, as he glanced into the students 'rooms. They were comfortable quarters, furnished alike with desks, chairs, and bookshelves. The beds had red wool blankets neatly creased at the top with crisp, white sheets and pillows.

The shiny wood floor was slippery on Jack's bare feet, which squeaked as he walked down the hall. Redvere went into a room and fetched a pair of boots under the bed. "These don't fit me anymore but they should suit you."

"Yer giving them to me?" Jack had never worn good boots.

"These too, if you'll take them." Redvere removed a bundle of clothes from a cedar chest. The breeches did not have any patches and the gray wool vest smelled clean, same as the white linen shirt. "Get dressed."

Decked out in the new duds, Jack met Redvere in the hall. The boots were knee-high and snug but not too tight. "These ain't bad." He stamped his feet, testing their strength.

"Calf's leather," said Redvere. "Sturdy as they come. The soles have honeycomb polymer at the heel. C'mon, let's get some grub."

With the coin purse tucked into the lining of his new vest, Jack trailed the student to a brick kitchen. There was a kettle over the fire grate bubbling with oat porridge. Redvere poured two bowls and gave Jack a wooden spoon. At a long pine table, he scooted out a bench.

"I'm curious how you got over the Orchard wall?"

Jack plopped down and ate greedily.

"What you did was worthy of top marks," continued Redvere. "Most students never figure the wall out."

"It weren't so hard," said Jack.

"Well, it got Allwise's attention. And Humfrey's."

"About him, er, 'Baldy'. Does he learn here too?"

"Humfrey? Not as much as we learn from him." Redvere slid a basket of apricots over. "He grew these."

Jack stuffed several into his mouth.

"Sweet, aren't they?" said Redvere. "Humfrey's an artist in the garden. A maestro, you might say."

"A what?"

"*A maestro.* You know, *music?*"

Jack shrugged. "I like songs."

"I figured as much." Redvere reached over an empty egg crate and produced Jack's little wooden harp. "Humfrey found this outside the wall where you climbed over. You don't strike me as much of a wandering minstrel, though."

"Jits, naw! I can't get rid of that strummer. Tried to sell it but no takers. Reckon it's a Fae harp."

"That's not the craftsmanship of the Fae, I can assure you. It's rumored their instruments are truly remarkable. Though, personally, I've never seen or heard any."

"I might've heard them. Don't really know." Jack felt the need to fib a bit. "Didn't make me all 'oohy 'or anything."

Redvere smirked, strumming the little harp. "Fae gals drive menfolk mad, they say. Womenfolk sure get jealous of them but I wouldn't mind stumbling across a faerie bower on a midsummer night, know what I mean?"

Jack had once spied a covey of faeries bathing in a forest stream. He knew exactly what Redvere meant but felt too red-faced to say so.

"These strings are a bit loose, but playable, I think," said Redvere. "Do you mind?"

Jack shrugged. "I don't play."

Redvere cocked his head and played. He actually made decent music and had a pleasant enough voice as he sang:

"Where are roses for my Rose,
Rarest of the rare,
I long to lay them by her side,
And soothe my Beauty fair.

Only thorns for my Sweet Rose,
No blushing petals pink or white.
On a bed of briars, red as blood,
Her years slip by, a long, long night."

Around her bed the Forest grows,
Her truth it guards and keeps,
The Silent One has promised hope,
And still the Beauty sleeps."

Finished, he put the harp aside.

"Nice poem." Jack, spit out an apricot seed. "That was about the Sleeping Beauty, right?"

"Do you pray to her?" said Redvere.

"Naw."

"Or to the Eight Great Spirits?"

Jack shook his head.

"But surely, you know about them. The Silent One? Earth, Fire, Light, Darkness, Wind, Water. The Green Mother?"

"Just the Green Ma. The rest kind of run together."

"The Mother of Everything. A good one to know. She's around us all the time, like nature. All of the spirits are, except the Silent One. He exists within yourself and comes when you need to see what's there."

"Fool-talk," said Jack. "That's what yeh do here? Learn about ghosts?"

"No." laughed Redvere. "Master Allwise loathes the Great Ones. In fact, it's all superstition to him. Under this roof, we study 'practical truths 'only."

"Then how'd an airy fellow like yeh come here?"

"I want to be a ranger and a scholar. Allwise, being a friend of my family, offered me a spot at the school. So, I accepted."

The sadness about Redvere grew. It seemed there was more to his story than he was letting on. "Of course, there was a disagreement with my father over it. We're from the capitol of the Horse Province, in Colterton. My father is Chancellor and I was to take his place.

Only, that's not for me." He pushed his bowl aside, nodding for Jack to finish what he had not eaten.

Jack wasted no time digging in to the rest of the porridge. "So now yer all learned, shiny, and happy?"

"It's been good here." Redvere grinned. "But my lessons are ending. I join Ardus Camlann and his Champions in less than a fortnight."

Jack put down his spoon and looked up in awe. "Really? "
"You know of them?" said Redvere.

"Sure, don't everybody? The Champions are the best of all the rangers. They ride on big horses and go around saving folks. Ardus Camlann is their leader."

"He is. He and his horsemen police the Great Forest and keep it safe from criminals. There's a search on now for the missing girls. Some say it was a dragon."

"Rangers hunt dragons?"

"When they present a danger. Lately, the real concern is ogre clans. Their attacks near the Red Ridge Mountains are growing more frequent. The rangers are helping to raise an army to defend against them."

"So, yer gonna be a ranger?"

"I am. Just like Ardus. He went to this very school. Did you know that?"

Jack did not.

Redvere seemed to brim with admiration. "He came here from the Mist Hills when he was young. He still returns to teach us from time to time. Ardus shares Allwise's dream to unite the

Forestland. So do I. The races must stand together. Men, dwarves, and elves. If not, the ogre army will crush us."

"Elves!" barked Jack. "Y'know, Redvere, yer mighty highfalutin' in this comfy kitchen but the real woods would knock yeh on yer butt."

"You're angry. Why? Do you think you'd make a better ranger?"

"Yeah, cause I know elves ain't decent. They're dirty runts that sling muck at yeh and then run off to hide in the trees."

"Oh, don't hate the elf tribes. That's exactly the attitude we want to change." "Shows what yeh know, schoolboy." Jack shoved the empty eating bowls away.

Redvere cleared them. "Well, I was handpicked by Allwise. I know what I've learned. I can speak five tongues, I'm a crack-shot with a longbow, and I compose music. Plus, I'm darn good with horses. What do you know?"

Jack replied with a loud belch.

"Good answer," said Redvere, opening the kitchen door. "Allwise is waiting. I'll let the first-year kids do our dishes."

Outside, the morning sun added color to the grounds. Orchard students crowded the yard carrying books, garden tools, and (more exciting) crossbows and swords.

Jack followed Redvere as the classes were held outdoors. A group in an exercise field practiced swordplay. The instructor called out, "One! Two!" The students 'movements were methodical. Back and forth, *CLANK!* Over and under, *CLANK!*

"Yeh *all* studying to be rangers?" said Jack.

Redvere just smirked.

Another group of boys were climbing tall oaks, using green ropes knotted to three-pronged arrows like the one Jack had found in the stolen satchel.

"What're them weird arrows called?"

"Grappling hooks," said Redvere.

A burly young climbing instructor, clapped and shouted at the boys, "Get up that tree, young rangers, move it!"

The students fired their crossbows and sent the anchors over a tree branch, slinging the weapons over-the-shoulder and climbing the lines.

"Master Cai is our most experienced combat instructor," said Redvere.

A pair of women in white aprons shook out fresh laundered sheets and hung them on a clothesline. "Good morning, Missus Linnie. God morning, Gert." waved Redvere.

They both smiled back.

Jack saw no other women. "Girls don't study here?"

"There have been exceptions but it's basically a boys school."

"Smart," said Jack, thinking of Ella. "Girls talk too much."

"And who ever knows what to say back, right?" grinned Redvere.

Humfrey was in a garden by himself, digging around a bed of yellow peppers. "Awbunk-bunk-bunk," he said, smiling and waving at Jack.

Jack continued following Redvere through different groves where fruit pickers had setup ladders and baskets. The two boys arrived at a house made entirely of paned glass.

"Here's the greenhouse," said Redvere. He rolled open a large sliding glass door. As Jack crossed the threshold, the heat nearly bowled him over.

"Phew. Hot."

"It's meant to be," said Redvere, rolling the door shut. "Come on, Allwise is waiting."

The greenhouse was a small forest unto itself. They walked between planter boxes of strange trees and plants, which were lined in precise rows. Some had tall, spiny trunks that stretched high to the rafters. Others were short and swollen, with prickly limbs that hung over the narrow walkways. Shrill *a-cheep-a-choos* twittered from birds not sprung from local nests. Glass aquariums held colorful fish and Jack wished he could read the handwritten labels on the sides.

Allwise stood at a trellis of thick green vines. He seemed pleased by Jack's appearance. "I barely detected you. A bathed thief is harder to notice than one who smells," he said with a nod.

"Where's Ma's stuff?" said Jack. The spice and mugginess stung his nostrils and the heat was making him woozy.

"This here, a plant of my own cultivation." Allwise drew a vine from the trellis and hacked it apart with a white knife. "*Cambria Boonis*," he pronounced. "Changing Beans."

The severed vine curled around his wrist. He plucked a pod and squeezed out a handful of gooey, black beans.

"These will grow quickly with a little moisture," Allwise said, showing the seeds. "Plant them, and in a couple of weeks they will bear fruit. Your mother should eat the beans with each meal. Raw is best but she may also cook them."

"Ma ain't gonna be impressed," said Jack. "Thanks for nothing."

"Trust me, they will do her wonders," said Allwise. "Incidentally, a lad of your talents might make use of the vines these beans grow on. They are unbreakable. Only a blade of bone, such as I have here, can cut them." He sliced the vine easily with the white knife. "I think we can spare one. Don't you, Redvere?"

"I know just the knife," said the apprentice, hurrying off. "I'll get it."

Jack reached for the beans but Allwise withdrew them. "Not so fast," said the old man, wrapping the pods with a cloth and stuffing them in his pocket. "Let's go outside, out of the heat. We still have a detail or two to discuss."

Allwise heaved the sliding glass door aside and Jack stumbled out, colliding with him as he pushed into the cool, fresh air.

"Are you ill?" said Allwise.

Sweat streamed down Jack's face. "It was too hot in there," he said.

Perdur approached with Jack's crossbow. "Recognize this?" he said, proudly popping the bow open. "It's restrung and new-polished. I brought life into the old girl by recalibrating the sights. I tried her out, hope you don't mind? She shoots better than ever."

Jack ran his fingers over the bow. "Trigger ain't stuck?"

Perdur grinned, "Not if you release the safety." He pointed to a switch near the trigger. "That's a weapon worthy of the best hunter." The student also handed him a small leather quiver, with six black arrows in it. "Can't hunt without good darts. I carved half a dozen for you."

Such generosity was overwhelming.

"What's the matter, Thief?" said Allwise, as if he had a card up his sleeve. "Your reward is well-deserved, is it not?"

A shadow stretched across the grass. It was Farmer MacDonald. He approached with a stiff gait and stern look under his hat. "I believe you forgot to give me something, young'un," he said, flatly.

Jack's heart pounded beneath the stolen coin purse in his vest.

Allwise spoke up. "You claim to be honest, Thief, or is that only when it's convenient for you?"

"Well?" demanded the farmer.

With a huff, Jack reached inside his vest for the coin pouch, handing it over.

"Bout time," said MacDonald, shaking the purse.

"I'm sure it's all there," said Allwise. "Sometimes my tests fail. I appreciate your cooperation in this matter, Dunkan. You know what young boys are like with all the sons you've raised."

MacDonald gave a sharp nod, plucking a long blade of grass to chew on. "Boys is trouble."

"That stupid cow were a test?" snapped Jack.

"You are in no position to complain," said Allwise. "If you still want the beans."

"Bunk to yeh and yer beans!" said Jack. He dodged past them shouting. "I want nothing from yeh, yeh old snake! Devils cheat! Yeh didn't learn me nothing!"

Redvere returned with a bone knife tucked in his belt and Jack plowed through him, storming towards the gate.

"Wait!" said Redvere. "What's the matter?"

Jack spun away, his eyes teary and stinging, but he ran on and never looked back.

"What could set him off like that?" said Redvere to Allwise. "I thought he might stay. Why did he barge off without taking this?" He patted himself, looking frantically down at his belt. "The bone knife. It's gone! The kid lifted it right off me and I didn't notice."

"How about that?" said Allwise, searching his own pockets. "The beans are missing too."

"He picked your pockets?" said Redvere.

Allwise retraced his steps back to the greenhouse door, Redvere helping him search. "They're not here," said the old man.

"Sir," said Redvere, "How did he do it so easily?"

"When he bumped me here at the door," the teacher grinned. "That is talent. Shame he has such a temper."

Farmer MacDonald scratched his nose. "Boys is trouble."

* * * *

"Now wait a dang second!" Jack said to the Silent One, snapping out of his past. His awareness of being on the cold mountain ledge returned. The ache of his bruised insides did not help his mood.

"I just saw what Redvere said to Allwise but that was after I ran away. How come I remember that? I weren't even there? Are yeh trying to trick me, Spirit?"

Warmth returned as the Silent One spoke. *"The whole past is known to you, Jack, whether you were there or not. Where your life has touched others, it is all now part of your story."*

"So, you mean that's true for things concerning Ella too?

"And your mother. Did she like Allwise's reward?"

"Naw. Guess yeh don't know Ma so good."

Chapter **7**

BEANS

" Beans!" cried Ma. "I ask for gold fruits and yeh bring back beans?"

Jack stood before his mother in the Thin Creek hovel wearing the new clothes and boots, with a polished crossbow hanging from his belt and a full quiver of arrows slung round his back.

"The other fruits weren't good for yeh, Ma. The old geezer said so." He unwrapped Allwise's bean pods and put them in her trembling hands. "The wizard said to eat 'em, and yeh'll feel rosy again."

~ 74 ~

"Yeh ungrateful kid! I gave up such lofty things to be yer ma."

"Yeh were a milkmaid," reminded Jack. "Yeh still could be if yeh git out and tried."

"Sweet Green Lady! How yeh backtalk me and look what yeh brought. A handful of beans." Ma threw the pods out the window and collapsed on her hammock like a sack of yams. "Yeh show up looking like a young prince, with new clothes and boots. My boy, all yeh did was look out for yerself."

Jack left the coins from Tinner on the cold stove, wrapped in the blue hanky and sidled out of the hut. "Be back then in a few days," he said, sulking. That is the way it always worked.

He set off for his secret hideaway, which was in a hard-to-reach cave deep in the woods.

"Allwise turned me out for a fool," said Jack, griping as he made his way up Thin Creek. "Cow-dung sniffing, bean gardner! He prob'ly told Big Bill what I done so now I can't go to Rivercross neither. Ain't going home. Maybe never. Gotta hole up like an outlaw."

The slow roll of thunder brought down a summer rain shower, siding with Jack's lousy mood. He veered through a fern field and moved to a large ash by a rocky bluff. Boulders that were too big to climb over were wedged behind the tree but Jack crawled between them and found his little cave. It was cramped and dark but at least it was dry. He lay back, exhausted.

"Allwise," he said. "Ol Goatbeard. He weren't gonna let me into his school no-how. Nobody helps me. That's why I took the farmer's money. Allwise weren't gonna learn me to ride no horse neither. Don't matter. I'll be my own ranger. Got a crossbow and arrows, don't I? Don't need a stupid school for that."

Jack watched and listened to the rain as it fell on the ferns outside. He could not sleep.

As he gazed out from the safe hideaway of his little cave, his mind wandered back to Redvere mentioning the spirits in the Orchard kitchen. It was not something Jack thought about much but as he considered things now, a strange scent wafted into the cave. Jack sniffed the air. "Whiff-o-spice smoke," he said. "Ain't nobody could light a fire in this downpour. Ain't a fire in here neither. What is this?"

A strange sensation tingled in his ears.

"Hello Jack," said a voice in the dark.

Now, Jack did not believe in ghosts but the hair on his neck straightened. He looked around. Nobody was in the cave with him.

Against the back wall was a pine box but he had placed it there himself. It once belonged to the Rivercross undertaker, who left his work shed unguarded at night. Jack had dragged the empty box up Thin Creek and stashed it here.

"Hello?" he said to the box.

Just to be sure there was no elf hiding inside, he flipped the wood latches and opened the lid.

"Nobody," muttered Jack, relieved. "But what did Redvere say in the school kitchen, when he talked of a spirit that comes when yeh need to see inside yerself?" He was straining to remember. "The Silent One. That was its name."

As he said it, the scent of spice-smoke grew stronger in the cave. Jack did not like this. Waving his hands, he said, "Jits! I can't stop my thinking. High time for an adventure."

From the pine box, he donned an old leather coat that had belonged to his pa, Jodd Spriggins. It was the only keepsake left behind by the good-for-nothing. Still too big and fusty smelling, it was Jack's only coat, so he filled the pockets. He added a flint stone and some rolled twine, a handful of fishing hooks, a hunter's flask for water, and a tiny bottle of lamp oil. All were things he had swiped from the Rivercross market square.

"Going real far this time. Somewhere nobody knows me."

Next, he dodged out into the wet and kneeled beside the creek, filling his flask with fresh water before he set off.

"North," Jack decided. "See where them far stretches of forest end."

Tired as he was, Jack was glad to be trudging through the rain, putting the past behind and pushing forward into the misty woods. Much of the day went by, one boot in front of the other, until finally his legs would not carry him further. The drizzle let up, so Jack stopped amid a stand of giant cedars. Thick ivy hung down from the trunks in long, dangly vines. Scattered sunbeams spotted the ground in streaks. "I give," he said, with a yawn. "Gotta sleep here."

He collapsed on a knoll of soft moss with Redvere's song still running through his head:

"Around her bed the Forest grows,

Her truth it guards and keeps,

The Silent One has promised hope,

And still the Beauty sleeps."

Jack was snoring so loudly he woke himself up. He also forgot where he was until he recognized the cedars and discovered he had a mouthful of gnats.

"Yuck!" he exclaimed, as he sat up coughing. He swigged water from his canteen and spit them out. Then he heard chirpy giggles in the trees.

TWING! Came a sound, zipping by Jack's ear, accompanied by a sharp tug on his arm. His shirtsleeve was pinned to the ground by a small, sharpened twig. "Elf twig!" He tried to yank free but a mud ball hit him in the face with a sludgy *THWACK!*

The air echoed with peals of elfin chatter.

"Yeh rotten elves!" shouted Jack.

Several copper-haired imps were skittering through the treetops, none bigger than a human child. Their nimble, tanned bodies were naked except for raggedy loincloths and feather collars. Full of wicked mischief, they aimed crude bows and flails at body parts Jack did not want fired at.

"Git out of here, yeh dirty runts!" he hollered.

The tiniest of the pack, a very bold elf, swung down from the high branches on a vine and squealed an uncanny imitation of Jack, squinting his eyes and getting the cracks in his chirpy voice right: "*Git out of here, yeh dirty runts!*" he said, aping to his chums by beating his chest.

The other elves exploded with guffaws. "Tylo! Tylo!" they cheered.

Mud-spattered and furious, Jack tore his sleeve free and pitched stones at them.

The tiny mimic, Tylo, scrambled to the treetops. He and his mates flung more mud balls, one of which struck Jack between the legs. "Ahh!" he grunted, doubling over. Remembering the crossbow,

Jack crammed one of the new arrows into the catch, yanking back the string until *CLICK!* He shouldered the bow, and fired.

His aim was awful. The elves howled with glee and dove from tree to tree, swinging off.

"Next time I'll shoot yeh dead!" swore Jack. "That's what I'll do. I'll be the best archer in the woods. Then it'll be my turn to laugh, when y'all be twitching against a tree, yeh blarn elves."

A tree stump stood nearby, about three feet high. "Elf-size!" Jack figured with a vengeful grin.

He loaded the crossbow again and lined up his sights. *FWISH!* The arrow missed. "Jits." He steadied his focus and fired another. *FLINK!* This arrow glanced off the side." Getting closer." The third arrow pierced the wood with a satisfying *THUD!*

"Yeehaw!" shouted Jack. "That's one dead elf." He retrieved the darts and continued practicing.

Rain showers fell throughout the day. Gales whipped the ferns but nothing swayed Jack from improving his shots. He learned to account for the wind and adjusted his aim. Nothing broke his concentration.

* * * *

"Minutes turned into hours, hours became days," said the Silent One, recalling Jack to the cold mountain ledge.

"I made the woods my classroom, just like always."

"What did you learn?"

"I'm a crack shot."

"You shot deer and rabbits."

"Lickity split, never ate better. No Allwise, no tricks, just me – Jack Spriggins. Turned into a ranger-o-the-woods, all on my own with nobody else around."

"Do you really believe you were all alone?"

"Reckon it was yer voice I heard in the cave, weren't it? Yeh said my name, sitting there in the dark."

"You knew me by what Redvere had shared."

"Yer the Silent One."

"But you thought of Ella as well?"

"Bunk. Nothing gets by yeh, does it, Spirit? Reckon I always think about her. Maybe yeh might show me what Ella was doing then. If that's how it works?"

"She was learning lessons of her own but they also had to do with you."

Chapter 8

THREADS

Ella sat with her chin propped on her hands, leaning on the third story windowsill of her family home. "I wish I knew if Jack got inside the Orchard." She searched the skies, hoping the wren would pass by with the news. "Nothing," she sighed. "An entire day has gone by."

Whispering Vine, where Ella Vintner lived, was a home unlike any other near Rivercross. The house was built like a grand chateau of the Coastlands where her parents were born. It stood three stories high, framed by stone turrets with wisteria spilling from the eaves in fragrant blue clusters. Plantation shutters framed the windows beneath red awnings.

"The rain stopped, so why hasn't the wren returned? Poor Jack. I wish I could have stayed with him. He doesn't realize how useful I can be."

Swallows returned to their nests, which were plastered against the eves. They twittered hello but carried no news. Ella felt an urge to tiptoe off into the shaded wonders of the woods that beckoned just beyond the vineyard fence. "Life under a ceiling of branches where time doesn't mean a thing and new adventures come as quickly as your next breath. That's where I wish I was."

Papa's foreman drove a wagon up the estate's carriage road, loaded with mercantile from Rivercross. The vineyard workers were finished for the day, heading home to small cottages scattered over the estate where they dwelled. From daybreak to day's end, they tended the grapes and crushed the harvest into a wine that was praised across the Forestland. The vintage was said to be the favorite of the Grand Count of Havensbend, who had once toured the cellars and dined as a guest with the Vintners.

A familiar chirp came from the sky and a wren landed on the sill.

"It's you!" Ella said. "Did you help Jack?"

The chittering bird was angry.

"Over the wall without a word?" Ella tried to reason. "Well, don't be upset he didn't say 'thank you'. I don't think anyone ever says it to him."

Mama came into the room with a sewing basket. "I'll thank you, daughter-mine, to get back to your studies, please." She walked slowly to a tall, comfy chair, where she resumed stitching a new hood for Ella's cape. "I'm sure you'll learn just as much from your history book as you will from that wren."

Ella smiled at the gentle scolding. Her mother was a graceful woman; always calm, with soft brown eyes. Lately, faint dark circles had appeared under them.

"Oh, Mama," Ella pleaded, trying not to stare, "I know I'm not being good but I was curious to see if my friend got in to visit Allwise."

"Is this the same boy your father went on about?"

"Yes. I'd say his name was *Jack* but Papa warned I'm never to mention it again. Oh! I just did. How can I have a friend and not speak his name?"

Mama put her sewing aside. "You can to me." She drew Ella close and began to stroke her hair.

"It's funny, Mama. Just last winter your hair was as thick and curly as mine, but—" she stopped.

"Now, it's not," Mama finished the thought. "I know."

"Is my cape ready?" Ella said quickly, fidgeting back to the window seat.

"Almost. The new hood should fit perfectly."

"My head hasn't gotten any bigger, has it?"

"It might if you read a little more of your history."

Ella rested her chin on the book. "The Great Forest is just outside bursting with history."

"Dear one, your father is right when he says the woods are no place to play alone."

"I'm never really alone, you know." Ella pet the wren with her fingers.

"It's not safe." Her mother pushed the needle into a pincushion and held up the red cape. "Let's see how this looks."

Ella put it on and flipped the hood over her head. "Well, what do you think?" she said to the wren.

The bird cocked its head, trilled, and then flew off.

Ella burst into giggles. "She told me I looked like a backwards robin."

"She's right," smiled Mama. "Now – ahem – back to your studies."

"I don't think Jack has ever opened a book." Ella plopped down on her seat. "I could teach him to read but I'd have to do it in secret. Why is Papa so hard-hearted? He never has a nice thing to say about Jack, the Orchard folk, or Old Gran in the Woods."

"Well, your father has a lot of concerns, Ella, and sometimes forgets his manners. We can forgive him that, can't we? And he has nothing against Hepkatee, the Crone, other than where she lives."

Ella sighed. "Deep, deep in the woods, I know."

"Hepkatee helped bring you into the world, remember. Your Papa was frantic when my time came. It was he who went and brought her here."

"Is she really a witch?"

"She certainly performed a miracle for us. You weren't all that keen on being born. The doctor in Rivercross was away at the time. If not for the Crone, we might not be talking to each other."

Ella closed her book. "That's why I like it better to call her 'Old Gran'. Tell me the story again."

"Alright." Mama set her sewing basket aside. "Let's see, as soon as you arrived, Hepkatee bathed you in my china basin and set you in your new cradle. A pair of songbirds flew to the window, just like that wren did. The Crone seemed very surprised. She made a circling gesture with her hand over you and the birds went on chittering. It was all very mystical."

"Then what did she say?" asked Ella, relishing every detail, which she knew by heart.

Mama lowered her voice, trying to imitate the Crone's rasp. "'Your daughter be favored by the Green Mother. She shares kinship with the natural creatures of this world.'"

"That's not how Granny sounds," Ella covered her mouth trying to hold in a new burst of giggling.

"Well, it's the best you're getting from me," chuckled Mama, who cleared her throat and then was overtaken by a coughing fit.

Ella patted her back, comforting her, and then closed the window to keep out the draft. "Old Gran knows about medicines and ways to make people feel better."

"She does." Mama dabbed her mouth with a lace handkerchief. "Come here."

They cuddled up together in the big chair. "I worry about you, Mama. Why doesn't Papa send for her now?"

"Because the Crone is not a doctor."

"*The Crone* – oh, it's dreadful to call her that – sometimes I see her gathering mushrooms and flower buds. She doesn't seem mean, like people say."

"People often talk foolishly when they know very little about others, sweetie."

"They really do." said Ella. "So, if I were to go to her cottage, she'd be glad to see me."

Mama gave her a look of chagrin. "Haven't you been listening at all?"

"Oh, Mama, before you say *no*, Old Gran might have a special tonic to make you feel better. If Papa won't go to her, I'd be perfectly safe. The animals will protect me."

"Not the wolves."

"Especially the wolves," Ella brightened. "Why, the man in the village said they liked me most of all."

Her mother raised a wary brow. "What man?"

"Mister Fen, the street performer, who has a wolf. Except, I think Jack scared them away."

"Good for Jack. Strange birds you can talk to. Strange men are another story. I'll thank Jack myself, if I ever meet him."

"Oh, I wish you would." Ella jumped to her feet. "Jack could use kindness from someone besides me. Say, he might know Old Gran. Maybe he'll take me to her cottage. Please, Mama? I'll go find him."

"Not tonight, my darling, and not by yourself." Mama rose stiffly from her chair. She pushed back Ella's red hood. "As for my little aches and pains, I'll be fine. Your father is bringing a new physician from Arborvale. He'll know just what to do. So, concentrate on your studies and be a happy girl. Now, I'll go see if Nessie needs help in the kitchen."

"Not alone, Mama. I'll help too."

They left the room arm in arm. Ella held on and kept her mother steady going down the stairs.

* * * *

Jack felt a fresh pang, not from his ribs but his heart. "Why're yeh haunting me, Spirit?"

"I see what you see. Feel what you feel."

"Well, seeing Ella and her ma like that made me think. All the silly things she says, being the chatterbox, it's Ella's way of being brave, ain't it? Braver than I've ever had to be."

"Brave enough to be your friend."

"Just imagine her worrying about me so much."

"She isn't the only one."

"Chee. Ma don't count. She was born to worry bout me."

"I meant Hepkatee, the crone of the woods."

"That musty ol witch?" said Jack." Naw. I ain't got anything to do with her."

"That's where you're wrong. She is aware of you, Jack, and as much a part of your tale as Ella or Redvere. Watch and learn."

A high mountain cloud passed before Jack's view, or perhaps it was another vision of the Silent One. Through the mist Jack began to make out the inside of a strange cottage more clearly than if dreaming.

Chapter **9**

CRONE

A pair of crooked, weather-beaten hands covered in age spots shook a small leather pouch and rattled its contents. With a thrust, out spilled eight smooth, flat stones into a circle of sand that was spread over the coarse wooden floor.

"Three-up, five-down," said a graveled voice with a trace of female to it.

Hepkatee, the Old Crone of the woods, squatted on her haunches to examine the throw more closely. She was ugly as a vulture; a hunched, gnarled figure draped in ratty green robes that reeked of smoke and herbs.

"Light the green candle, Ganzil, and burn the incense," said the crone. "There must be a veil of smoke for the Spirits to speak freely."

"Yes, Gran," said Ganzil, a fifteen-year-old witch-apprentice, who was minding a strident red cardinal in a wicker cage. She shut its door and crossed the room for the matches.

The Crone mumbled an incantation in *palagot*, the enchanter's tongue. She passed her palms over the runes.

The cottage was not creepy as one might expect. There were no spider webs and all eye of newt was kept in neat, glass jars. A patchwork quilt was draped over a rocking chair by the hearth.

"What do the runes say?" said Ganzil, who withdrew a cone of incense from a tinderbox on the mantel.

"Nothing without respect," snapped the Crone. "Hold yer tongue and mind yer eager ways."

The look of the crone's sand-blind eyes warned she could cause ills just as easily as cure them. Bubbling cauldrons hung on the fire grate, spicing the air with ginger and pepper. By the door a strung hourglass swiveled on a horseshoe frame. Ganzil watched the sands funnel down the pipette.

"The gingerbread don't need pulled from the brick oven yet," barked the Crone. "Don't tarry. Keep yer mind clear, stay present for the reading of the runes."

"How do you read them without eyesight?" said Ganzil, who lit the wick of the sacred candle.

"O, Ever-giving Mother," chanted the Crone over the runes, "Use me as a vessel to read yer will and carry out yer wishes."

She reached to the floor and discarded three stones that were already exposed. Then, with clawing fingers, she turned over the first mysterious chip. "Ah, from the Fire One," she said. "Cherry red. Speaks to me of a girl blessed by the spirits. Ella of the scarlet cape. Midwifed her birth eleven springs ago, I did."

Ganzil gave a jealous sniff. "Why does little Miss Ella have anything to do with the red stone?"

"Her fate be tied to a boy. An important hero."

"I don't see why a red mark means Ella's hood. It could mean my pet red cardinal."

"Hush. The Spirits speak to me through the stones, not yeh.

"Fine. So, why do we need a hero?" said Ganzil.

Hepkatee flipped another stone. It showed the black crescent moon. "The Spirit of Darkness be warning me about shadows."

"You see them again."

The Crone pulled a handful of bilberry reeds from a bundle off the wall and tossed it into one of the smaller cauldrons. She added a sprinkle of nettle powder. The cauldron hissed. Steam wafted into her face. Her white eyes never blinked.

"What does the black stone mean?"

"Demons, I see, gathering like a black cloud to cover the woods in shadow."

The room began to shake. It was only a slight tremor made by a herd of moose charging through the meadows, but the rattle of glass and clanking cauldrons aroused a sense of dread.

"Does it say who the demons are?" said Ganzil.

"Nay, their faces be cloaked," said the Crone. "I see red eyes. Bones of the dead." "Why do the runes conjure them?"

"Hush! I hear howls of a wolf pack, echoes in the dark, screams of young girls." Spellbound, the Crone clutched her head and issued this prophecy:

"A shadow prowls the girl of the scarlet cape,

the voice they share, of beasts, will lead astray,

when a stolen name lures in fanged shape

a thief, the dark, will snipe an arrow's way."

The Crone recovered with a long sigh. "One of the demons means to prey on our Red Riding Hood," she added.

"And murder her?"

"He'll devour her, if he can."

"You mean Miss Scarlet?"

"Get a featherbed ready, Ganzil. The dear girl will arrive here, sick with a fever. She'll need a place to sleep."

"Does the black stone say who the demon is?"

"I have protected yeh from him, child. Yer charms be just the kind that bring him out."

Ganzil leaned toward her own reflection on a glass jar. Her features were rare and lovely, more so than most girls ever possessed, with blue-green eyes and silken gold braids. "Is he the reason I must stay closed in, without so much as a hand mirror for comfort?"

"Beauty brings out beasts," said the Crone, thumbing a wart on her crooked nose. "That, and being too vain."

"So, what do the other stones say? Are we to save little Miss Scarlet?"

Hepkatee looked surprise as she overturned the third stone. "Tis the blank symbol of the Silent One. Tells me no. 'There be another chosen for that."

"Who? Captain Ardus Camlann? Will he be the rescuer? Or, Allwise of the Orchard?"

The Crone turned with a shriveling glare. "Never speak that name under this roof! There be nothing wise about that apple-picker. He denies Green Mother her due, scoffs at our ways. Yer my foundling, not his."

"Yes, ma'am." Ganzil shrank behind the cardinal's cage. "But you never answered the question."

"The fourth stone will tell." Hepkatee shook her head, reading the fourth rune stone again. "How be this? It is the stone of the Earth One, covered in cracks. He is the Spirit of all that is brave and is pointing me to a pair of yellow eyes. Ach! Can he mean that wretched boy who steals berry tarts from my oven and then hides by my woodpile?"

"I've seen him," said Ganzil. "He comes from that hut by Thin Creek and smells like a wet rat. He's the hero?"

"He be chosen, that's all," sighed the Crone. "Question the Great Ones and yeh'll not get answers again." She scooped up the stones and waddled over to the hourglass. "The Sight be pulling away. Leaves my bones aching."

"But what about the last stone, Gran?"

"Three curved lines. Symbol of the Wind One."

"What did She say?"

"Far-off hokum about the boy and giants. Bah. Those degenerate fools left the woods a hundred star-passes ago. They will not help."

~ 92 ~

"I don't see why we would need the help of giants unless – the black cloud means war?"

Hepkatee groaned as a vision of power forced her to speak:

"A snake devours the great gate, the stone, and hoof;
war, people, possessions, to cinders lost;
striking hard, hope will fail, the trees will burn,
blue-tattooed raiders, when curved blades return!"

"It's ogres then," said Ganzil.

"They will come," interpreted Hepkatee. Another distant rumble shook the bottles on the mantel. She fumbled for one and took a sip of the tonic.

"You're drained." Ganzil slyly took the runes out of the old Crone's palm. "Rest. I'll clear out the smoke and sweep the sand."

"Don't forget the gingerbread, child," the Crone said, "This batch be for the Arborvale orphans."

"I'll see it gets done."

Ganzil slipped outdoors with a shrewd smirk, pocketing the stones.

Aside from Ganzil's red cardinal, the Crone kept a covey of messenger finches and a black raven. The large black bird hobbled about the rafters, and often served as the Crone's eyes.

"Tsk," said the Crone. "Over-reaching lassie, wants to cast them herself soon as I fall asleep but her throws will all be empty. I brought her to my cottage too soon. Back she'll go to Arborvale til she's humbled."

Alone, the Crone watched the flames lick at the cauldrons. She exhaled a long, rasping breath. The glow in the room dimmed, the cottage grew dark, woeful. The cauldrons spat. Then came another vision of power:

> *"Misfits to the guardian sort, chosen, not anointed;*
>
> *a girl in the red hood, a boy with yellow eyes,*
>
> *he wiser seeks the demon bones, in hollow wooded belly*
>
> *when a wild goose is slain in vain."*

The Crone's attention returned to the cottage. "Sersi, my faithful friend, where be you?"

From the rafters the crow cawed.

"The girl needs our help. Find her." Obediently, the bird flew out the window.

"Oh, Spirits, I grow old, withered," said Hepkatee. "You need strong warriors for your battles. Yet, you send me mere babes in the woods. Guide them I will, if that be enough."

* * * *

Caught by a mountain gust, the scene in the cottage flickered and vanished like a blown candle. Jack hissed through his wind-chafed lips in disgust. "Sure, Spirit," he said to the Silent One. "That wicked hag seems real friendly. Like she couldn't figure whether to roast me in her gingerbread oven or hex me into a lizard and then feed me to her crow."

"She wants to believe in your courage."

"She wants to believe her big hero is someone else."

"Like a Champion ranger?"

Jack sighed. "Yeah, I knew the rangers would come up sooner or later."

"Just when you mastered your crossbow, they gave you a new reason to use it."

Chapter **10**

CHAMPIONS

After two weeks alone in the woods, Jack Spriggins emerged on a soggy trail in the Swamplands putting Thin Creek, Rivercross, and the Orchard long behind. He pitched the last of a roasted rabbit's thigh into the bog.

"No more thieving," he said, licking his fingers. "I'm a real hunter now, making my own way."

The only real holdup was a pang to check on Ma and make sure she was all right. "Them beans were a bad deal," he said, still sore at Allwise. "Phony wizard. Reckon Ma gathered 'em up by now. She's gotta eat."

The swamp air was clammy and hot. Mosquitos, gnats, and horse flies were so ornery that Jack's neck had grown sore from smacking them. "Oof! This bog is full-o-gunk," he groaned. "Figure I'm close to Big Pine Lake."

His next step went thigh deep into the mud. Several yards ahead, a gator stirred.

"What're yeh looking at, scaly-snout?" Jack said, wriggling to get unstuck.

There was a vile scent on the air.

"Phew, that's more than just bog stink."

A rumble shook the ground.

A flutter of ducks took flight from the sedge grass. Muskrats floundered, digging in beneath the reeds. Even the gator slipped into the marsh. A man's scream ripped through the woods. It was not a yowl of terror but a battle cry. Jack could not see through the tall grass but he made a break for the trees and shimmied up the nearest pine, his pulse throbbing in his temples.

Then he saw the dragon.

It was a monstrous lizard, twenty-five feet long and as thick as an oak. "Reeks fouler than rotten eggs and skunk," said Jack.

The reptile thrashed on four squat legs, flattening the swamp grass behind with its pointed tail. Its skin was coarse as slate with gray bumps. The eyes were jewel-like with black slit pupils. For a brief second, they fixed on Jack but the creature moved with alarming speed toward the lake.

Another bloodcurdling cry blared as a huntsman bounded from the woods. He was a fierce man in a leather vest and buckskin pants. He had wide shoulders and a broad chest but a thin, almost girlish, waist that gave way to legs so muscular they had to keep splayed to run.

"A Mist Hills ranger," muttered Jack. He had seen travelers from the north making trade at Rivercross who had the same rough look. "A dragon hunter."

The warrior swung a long, broad ax over his head and bellowed like a madman, revealing his dark furious eyes. One, two, three times around and he let the twibill go with a mighty heave. The ax whirled through the air and struck the monster at the neck only to glance off its scales.

With a low, horrifying hiss the dragon spun round and charged at the ranger.

The man bolted for the tree where Jack was perched. The ground rumbled as the creature closed in fast. "He's doomed," said Jack. Somehow, the ranger dove free of the snapping jaws. The dragon struck Jack's tree with tremendous force.

The blow was like a quake. It brought down several branches and a shower of pinecones, but Jack held on.

Below, the dragon upended itself. It whipped its tail violently, trying to turn back over. Another awful hiss exposed jagged teeth and a slimy blue tongue.

"Grist and bone of Father Ter!" cursed the wild man, in a heavy northern accent, "I'll rip the scales from yeh one by one!"

Madness drove the ranger to leap onto the beast armed with just a hand ax. His weapon was raised and poised to strike but the monster's tail lashed him to the ground. The dragon twisted to its feet. The mighty northerner got up and dove onto the dragon's back, hacking and hacking, but his ax would not pierce its rocklike skin.

The dragon arched its back.

"No yeh don't, yeh spiky wench," he shouted, diving away.

A dozen bony horns popped out along the monster's spine as the ranger leapt free. When he landed on the ground, the dragon's tail clubbed him like he was a rag doll tumbling across the glade.

"Umph," grunted the man, landing in a heap of grass. He got up with blood streaming down his face. "Try that again, little princess." Raw energy shook his voice. He clenched a knife between his teeth, ready for the next charge.

For once, Jack was watching someone he truly wanted to meet. "That's a fight for yeh," he muttered.

"Not by yourself, Gwachmai!" boomed a new voice. A tall ranger with wheat-colored hair ran across the glade. He held a steel musket. "We attack this fiend together." There was a natural authority to the way this one spoke.

The dragon rolled its lizard-eyes from one ranger to the other, wary of both.

"I was doing fine by myself," said Gwachmai.

"Together, brother," commanded the shooter. "You never wait."

"Well, it's about time yeh joined the fight," said Gwachmai.

The dragon rasped at them. The two men scrambled to avoid its lashing tail.

"I'll be a ranger someday too," said Jack, watching them from the tree.

"C'mon, ugliness," said Gwachmai to the dragon. "Gnaw me into mash if yeh can." The beast spun and clubbed him again. His axe pitched out of reach into the mud. Gwachmai now lay perilously close to its snapping jaws. "C'mon then! Let's see who's got the meaner bite, milady." He took up his knife.

The second ranger fired his musket. The gun's deafening crack made a spark but the musket ball glanced off the dragon's hide, which turned to face the shooter.

"Yeh'd better fire again, Arto," warned Gwachmai.

"Blasted weapon," cursed the leader, struggling with a powder horn strung at his side. Quickly fed up, he abandoned the musket and pitched it away. Reaching both arms behind his shoulders, a silvery scrape rang out as he unsheathed a pair of swords and uncrossed them over his head.

"Now that's a proper fight coming," said Gwachmai.

"On your feet, Gwach!" said the swordsman, clanging his weapons together. The dragon locked its attention on him.

Its lashing tail whipped round and he ducked, climbing swiftly onto the dragon's back. The swordsman's blades plunged but the dragon's impenetrable hide blocked the strokes. He too was bucked onto the grass.

Jack fumbled for an arrow but before he could fire, an archer sent a bright flare across the glade, which landed with a burst near the dragon. The beast shrank from the flame, hissing.

The archer entered the fray at the edge of the trees, armed with a longbow. Dressed in black, his moves were graceful, as if coaxing a stallion rather than a vicious reptile.

"Easy, shh, shhh," he cooed. "Easy, big fella."

Jack knew the archer's voice. It was Redvere, the Orchard apprentice.

~ 100 ~

"Excellent work, Redvere," said the leader. "Keep your distance, don't get closer."

Jack could not have been more surprised. "Pretty-boy said he was joining the Champs. That means the leader there is Ardus Camlann." (Jack had never been near anyone famous before.)

"What's next, Captain?" said Redvere.

"Keep it entranced," said Ardus, reaching under his cloak and unfurling a mesh. "I need only a moment."

The dragon remained spellbound by Redvere's flaming arrow as Ardus crept behind it with the grappling net.

"Captain, do not kill the creature," said Redvere, glancing at him.

"Don't turn away!" said Ardus, too late.

The dragon spat an orange glob of steaming gunk onto Redvere's face. The young knight dropped with a shriek, clawing at the thick slime.

As the angry dragon bolted beyond reach, Ardus hurled the net in vain.

"Oh, that worked real dandy," said Gwachmai. "Get the slather off the boy before it burns his pretty face."

"Mind the dragon," said Ardus, who was busy yanking Redvere out the way.

Gwachmai's feet were swept out beneath him by the dragon's tail, which hammered down on the grass as he rolled aside.

"My turn," exclaimed Jack, who wrapped his legs around the tree and fired. His bolt pierced the dragon in one eye. The beast let out a horrid rasp as it reared, shaking its head.

A splintering crack came from the woods and a large pine was sent crashing down on top of the dragon.

"What was that?" Jack wondered.

A warrior unlike the others charged in. His skin was dark as black walnut. The man's boots and breeches were made of spotted hides. The forward point of his spear was sharpened stone; the other end, a straight ivory tusk. The warrior had the grace and power of a wildcat and joined Gwachmai, badgering the pinned dragon.

"Take your time, Ootan," said Gwachmai. "Were yeh gathering flowers?"

"Do you ever stop talking?" said the black ranger, whose voice was very deep. He jabbed the stone point of his spear at the beast and Gwachmai swung his axe. The dragon threw the trunk aside with its tail and lurched onto its stumpy legs.

"Spit of the Wet Codger!" cursed Gwachmai. "We gotta pierce her in the belly. Only place soft enough for the kill."

"Must we kill it?" said Redvere.

"Yeh want more village gals to die?" said Gwachmai.

"We were sent to kill the dragon," said Ardus. "So do your duty."

The monster took off across the glade but Ootan rushed forward and blocked its path. The beast hissed at him.

"Good, Ootan," said Ardus. "We'll never catch her if she reaches the lake."

Jack readied an arrow, intended for the creature's other eye. However, the dragon tucked its head, turtle-like, behind hunched shoulders. The rest of its body and tail stiffened.

"What's she doing?" said Jack.

"Heed!" shouted Ootan. "The devil's gonna spin."

Like a tumbling log, the dragon hit the ground and barreled towards the Champions. Chunks of mud and grass whirled through the air, the crush of its weight mashing a level path in its wake.

Jack was grateful he was high in a tree. He saw no escape for the Champions, who were in danger of being squashed. Gwachmai reacted by sprinting at the rolling dragon. He sprang over it with a swing of his ax, narrowly missing the belly as it bowled by.

Ardus struggled to pull stricken Redvere out of the monster's path. "Ootan, throw your spear!" he shouted.

Ootan leapt and hurled the weapon high over the beast, its stone point landing in front of Ardus. The sharp, ivory tusk stuck out from the grass, pointing at the barreling dragon.

As the monster rolled over the spear point, it issued a gruesome roar, skidding onto its back with its pierced underside exposed.

"Now, taste my axe!" said Gwachmai, hacking into the soft belly. Purple blood and scaly flesh spilled into the clearing. Ootan jumped in and drove his spear deeper. The dragon gave out and collapsed on the grass.

With jitters of excitement, Jack wanted to hoot. "Better keep quiet and stay put," he decided.

"How are your eyes, Redvere?" said Ardus with relief.

"They sting," Redvere said. "But not as much as my pride."

"Yeh did just fine, boy," Gwachmai said, dropping his bloody twibill. "It weren't easy with only yer wits between yeh and that devil's jaws."

Redvere squinted. "You killed it?"

"A necessary death," said Ootan, pulling his spear from the carcass. "The beast's life for yours."

Ardus tapped one sword against the carcass and smiled. "Dragon's scales. Allwise knows how to fashion soldiers 'vests from it. We shall have better armor soon."

"And roasted dragon's meat for supper," said Gwachmai. "Ever eat dragon, pretty boy?"

"Can't say I have," said Redvere, turning away.

Ootan plucked Jack's arrow from the dragon's eye. "A curious dart. This is not an arrow from Redvere's bow."

"Who shot it?" Ardus said.

Ootan pointed to Jack, who was still up the tree.

"Climb down here, boy," said Ardus. "Let us see you."

Jack was cautious. He wanted to meet them but felt a bit afraid.

"The only one that would harm you lies dead," said Ardus, pointing at the dragon. "Thanks to your help. Why don't you come down and tell us your name?"

Jack shouldered his crossbow and slid down the trunk.

"Why, I know you," said Redvere. "You're the thie—"

Jack glowered at him. He knew the word 'thief 'had gotten stuck in the pretty-boy's throat.

"I mean, the kid who climbed over the Orchard Wall," Redvere finished.

"Is that true?" said Ardus, raising an impressed brow. "What's your name, son?"

"Jack Spriggins."

"I'm Ardus Camlann. We Champions are indebted to you." He held out his hand.

Jack felt awkward. He had never accepted a handshake.

"It's fine, Jack," said Redvere. "Shake his hand."

Ardus clasped his wrist with a firm grip. "You're a good shot with that crossbow. We would be honored if you would share our food and fire tonight."

"Reckon I'm obliged," Jack nodded.

Gwachmai burst out with laughter. "Jack the Dragon Slayer! And he done the deed with a crossbow, no blasted length of pipe, pellets, and gun powder." He kicked the musket that lay in the grass.

"Firearms need perfecting, yet," said Ardus, picking up the heavy gun. "But we will need them. They aren't going away." He looked towards the sky. Ravens already circled overhead. "Quickly, let's get to work on the remains."

The rangers, all except Redvere, unsheathed daggers and began to skin the carcass.

"We tracked the beast from the woods near Rivercross where another girl went missing," Redvere told Jack. "Its tracks led us out here. I expected we'd just capture it, not slaughter it."

"Yeh ain't proud to kill a dragon?" said Jack.

"I'm not sure it deserved to die."

Jack rolled his eyes. "Why don't yeh write it a poem or sing it a song?"

"He prob'ly will, Dragon Slayer," said Gwachmai, who tossed a hunk of skinned carcass aside. "There's no feeling sorry for a dragon. It be the killer of them missing girls."

An image of Likov Fen flashed in Jack's mind. He looked at the dead dragon and knew a mistake had been made. "Hold up a sec," he said. "Yeh say a girl was snatched from the village? Ain't ever seen a dragon near Rivercross."

"That's what I mean," said Redvere. "Varnagators sometimes stray near villages, like this one, but they've not been known to kill there."

"Oh, a *varn* is it, schoolboy?" said Gwachmai. "Did yeh hear that, Arto?"

"It's quite correct, brother," said Ardus. "*Varnagator* is this dragon's proper name."

"Just call a dragon *a dragon* and be done with it," said Gwachmai.

"A varn swallows everything, bones too," added Ardus. "No other creature could have snatched so many girls and left no trace."

"Now it's dead," said Gwachmai.

Again, Jack recalled Likov Fen, who had crooned morbidly before the moon a fortnight earlier. "This ain't no killer of girls," he said softly.

Ardus shrugged. "We had a fresh trail to follow from the last one who went missing, so we ran it down."

"Don't yeh Champs ride horses?" said Jack.

"We do, but Varns spook them too much," said Ardus.

"They also eat them," said Gwachmai, as he ripped the jawbone from the dragon's remains.

"We left the horses at Whispering Vine, the Vintner's estate," said Redvere. "It was in those woods that the girl went missing. We picked up the dragon's trail from there."

"But where is she?" said Jack.

"Mother Green!" said Gwachmai. "It's got bones in its belly." With a squishy yank he pulled out what looked like a ribcage.

"Not human," said Ootan. "Those are the bones of swine."

"Ha!" laughed Gwachmai. "That's just great. It had a pork dinner and didn't even invite us."

The hair on Jack's neck stood straight. "A vintner's one who makes wine, don't he?"

"That's right," said Ardus. "His eleven-year-old daughter went missing."

"She was a delightful child," added Redvere. "You may have seen her in the village. She always wore a bright red cloak and hood."

"Ella?" said Jack, queasy. He bent over and was sick.

Redvere patted his back. "It's alright," he said, "This slaughter makes me ill as well."

Chapter **11**

CAMPFIRE

" This bad news don't reckon," muttered Jack. Ella's disappearance was staggering but he kept busy with the work at hand.

The Champions butchered the dragon quickly. Ootan handled the skinning while Gwachmai broke down the body. Jack helped Ardus and Redvere pack the meat in deerskin wraps. Then, they lugged as much of the heavy hides as they could carry to camp.

"Ella ain't dead," said Jack at last. "I'd know deep down if it were true."

"I understand your hope," said Ardus, glancing back. "But the girl's tracks led into the woods."

"We picked up the dragon's tracks after we lost hers," said Ootan.

"But her red cape weren't in it's belly," said Jack. "That don't tell y'all enough?"

"We've searched for days, Jack," Ardus said. "I'm sorry, your little friend is gone. Now, the heavy task of telling her folks falls to me."

Just before nightfall, the men slung ropes over an oak branch and hoisted the hides several feet off the ground.

"This'll keep the wolves and bears off it," said Gwachmai.

A short distance away, they made camp. Once a pit had been dug and a fire struck, Redvere was placed in charge of roasting the dragon meat. He stacked rocks on each side of the pit and used his long arrows for skewers, then seasoned the meat with pepper and thyme from his satchel.

"Smell that delicious roast," said Gwachmai, rubbing his hands.

Jack shared the fire but kept badgering the pigheaded Champions. "Ella ain't dead," he said. "No matter how long she's been missing."

"You knew her, Jack," said Redvere. "That's hard news."

"When yeh been soldiering long as me, boy," said Gwachmai." Yeh learn to look death in her cold face and not blink. Ain't saying it's easy, yeh just get used to it is all."

Ardus was off by himself, wiping his blades with a piece of leather. Jack noticed his lips were moving, as if talking with an imaginary person. Each time that he murmured he tried a different gesture.

"What the spit's wrong with him?" said Jack.

"I don't envy Arto," said Gwachmai, between swigs from a goatskin flask. "He's got to break the sad news to her pa. I'd rather face a thousand dragons than tell folks their child is gone."

"Yeh mean, he's practicing for Ella's folks?" said Jack. "Only, no dragon ate her, I been telling yeh."

Gwachmai hung his head. "It's what dragons do, boy."

"All yeh found was pig bones," said Jack. "Y'all don't understand."

"That was a fresh kill," said Ootan. "The fire in a dragon's belly needs only hours to waste those bones."

"What fire?"

"He means the acid, Jack," said Redvere. "The strong stomach acid melts everything they eat, very quickly." The young ranger poked at the broiled meat. "It wasn't like I thought it would be, the dragon, I mean. I always pictured them more colorful, red or gold, with wings and magnificent fins."

Gwachmai snorted. "Yeh wanted a pretty monster, eh?"

"No, not at all," said Redvere. "I simply thought a dragon might be special."

"That's because yer a poet," said Gwachmai, sounding tipsy with wine. "Yeh'd like it if things had a good side yeh could sing songs about. Well, listen up, boy. Bad's bad. See it for what it is. Ain't no good being a Champion if yeh cannot face the bad."

Ardus joined them and squatted by the fire. "Too much wine, brother," he said. "It only stokes your temper."

Gwachmai downed another gulp.

"As for dragons, Redvere," Ardus continued, "There are many kinds." He lifted a skewer from the flame and blew on it for a taste. "I've never seen the ones you described, but that doesn't mean they don't exist. Remember to approach them all with caution, like our friend Jack did."

"I'll try, Captain," said Redvere.

Gwachmai leaned close to Jack; his breath reeked like a wine barrel. "Get Redvere," he said. "The singing poet who wants to be a ranger."

"We are lucky to have him," said Ardus. "Redvere's one of Allwise's finest archers and a good soldier."

"Ah! Ain't he the lucky one to have us?" slurred Gwachmai. "He ran away to become a ranger because he fell in love with his brother's bride."

"That's enough, Gwach," said Ardus.

Redvere skewered a fresh hunk of meat and thrust it over the fire, glaring at Gwachmai.

"Born a Celot, son of the chancellor," ranted Gwachmai. "Wealthiest breeders in the Horse Province. The whole works could've been his, but got his heart so broke he ran away. Sweet Shaina, don't it make yeh wanna cry?"

Jack watched Redvere across the fire. The archer's eyes were downcast and the sadness Jack had seen before now made sense. He admired Redvere's composure.

"If you're going to gossip," said Redvere. "At least tell the story right." He lifted the cooked skewer from the fire and shoved it towards Gwachmai. "I became a Champion to fight for the good of the Forestland. Same as you."

Gwachmai bit down and tore the meat off the skewer with his teeth. "I just did it for the fine food," he grinned with a sloppy mouthful.

"Count your fingers after you feed him," joked Ardus, slapping Redvere on the back. Then, he pulled a harmonica from his pack and tossed it over. "Redvere, play some music. Lighten the mood. The sad tidings of tomorrow can wait."

"But Ella ain't dead!" said Jack. "Can't just sit here. If she's lost, then she needs help. Or I bet that wolf man I seen in Rivercross done something bad, made off with her."

"Wolf man?" said Ootan.

"Fen. He's got a wolf for a pet, wears another as a coat. He even smells like wolf. I bet he snatched all them girls."

Ootan seconded, "The old hag spoke of this man."

"The Crone?" Ardus rolled his eyes. "She spoke of a man who becomes a wolf by the full moon. That old woman's batty, just like Allwise warned."

"Yeh cannot trust a witch, Ootan," said Gwachmai. "She be smoking herbs and eating frog's brains. Hocus pocus stuff. I'd just as soon cram her in that brick oven."

Ardus turned to Jack. "The man you described is an actor. Don't be fooled by his theatrics. The dragon was the culprit, son. The girl's tracks led us right to it."

"A dragon that just takes girls?" said Jack. "It don't figure."

Wolves began to howl out in the dark.

The captain pointed in their direction. "Hear that? We all know this wilderness. If the dragon did not get her, then something else did. No eleven-year-old girl could survive for ten days alone."

"This one could," said Jack.

"Maybe elves took her in," said Gwachmai.

"Careful, Gwachmai," said Redvere. "Jack Spriggins feels about elves the way you do about giants."

"Ach!" Gwachmai nearly choked on the wine. "Don't get me started on giants. Big, miserable snots." He turned to Jack. "Yeh ever met one?"

Jack pointed at Ootan. "Just him."

Gwachmai howled with laughter.

"I am not a giant," said Ootan, raising his eyebrows with amusement. "Just a man."

"He is from Zan," chuckled Ardus. "A land beyond the seas."

"Ootan ain't greedy like a giant, neither," said Gwachmai. "Giants keep holed up in the East Mountains – Broog's Range – hoarding their wealth in two big cities. They see the forest as dirt beneath their feet."

"Captain and Gwachmai already asked the giants for help," said Redvere, "To fight the ogres if there's an invasion."

"Giants turned us down flat," said Gwachmai.

"To have an alliance with giants again would be a boon to our cause," said Ardus.

"If they had seen the bloodshed at Hedgewall, they might change their minds," said Ootan.

"Where's Hedgewall?" said Jack.

"The northern fortress in the Red Ridge Mountains," said Redvere. "It's on the border gate of our Great Forest, where skirmishes with the ogres have become a regular occurrence."

"It would not make any difference, Ootan," said Ardus. "Giants have grown too comfortable in their mountain valley. The troubles of our world seem far below them, easy to ignore."

"Now, here be a question I ask myself daily." said Gwachmai. "Why are the best fighters in the land still sitting by this fire, not lending our blades at Hedgewall?"

"If the ogre threat escalates further, I'm sure General Steelhouse will call upon us," said Ardus.

"I'll tell yeh why," said Gwachmai. "Because Steelhouse is afraid yeh'd make a better general."

"Lay off the wine, Gwach," said Ardus. "You're talking too much."

Ootan and Redvere chuckled.

"Are ogres monsters?" said Jack.

"Nay," said Gwachmai. "They're men. Spiritless, savage murderers, trained with curved swords from their first steps to have no pity. At their wicked hands, not even babes and their mamas find mercy."

"That is true," agreed Ootan. "The ogres want only to conquer and dominate. The harsh sand of their desert home has wasted their people, bred them to live without hearts."

"So yeah, they're monsters," said Gwachmai. "They file their teeth to pointy fangs."

"Really?" said Redvere.

Ootan nodded. "It is common among their warriors."

Jack took the ogre brooch from his pocket and held it up to the others." I found this." The bronze and blue snake gleamed in the firelight.

"Where'd you get that?" said Redvere.

"Keepsake off some lost travelers," said Jack.

"May I see it?" said Redvere, taking it. "It bears the sign of *the Ogrelun*. The Desertland Serpent, the blue snake of the ogres. It's their god. Ogre warriors tattoo their bodies in honor of its power to devour the world."

Ardus looked away from the brooch as if it were an ugly wound. "In the Mist Hills, where Gwach and I come from, our people were ravaged by the ogres. They destroyed our family. Now, they are a threat again. I will never let that serpent devour the Great Forest if comes to war."

"Put it away, boy," said Gwachmai. "Lell's Curse be upon the giants, and any forest race who does not join our fight against them."

Redvere passed the brooch to Jack, who pocketed it.

"Only the giants have shunned us," said Ardus. "There is still hope for uniting the others."

"Oh?" challenged Gwachmai. "And exactly which forest race gives yeh hope, brother?"

"The elves are still our allies."

"Elves? They're the size of wee boys, with brains like squirrels, singing and prancing about the trees. A lot of good they'd do in a fight! And yeh can forget about dwarfs, the nasty-tempered dirt-diggers. Who can say when they last saw the light-o-the-sun?"

"Why not the Fae?" smiled Redvere.

"Oh sure, lover boy. Any man of red-blood knows what trouble faeries bring. Just ask, Arto," winked Gwachmai.

The captain's face appeared to blush then shifted his eyes to Jack. "My only gripe is with giants."

"Giant snobs," said Gwachmai. "Think they're the Chosen Ones. By the rays of Fair Shaina, giants say the Sleeping Beauty is *a giantess.*"

"All the forest races claim She's one of their own," said Redvere.

"Well, she ain't! She's our kind," said Gwachmai. "The Beauty's a woman, my kind of woman. A lovely princess with golden hair and silky skin, and the kinda eyes that when She opens them, yeh'll forget yer troubles and swear peace that day forever."

Ootan shook his head. "Such feverish devotion from you, my friend. Very interesting."

"Yeh don't believe in the Beauty where yeh come from, Ootan?" said Gwachmai.

"In Zan, my people know the lore of your sleeping princess," said the foreigner, "But it is a tale of your gods, not ours."

"A tale? Did yeh hear that?" Gwachmai teetered, waving his hands at the sky. "O Great Ones! Blessed Father Ter, Gentle Shaina, Quick Master Red Eyes, Dancing Mad Mariah – forgive and be merciful. If yeh strike him down, spare me."

Behind him, Ardus delivered a swift knock to Gwachmai's head. The drunken warrior's eyes crossed as he keeled over.

"Excuse my brother," said Ardus, lugging the unconscious man away from the fireside. "Wine brings out the zealot in him. He often forgets that disharmony among the forest races is what truly keeps the Beauty asleep."

"A good sleep can also bring peace," said Ootan.

"Fill your bellies, gents," said Ardus, who covered his snoring brother with a cloak. "Then get some rest. Tomorrow is a long journey back. Redvere, keep the first watch."

"Yes, Captain."

It was pointless to speak more of Ella, so Jack spread out his coat and watched the stars until he fell asleep. A feverish dream took over his thoughts:

Ella was skipping through the woods in her red cape. "Hello, Jack," she said, picking him a flower. Likov Fen stepped out from the trees, hairy and fanged, with razor claws bursting from his fingers. Jack took aim but his crossbow was empty. "Puny mongrel," laughed Fen. The killer sprang and tore Jack's vision, pulling blackness down over his eyes.

"Jack," said Redvere, giving him a shake. "Jack, you were having a nightmare."

Embarrassed, Jack shoved him away. The campfire had dimmed to orange embers. The white crescent moon shone through the trees. The others were still asleep.

"Yeh go on and sleep," said Jack. "I'll keep watch for yeh."

"No, I'm fine."

"Go on, Red, I ain't tired," said Jack. "I want to stay up a bit."

"Alright," said Redvere. "If you change your mind or sense any danger, give me a shake."

Jack waited until Redvere was asleep, then quietly gathered up his things. "Ella's out there. Fen's out there too. Gotta hunt to make. Going to find Ella and keep her safe. See yeh, Champs."

As the rangers slept, Jack stole out of camp.

Thin Creek was a long way off but Jack could get there if he kept running until morning, and he was driven by a hunch to protect Ella. "She's still alive." Just saying it gave him strength. He also had a good sense of her whereabouts.

"Little pest is always too close to trouble but never far from the Crone's cottage. Ella likes that ugly ol' witch."

He ran through the night, pausing only to fill his canteen while fording streams. The wetland swamps gave way to the cedar forest, then thicker woods as he drew closer to home.

"Get to the creek," he panted. "Run south. Fastest way in the dark." His breath was steady like his steps. "Smell, listen, look." These were words Jack used to keep alert.

Dropping to the ground, he drew a deep breath. The dark terrain smelled familiar. "Evergreen firs, blackberry, wild fennel. Getting close to the stream. It'll be morning soon." As he ran on, he knew what to listen for next. "Trickle-o-water," he sighed. "Upper Thin Creek!"

"Can't rest while Ella's alive." He saw her face, her red hood, even her smile. He wished to hear her pesky voice say, *"Hello, Jack!"*

"The Champs were wrong. I can prove it. Ain't gonna rest until I find Ella."

* * * *

"Yeh see?" said Jack to the Silent One. "Told them Champs what I knew, but they gave no help. They wouldn't listen."

"You followed your instincts."

"Can't say why, but I knew Ella needed help."

"The Crone spoke of her fate being tied to yours."

"I'm always fetching Ella outta trouble. Ain't letting Mister Wolf get his paws on her."

"You know a monster when you see one."

"Always have," Jack said. "If I'd known Ella was gonna be in danger, I'd have stayed closer, not journeyed so far. I'd follow her and keep her safe. Still dunno why she let that wolfman get near."

"Her lesson still had to be learned," said the Silent One. *"Let's follow her, see where she went together."*

Chapter 12

SCENTS

Shaina's Window was a glade in a peculiar stretch of the
Great Forest between the Swamplands and the Briar, not far from the
Old Crone's cottage. Ella loved visiting there. It was a sunlit belt of
green marsh where gentle streams wove through beds of wavering
flowers. Long strands of pink, purple, and yellow blooms bent over
the reflecting pools as if preening in a mirror. The unspoiled serenity
was broken only by the occasional patter of a dragonfly or, on this
morning, the humming of an eleven-year-old girl in her scarlet cape.

"What beauties," said Ella, frolicking in the grass. She sniffed bouquets of fresh-picked flowers and placed the stems in her basket. "Heavenly."

"The same words could be used to describe yourself, little Miss Vintner," spoke a man with a heavy but familiar accent.

A cool breeze rippled across the glade with an unpleasant scent like cigars that reminded Ella of her papa's parlor. She shaded her eyes against the morning sun. Likov Fen, the wolfish showman, was leaning against a birch, packing a long pipe with tobacco. He was alone and easy to recognize wearing his wolf-skin cloak. Judging by his casual manner, he had been watching her for some time.

"Why hello," called out Ella with a smile. "We met in Rivercross Square, didn't we? Where's Lobar, your pet wolf?"

"With a good friend," he said.

Ella kneeled to pluck some irises. "This secret glade is far from the village. What brings you here?"

The foreigner chuckled. "I might ask you the same question." He struck a match and lit his pipe.

"I'm gathering a special kind of flower for Gran," she held up a hawthorn floret. "See these? They only grow here. Not to mention all these other sorts. Many of these flowers are so rare, they have no names. Ol Gran is going to help me brew them into a healing tea for my mother."

"Your family," said Fen. "Do they know you are here?"

"Yes, they should by now. Gran sent them a message."

"Ah," Mister Fen exhaled between puffs, "A message may easily go astray."

"No, I don't think so, Gran's finches are very reliable."

"Nothing to worry about, Tender One. Now, you are no longer alone." He flicked the matchstick into the grass.

Ella felt a bit nervous. "Papa's sure to be cross with me. You see, I was on an adventure, like my friend Jack Spriggins, but I got sick. So, I went to Granny's and she took care of me. Anyway, I'm well now and it's such a lovely day. I thought I might find Jack before I went home. Do you remember him from that night in Rivercross?"

"Is he nearby?"

"I haven't found him and none of the animals have seen him."

Mister Fen said nothing as he toked his pipe.

A warning tingled in Ella's fingers and toes. "I wish Lobar was with you."

"Yes, everybody likes the wolf. He's a good pup."

"He's very grown for a puppy."

"True, but I still call him *pup*." The foreigner returned a smile. His eyes remained fixed on her.

"I should be getting back." She did not feel all that comfortable. "It was nice to see you again. Say 'hello 'to Lobar."

"You should not be in the woods alone, Tender One," pressed Mister Fen. "Have you not heard of the pretty young maids that have gone missing?"

Ella's heart began to race. "I'll go straight to Granny's where I'll be safe." She turned and started walking away.

"You will not find Gran at her home," said Fen.

Ella looked over her shoulder. "What do you mean? "

"Have you not heard?"

"No."

"Then I will share with you the news." Mister Fen tilted his head back and blew out a thin trail of smoke. Then, he cast a desperate glance. "First, if you would be so kind, pick one of the yellow beauties for my waistcoat."

"Please, just tell me," said Ella.

Fen indicated his empty buttonhole, "We share so much together."

"Do you mean how we both can talk to animals?" She snapped the stem of a daffodil.

"We are both so different from the others. So misunderstood."

"You're right." Ella held the flower out to him. "I was being silly. A boutonniere would look dapper."

The showman bent down with a tip of his hat and gestured, rather playfully, to his lapel. "Do me the kind honor, Miss Vintner."

She put the flower in the buttonhole, though her hands were trembling. "Do share the news."

The man knit his thick brows together with a troubled frown. "Your poor Gran is in peril."

"How can that be? I only just left her cottage."

"It's a good thing you did. The villagers have attacked it."

"Why did they do that?

"They were looking for you, Tender One."

"For me?"

"Your papa claimed Old Gran kidnapped you."

"No, I wasn't kidnapped. Granny's a friend!"

~ 123 ~

He took her hand, covering it with his own. "Of course. I got there ahead of them, and kept her safe. I can show where she hides. She asked for you. I said I would come, so here I am to take you to her."

"Why didn't you say so?"

"To be certain you were alone."

"Where is she?"

"Not far."

"What about Ganzil?"

"There was no Ganzil."

"Ganzil is the girl who lives with Granny. You couldn't have missed her. She's as pretty as any of these flowers."

"I would not have missed such a one," he shrugged. "Gran called only for you. Such a dangerous mob. I arrived ahead of them to protect her but there was no time. Ganzil must have run from the angry villagers. Gran's old heart was beating so fast. She bid me to seek you in this lovely place."

"Oh no," cried Ella. "This is my fault."

"She looked ill. Perhaps, she needs the flowers of healing for herself." Fen started to take the basket off her arm. "Allow me to carry the blooms."

Ella pulled back. "No. I'll go by myself."

"Too dangerous. I must keep you safe. Shall we go to her?"

"Yes," Ella decided. "If Gran is in trouble, let's hurry, please. Papa was wrong to have accused her so unjustly."

"Very well." Fen took the pipe from his mouth and knocked the ashes out against the birch. "I must warn you – the cave is dark."

"Did you leave Gran there?"

"For safety. Brave soul, she waits."

Ella pulled the red hood over her head. "I'll be brave too."

With that, Likov Fen led Ella from Shaina's Window. They moved swiftly, darting down a narrow-wooded path. Her breath quickened as she tried to keep up. Many of the flowers jounced out of her basket.

"Please, you're going too fast," said Ella, as birds in the trees began screeching." Those birds think someone's in trouble."

"Perhaps we're already too late," said Fen with a strange growl. Ella thought he seemed angry at her for being too slow. She clung to his cloak. His strides were powerful. The going was difficult and she nearly tripped.

"Have we far to go?" Ella was out of breath.

"Nearly there, Tender One," he answered, panting.

They rushed into a ravine and down a slope until the path ended, where the man stopped so abruptly that Ella stumbled and fell, scattering flowers all over the ground. Embarrassed, she gathered them up.

"Now, Tender One. We are there," said Fen.

Two dark passages loomed before them. Side by side, the caverns looked like eye sockets in a skull of rock. A dull, rotten stench crept out. Ella covered her mouth and nose. "Where's Gran?"

"Inside." The man's sweaty skin had paled and his stare seemed ravenous.

"Are you feeling ill?" said Ella.

"I will be fine," he insisted, fixing his collar. "Go, Gran waits for you."

Ella approached the cave entrance. "It smells foul, are you sure she's there?"

"Yes, it's safe, go in."

Wolf howls echoed above the ravine.

"Wait," said Ella. "The wolves."

"What about them?"

"They're warning us of a threat that approaches."

Mister Fen suddenly let out a howl of his own that peeled through the woods. The wolves answered back.

"Strange," said Ella. "I didn't understand that. Who do they say is coming?"

"A villager. One has picked up our trail."

"Oh no, we must get Gran." Ella then called into the cave. "Gran?"

There was no answer. "She's not in there."

"Allow me, Tender One." Mister Fen stepped in front of her. "I shall go see to her and have Gran call out. Then, you come." He pushed his fur-cloak off his shoulders and entered the cave. Turning with a smile, he backed into the cavern until all she could see was gleam of his teeth. "She will call. Then you come."

Ella clutched her basket, waiting. "Gran?" she called again into the cave. "Are you safe?"

Gran's voice crackled out from the black, "Have you brought me flowers, Sweetness?"

Chapter 13

WOLVES

Somewhere in the woods a wolf howl broke the morning's stillness. Then, a bird chirruped. Dawn's pink rays seeped into the sky and sparkled on the stream, which Jack followed south.

"Smell of smoke. Wood burning. Gingerbread!"

The Crone's ivy-covered cottage lay not far from Thin Creek, tucked within a chestnut grove. A large brick oven stood across the yard, puffing a comforting smell of burnt apple wood and gingerbread from its chimney.

"Ol' Ugly chased me outta here plenty of times."

Winded and aching, Jack slipped through the fence boards into the witch's herb garden. Rabbits scampered off as he snuck over and hid behind the woodpile next to the oven.

Whatever was baking smelled delicious. "I'll just grab one cookie." He reached in and took two, started munching. He had been walloped many times by the Crone's broom when she chased him off.

Above, a raven cawed.

"Aw spit!" Jack hated that black bird. "Yeh always seem to spot me before Ol' Ugly does. Yep, there she be."

The bony witch was on her porch, leaning against the broom in a tattered, green shawl. Her white hair was pulled back and, in the pale morning light, the warts on her face looked hideous.

"Yeh ain't blind, yeh old prune," said Jack. "Always watching me like a hawk. Prob'ly hex me. There yeh go, pointing a finger. Make my teeth fall out or something."

The crone did not speak. Her cloudy-white eyes stayed fixed on him and she pointed to the west.

"Yeah, yeah. I was just leaving," he added. This was usually where she chased him off the yard, but not today.

Jack stopped. "Yeh ain't mad at me?"

Her bent finger pointed beyond the fence at a line of trampled grass leading into the woods, where the morning dew was brushed away.

"Yeh know where Ella is?" he said.

The Crone leaned on her broom without a word.

Through the fence Jack pushed some of the grass aside, looking at the footprints. "Small, slight at the toe, girly kind-o-stance." He caught a fresh scent. "Honeysuckle – like Ella!"

Not that Jack wanted to say "thank you" but when he stood, the hag had gone inside." Ol' Ugly's been a help."

He started running. Not far along, Jack discovered new tracks that fell in behind Ella's. "Bad scent. Tobacco. Wolf-stink. Likov Fen!"

He followed the path to Shaina's Window where the tracks broke off and went in separate directions. "Reckon he didn't want her to know she were being followed."

Ella had crossed through the grass, where several broken flowers were snapped off at the stems. Jack kneeled. "Fresh, milky sap. Her scent still clings here. His too."

Their tracks met in the glade and led away together. "She went with him," exclaimed Jack. "Stupid girl." If Jack's thoughts could have burned, they would have roasted the backs of his eyeballs.

"Wolf hunt! I'll kill him if she be hurt."

There was a ruckus to the north of screeching birds. Jack charged on the trail past flowers strewn by the wayside. "Ella's footprints ain't right. Looks like she got pulled along but not putting up a fight."

A wolf cry pierced the woods. Jack stopped in his tracks.

"Smell, listen, look! Wolf-stink coming from all sides." A low shadow with two eyes moved through the brush. The patter of paws and other dog-like pants closed in. A strange howl bayed in the distance. "That weren't one wolf. Fen's got a wolf pack and they're guarding his lair."

At this moment, a large grey wolf crashed through a thicket on the trail ahead. "Lobar! Ain't so friendly now, are yeh, furball?" The wolf, no longer a performing pet from Rivercross Square, snarled and bared its drooling fangs. Jack whipped off his buckskin coat and twisted it between his hands, ready if it sprang. "Ella must be close, wolfy. Now git!"

A new rustle came behind him. Over Jack's shoulder he saw a black wolf jump on to the trail.

"Jits! A trap."

He threw the coat aside and went the only way he could.

"Up I go!"

The wolves sprang.

With the crossbow slung over-the-shoulder, Jack leapt onto a pine and dug hands and heels into the bark but with tired legs, he did not climb well. The black wolf caught his heel and shook violently, its jaws clamping down.

"Ahh!" cried Jack, with a tenuous grip.

Lobar leapt and tore at his shirtsleeve. Jack kicked and clamored higher but the black wolf would not let go. "Git off me!"

Lobar leapt, snapping. It was a ferocious contest between the two animals to bring Jack down and tear him apart.

Jack swung his bone knife, wriggled, and finally kicked free. The strong boots spared his foot but his heel was injured. "Outta my way, furballs!

Higher up the tree, Jack pulled an arrow from his quiver, clung tight with his legs, loaded and aimed the crossbow. His shot caught the black wolf. There was a yelp as the beast tumbled to the ground, an arrow sticking out of its pelt.

"Chew on that!"

The black wolf did not even twitch. Lobar leapt fiercely trying to get at Jack.

"C'mon, Snarly, yer next." He hooked an arm around a branch but it gave way and he fell out of the tree, landing on top of Lobar with the broken bough. The wolf snapped through the limbs at Jack's throat. Using his crossbow to fend off the attack, Jack's weapon was wrenched from his hands by Lobar's jaws. Then the wolf sprang. Jack pulled the bone knife from his belt and slammed it home in Lobar's side. Another yelp.

The beast whimpered and sprang away. Jack got his crossbow and quickly fixed his sights.

Blood dripped from Lobar's pelt but the wolf still had fight. "Spring again and yeh die, show-dog."

Lobar lunged. Jack fired.

THUNK! The wolf spun in the air and hit the ground; an arrow stuck in its hind leg. It snapped at the wound but Lobar's rear legs buckled.

"Keep yer hiney down or I'll finish yeh."

With an arch of its neck, Lobar gave a low howl and then hobbled into the brush and disappeared.

"Where's Ella? I gotta be quick."

The tracks led downslope into a gulch. Jack snatched up his wadded coat. Now limping from the pain in his heel, a faint smell of honeysuckle grew stronger so he quickened his gait. "That's Ella's scent."

More panting drew his attention to the ridge above. "Fen's got a whole pack-o-wolves guarding him."

Through the trees, Ella's voice called. "Gran? Are you there?" Elms blocked Jack's view but a flash of red made him stop.

"Ella's alive." Veering off the trail, he ducked under tree cover. "Where's Fen?" Jack lifted his bow. "I can't see him but his stink is near."

Ella crept forward towards the cave. She had a basket on her arm filled with long, pink flowers.

"Gran?" she called. "Are you safe?"

Then, a voice that sounded like the Crone's crackled from the cave. "Have you brought me flowers, Sweetness?"

Jack felt a shiver on the back of his neck. "That ain't the Crone. It's Fen," he realized. "He's doing that stage trick with his voice."

"Why do your eyes shine red?" said Ella, taking a step back.

The crackling voice answered, "I have cried too much waiting to see you, Sweetness."

From the clustered elms Jack aimed his bow, hobbling closer.

"Why do your teeth gleam?" said Ella, trembling.

"I have gnashed them together waiting—*TO EAT YOU, SWEETNESS!*"

She stumbled back and screamed. A wolf-shadow lunged from the dark cave.

Jack fired his crossbow rushing forward. A shriek echoed like a man's voice but then rose to the pitch of a wounded animal.

"Jack!" said Ella. "He was a—"

"A wolf, I know!" Jack stood in front of her and fired another shot. Another yelp and the baying withdrew deeper into the cavern.

"Don't get too close," said Ella. "He might not be dead."

Jack tore his tattered shirtsleeve off and with the bottle of lamp oil from his coat pocket, doused the rag, wrapping it on a stick. Lighting the torch, he marched inside.

"I'm going to make sure he is."

In the cave, the ground crunched beneath his feet. Jack waved the torch low and grimaced. "Bones," he said, finding a girl's bonnet and torn clothes. "It were no dragon," he muttered. "Fen was the killer. He brought them here to these Dead Bone Caves."

The small rag burned quickly and his torch began to flicker. By the wall, a large black form lay on the dirt, issuing a low animal-like groan and panting heavily as if struggling to breathe.

"Yer dying, wolf man," said Jack, creeping forward. "My arrows got yeh. Remember me?"

The shadows played tricks on Jack's eyes as the misshapen, hairy form convulsed. "Yeh can't be a real wolf. How come fur grows on yer hands? Why yeh got a snout beneath yer hat?"

The motionless shape lay still and Jack poked it with the torch. "Yeh dead?" The impossible notion that Fen had turned into a wolfman became real. "That ain't yer wolfskin cloak," said Jack, disbelieving his eyes.

As he held the torch closer for a better look at the villain's face, the flame died. "Spit! I'm gettin' outta here."

He called to Ella as he stumbled out of the tomb. "Yeh ain't gonna believe what I seen," he said, but then something new stopped Jack cold in his tracks.

The wolf pack had Ella surrounded. She stood calmly among them. Jack yanked his weapon and aimed before realizing there was no threat. "Six wolves just sitting, not pouncing? Panting like loyal pups." He lowered the bow. "How'd yeh do that?"

Ella put a finger to her lips with a shy smile. "Likov Fen was a terrible brute," she said. "His will made them slaves. Their dignity as a wolf pack was taken from them." She turned and addressed the animals. "Your cruel master is dead."

The wolves yipped and howled in obedient response.

"Yeh weren't making it up," said Jack, "Yeh really talk to animals."

She pointed at him, addressing the wolves. "This is Jack Spriggins," she told them. "Remember him. He freed you."

"Git!" said Jack. "Shoo!"

The wolves scattered, Lobar trailing behind with a limp. The fletching of Jack's arrow still stuck in the hind leg but had been chewed until all that was left was a broken shaft.

"Oh Jack! You're the last person I expected to see," said Ella. "Though,I don't know why. After all, it seems I can always count on you when I'm in trouble."

"Hunt's over," he said. "Yer safe, and so am I."

Chapter **14**

HERO

" Why, Jack you're limping," said Ella. "And your poor arm has blood on it."

As usual, Ella did enough talking for both of them. Jack led the way, hacking at the tall summer grass with a sharpened stick.

"I wanted to find something to make Mama feel better," she went on, "That's why I came to the woods. Gran said these hawthorn blooms would help."

Jack glanced over his shoulder. Ella was tucking flowers from the basket into her sash. "Witches brew, huh?" he sneered.

"I hope Gran isn't hurt. Let's go to her cottage and check on her."

"I'm taking yeh home."

"But wasn't Gran attacked?"

Jack spun round. "Everything that wolfman said to yeh was a lie. Yer folks think yer dead."

"Dead?" The color drained from her cheeks. "But they should have gotten Gran's message."

"Never did, I reckon."

Ella shivered. "Likov Fen knew just what to say to trick me."

"The best liars always do."

"But I don't want to go through life not knowing if I can believe anyone."

"Just gotta be smarter." Jack looked her in the eyes. "Yeh gotta figure what folks really are, see? Ain't hard if yeh try."

"How?"

"By using this." He struck his gut with his fist. "Yer sense. Get it?"

"I think I do." Ella nodded as if, for once, she had truly listened. "Mister Fen said things that felt like danger, but I only wanted to hear what was good. I missed the bad things. The true things."

"Yeh sure did."

"Animals are so much simpler. They always watch out for me in the forest. Mama and Papa should know they'd keep me safe."

"Yer lucky yeh ain't a goner."

"But Green Mother's spirit gift—"

"She didn't save yeh. I did."

Ella lowered her head.

"Yer just a girl to most folks," Jack tried to explain. "Just like them others who got snatched by him. What's somebody with no spirit-gift supposed to think?"

"Papa always tells me not to talk about my spirit gift."

"Sure he does! Yeh wanna be stared at like a goat with two heads? Have folks tease yeh? Feel afraid of yeh? Yer secret's gotta stay a secret."

"I just wanted to fix Mama's trouble." Tears welled in Ella's eyes. "I've only made things worse, haven't I?"

"Well, yeh never went missing so long before this." Jack stamped his feet and thrashed hard with his stick.

"Why Jack, that was the longest speech you ever made," said Ella. "Why are you hitting the ground so hard? Are you angry?"

"Naw, it's for trigger snakes." He went on stomping. "They go blind this time of year. I'm telling em to get outta the way." In truth, Jack was riled up. Ella had gotten too close to death this time. He paused, squinting at her. "Maybe yeh can warn the triggers yerself, cause yeh ain't gonna tell me triggers ain't dangerous."

"No. A snake is still a snake. And a wolf is a wolf. "

"Reckon so."

Ella stamped the ground a bit herself. "Did you know the Crone's almost completely blind?"

"Did yeh know I don't care?"

"Jack Spriggins! You may act like you don't but I know you do." She put her arms on her hips. "And your mother knows too."

"Ma?"

"I paid her a visit."

Now, the color must have drained from Jack's face. "Yeh met Ma?"

"Why, yes. I went to your house."

"How'd yeh find it?"

Ella smiled. "Any bird, squirrel, or tree toad on Thin Creek knows where you live, Jack. Oh, your mother went on and on how proud she is."

"I knew it." Jack twisted his face. "That weren't Ma yeh met, nuh-uh."

"You're being shy."

"And yer being a loon."

"I really do want to get home now." Ella took up a long stick to help whack the underbrush. "Oh, where's a bull moose to help thresh when you need one?"

Jack led Ella through the summer fields back to Whispering Vine. She chatted nonstop about the Crone, the black raven, and this other girl, Ganzil, who she had made friends with at the cottage.

Grateful to finally reach Ella's property, Jack stopped at the edge of the vineyards. "Where are them workers yeh usually got tending the grapes?"

"I'm not sure," she said, plucking one. "The harvest is a way off yet, but I'm feeling hungry."

"C'mon, I'll see yeh get to the house."

As they followed the tree line around the property, the chateau came into view. Jack recognized a group of rangers by the front steps, greeting Ella's parents. "The Champs," he said. "They beat us here."

"Look!" said Ella. "There's Mama and Papa."

She started to run but Jack held her back. "Keep hid a sec," he said, "In the shade of the trees."

"How come? I must let them know I'm safe."

"Just wait," he said, smirking. "I wanna see what them rangers say."

"But that's Captain Camlann."

"I know. I shook his hand."

At Mister Vintner's signal, a stableman brought the Champions their horses. Ardus spoke to the parents, while the others loaded the satchels of dragon hides onto their saddles.

"What's the captain saying to Mama?"

Missus Vintner's expression went pale and she slumped into her husband's arms. A stout housemaid rushed forward to assist.

"Oh no," said Ella, who grabbed Jack's hand and pulled him into the sunlight. "Papa, Mama, I'm home!" she shouted, running to them and dragging Jack along.

"Ella!" erupted Missus Vintner with tears. The woman reached for Ella and buried her in her arms. "My angel! You're safe."

"Jack saved me," said Ella. "There was a wolf. Not a real wolf, but a bad man. He tried to take me away, and Jack stopped him."

Mister Vintner joined them, holding his daughter's face in his hands. "For days, we have searched," he said, sobbing. "Day and night, we could not find you."

"I went to Gran's cottage but I caught a chill and lost the way. Then I came down with a fever, so I slept in a fallen juniper log. Then I heard Sersi call my name."

"Who is Sersi?" said Ootan.

"The Crone's raven," said Ella.

"The bird never really spoke her name, of course," added Mister Vintner, clearing his throat.

Ella glanced at her father. "Well, it cawed. I woke up on a soft featherbed at Gran's. I don't remember how I got there but she and Ganzil took care of me, fed me soup and tea until I got better."

Ardus stepped forward. "We went to the Crone's cottage," he said. "She had not seen you."

"She told me you had come," said Ella. "But that was before Sersi found me. Oh Mama, Papa! Gran sent a message, I'm so sorry you didn't get it."

"The man who tried to harm you," said Mister Vintner. "Who was he?"

"Mister Fen, the showman," said Ella. "He did tricks with a wolf named Lobar. He could speak to wolves, just like I—" Ella stopped short of finishing.

"Did he harm you, child?"

"No, Papa, but he would have if Jack didn't save me."

Ardus glanced at Jack. "Where's this man now?" he said.

"Dead," said Jack.

"How? You killed him?"

"Captain, Jack really had no choice," said Ella.

"Where did this happen?"

"A dry gulch north of Shaina's Window," said Jack. "You'll find the Dead Bone Caves. Fen ain't all you'll find in there."

"The missing girls," said Redvere. "Any other's alive?"

Jack shook his head.

Mister Vintner pulled his family close and melted into grateful sobs.

"Thank you, wonderful boy," said Missus Vintner, who reached out and swept the hair from Jack's face. "I'll bet you're hungry."

"Indeed, you must all be," said Mister Vintner, "Nessie, prepare a banquet for our Champions!"

"I'll get the stoves lit," said the cook, clapping her hands to the other house servants.

Gwachmai bear-hugged Jack, "A dragon-slayer and wolf-hunter! And yeh don't have a whisker yet to shave."

"The townsfolk must be notified of the news," said Ardus, who prepared to mount his horse.

"If you'll permit me, captain," said Mister Vintner, holding his arm. "I will send riders. We prefer very much to have your company at our table."

"I am honored," said Ardus, "To celebrate the heroism of Jack Spriggins."

Riders went out from the stables and field hands were summoned to the banquet. With the strike of a fiddle, the party sprang up. A table was set out and a hero's feast was prepared in the chateau's kitchen.

Jack squirmed from all the attention. "I should prob'ly git," he said.

"No-no." Nessie the cook led him by the scruff of his coat. "This is your place of honor, Jack Spriggins." She sat him down at the head of the table. "Don't be so shy. Captain Ardus, keep our hero company."

The notion of making table talk was not the same as bragging over a dead dragon and Jack stared uneasily across the table to avoid chitchat. Ardus sat next to him, content to thump his fingers to the fiddler's tune.

Ella glided around the yard in her father's arms as Gwachmai hoisted one of the serving girls into the air.

"Yeh'll make as fine a dancing partner as any man could ask for," he said to the blushing woman.

"Put her down," shouted Nessie, who rushed over to grab the girl. "I need her help in the kitchen."

"Let them dance, Nessie," said Mister Vintner. "It's right to celebrate."

"Ooh, just one dance, then," she said. "A lot of mouths need feeding here."

"Yes, ma'am," said Gwachmai, winking. "Yeh save me a turn later too?"

"We'll see about that," said Nessie, smoothing her skirt as she marched to the kitchen.

Redvere proved rather shy and stood by tapping his foot to the music.

"Where's Ootan?" said Jack.

"One never knows," said Ardus. "He slips in or out of sight like a panther. "Always with good reason though."

Servants carried trays bearing fresh cornbread muffins and honey, scrumptious cheese and fruit. Wine flagons and goblets were set out. Wonderful smells came from the chateau.

As the guests dug in, the captain spoke to Jack. "I remember the first time I killed a man," he said quietly. "I was your age. I'll never forget."

"I killed no man," said Jack. "Fen was a monster."

"I was wrong not to listen to you. You're wiser than I gave you credit for. I apologize."

The words made Jack feel tall as the stone spire at the Orchard. "I'm a thief, not a liar."

"I'll remember that," chuckled Ardus. "You know the forest as well as any of us, I suspect. Your instincts, not to mention your skill with that crossbow, I admire very much. Where did you learn to shoot?"

"The woods. Taught myself."

"You are full of surprises; I'll give you that."

When the fiddler's song was played out, the dancers sat and joined them at the table.

"For the sake of the families whose daughters were lost," Ardus added, "Will you share what happened?"

The Champions, Ella's family, and the workers all eagerly awaited his story. Jack fumbled for courage to find the words. The blood rushed to his temples and his mouth went dry and gummy. "Um," he smacked. Even his lips stuck together.

"Captain, let me tell you," said Ella, just in time. Utterly gifted with being a chatterbox, it was her turn to save Jack. "That is, if Jack doesn't mind."

"Huh-uh," he said, slumping back with relief. "Yeh tell it."

Ella shared all that happened, building on Jack's heroism with embarrassing glee. She wisely left out her talk with the wolves.

"What is in the caves?" said Ardus.

"I really don't know," she said. "Jack had the courage to go in."

Jack shook his head to Ardus. "Ain't table-talk."

"Very well, then."

"So, why be it the Crone's message never arrived?" said Gwachmai. "Ain't that suspicious?"

"Oh, but Gran really did send a message."

"It never got here, Riding Hood," said her father. "And let me remind you, Hepkatee, the Crone, is no relation. You know how I disapprove when you call her *Gran*."

"Treacherous harpy," said Gwachmai. "We should bind her lying tongue fer keeping the girl hid."

"Oh no, sir! Please don't blame Gran. She wouldn't mislead you," said Ella.

Ordinarily, Jack might have sided against the Crone but Ella was right. The old hag had some decent points.

"Young miss, you speak true," said Ootan, who approached with his large hands cupped. "I found a finch entangled upon the grapevines."

He opened his palms and revealed the mangled form of the dead bird. Tied to one of its bent legs was a tiny roll of parchment.

"The message," exclaimed Ella.

Mister Vintner took the scroll to read it.

Ella came to Ootan's side for a closer look at the finch. "The poor darling," she said. "What happened?"

"Hawk prob'ly," said Jack.

"No," said Ootan, holding up a red feather. "A cardinal." With his fingertips, he brushed the lifeless creature and drew more fuzzy red fragments from its plumage.

"The message?" said Ardus.

Mister Vintner looked up from the note. "It is indeed from the Crone and Ella was in her care."

"The finch, sir, please," said Ella. "Let me bury it."

Ootan gently passed it to her. She walked toward a nearby garden but paused before Gwachmai, who took a seat. "Sir, be kind what you say about Gran," said Ella, "She always looks out for me."

Gwachmai waited until Ella walked away and then half-snorted, placing his hands on his knees. "May my vitals be an ogre's breakfast if I ever trust a witch."

At Mister Vintner's signal, the fiddler resumed an airy jig. More wine was brought and a pouch of tobacco. The Champions took out pipes and smoked. Even Jack, when offered, enjoyed a puff of Gwachmai's pipe.

Soon, a pouch jangling with coins landed on the table before Ardus. "Payment," said Mister Vintner, "As promised."

"The reward belongs to Jack Spriggins," said the captain.

The smile dropped from the winemaker's face. The fiddler struck a sour chord. Mister Vintner reluctantly passed the reward to him. "Our gratitude for returning Ella home," he said, with a nod. "This belongs to you."

Jack was so tickled he thought his ears might pop off.

From the rose garden, Ella could be heard singing Redvere's song to the buried finch:

"Where are roses for my Rose,
Rarest of the Rare?
I long to lay them by her side,
And soothe my Beauty Fair."

Mister Vintner wiped tears from his eyes. "Forgive me, none of you know how precious a daughter is."

"I can imagine," replied Ardus, lowering his head.

A dinner bell rang.

"Hot roast!" said Nessie. Platters of beef and lamb were served. Jack smirked and Gwachmai rubbed his hands together, as they feasted. Steamed vegetables were brought out, and pudding, molasses, and fruitcake dessert.

Across from Jack, Missus Vintner was seated, assisted by a housemaid. "Nessie," she summoned. "Be sure Jack Spriggins has everything he desires."

"Of course," said Nessie.

Ella's ma looked frail but her soft voice carried irresistible kindness. "Friendship is a marvelous gift, Jack," she said. "I'm glad Ella has yours."

Halfway through the meal, an unexpected guest arrived. "What's Allwise doing here?" Jack said. "Is the fat-bellied meddler selling beans?"

"Don't hold a grudge, Jack," chuckled Redvere. "You know he was trying to help you?"

"Chee."

Allwise drove a hay cart pulled by two mules. "Whoa," he said.

"Welcome Allwise," said Mister Vintner. "Please join us."

"I met your riders on the road and came straightaway," said Allwise. "Excuse my intrusion but I also have urgent news from Hedgewall."

"Was there another skirmish?" said Ardus.

"The news is sobering." Allwise placed a parchment on the table. "My scouts report we are facing an invasion."

Ardus read the message. "The ogres have broken through and overrun the defense at Hedgewall."

"Impossible," said Redvere. "The garrison was four hundred men. The forest's best archers were stationed there."

Allwise shook his head. "The gates are smashed and the citadel has been burnt to the ground."

Ella's ma got up from the table, "Come Ella, please assist me." Together, they walked back to the manor.

"The invaders already have marched on Briarslate and Nethervil," added Allwise. "Many soldiers and good folks were killed or forced to flee."

"How large is the enemy force?" said Ardus.

"Four thousand when it began."

Gwachmai spit wine halfway across the table. "By Lady Lell's shadow!"

"The ogres have never waged such an assault," said Redvere.

"No, not like this," said Allwise. "Their art in war has also advanced. They bring siege engines."

"Siege injuns?" said Jack.

Ootan explained, "A slingshot, high as a tree, that flings rocks large enough to crush a house."

"General Steelhouse ordered retreat?" said Gwachmai.

"No," said Allwise. "The general was killed in the invasion."

Ardus crumpled the message. "We should have been there. This report is three days old. Why were we not summoned to the front?"

"Our line is scattered and our marshals are few," said Allwise. "We must rally a defense of the Forestland."

"A real war?" said Jack, sitting forward. He felt jitters of excitement, imagining he would now join the soldiers and become a ranger.

"Who leads the ogres?" said Ardus, as he paced the length of the table.

"The chieftain's name is not known," said Allwise, "His army is disciplined, more than any ogre force of the past, but his taste for slaughter is ruthless. Common folks who are unarmed are being cut down same as soldiers."

"Aye, that's the ogres way," said Gwachmai, who slammed his fist on the table. "Serpent-lovers! We'll give em a fight, turn em back to the infernal sands they come from."

"We need to muster men and horses," said Ardus. "But this ambush leaves little time."

"I have sent word to Chancellor Celot," said Allwise.

"My father?" said Redvere.

"He promised two hundred mounts. His finest riders arrive tomorrow. The Count of Havensbend and his guard are also joining us."

"There's three hundred good riders," said Ardus. "And his infantry is five hundred strong."

"We are still awaiting word from Arborvale, but bands from all the local villages have been called upon."

"Any word from Lothur of the Crokees?"

"He has already marched," said Allwise. "His clansmen are barricading the road at both Terac and Rudd. Well over a thousand men will be ready to march with you from Forks crossroad. The rendezvous is set; meet there in two days. A new commander must be chosen from among the captains."

"We all know who that will be," said Gwachmai. "Nobody's better fer that than my little brother."

Ardus seemed to ignore the suggestion. "Only a thousand men? We're badly outnumbered."

"For now, the army will grow as word spreads," said Allwise.

"And who knows these woods like we do, Arto?" said Gwachmai. "No ogre's gonna match us fighting beneath the boughs of the Green Mother. By the brawn of Father Ter, we'll sharpen our blades on their stony hearts."

Ootan patted Ardus on the shoulder. "Time, my friend, is not a patient warrior."

"Let's get ready," said Ardus, turning to Allwise. "Any luck with the dwarfs?"

"Not for fighting," said the mentor. "They offered help by way of armaments. Fifty swords are on the way."

"That was gracious," said Redvere.

"It was business," said Allwise. "The Count of Havensbend is covering the expense. If the dwarf clans or giantdom would join us, we might be assured victory."

"The giants would not even let us pass their borders," said Ardus, pulling on his riding gloves. "Not even for discussion."

"Then why discuss it now?" said Allwise.

Ardus nodded toward the horses. "We have a dragon's hide."

"Ah-hah," Allwise grinned. "A new set of ranger's vests and leg plates."

Mister Vintner signaled his foreman. "Men, load those hides onto the wagon."

"Obliged," said Allwise. "And consider it done, Captain. I will send the new armor soon as it's ready. Farewell."

"Drink up, gents," said Ardus. "We ride for war."

"High time," said Gwachmai, jumping to his feet. "A battle for our Great Forest awaits."

The rangers clanked goblets and drank.

Jack fidgeted at the end of the table, wondering how he might go with them. He failed to notice Allwise had slid over beside him.

"So, *hero* now, is it?" said the old man. "Well, you'll always be *'thief'* to me. Affectionately, of course."

"And yeh'll be Goat-Beard to me," said Jack.

"A clever new title," said Allwise, proudly stroking his own goatee. "You rescued the girl, nice work."

"Better than yer Champs did."

"Yes, well, there's much work to do."

"I heard yer talk," said Jack. "Yeh want me to fight?"

"I want you to return with me to the Orchard. We have much to teach you at my school."

"School?" laughed Jack, spitting out a watermelon seed. "Yeh just said there's a war."

"Soldiers are trained," said Allwise, handing Jack a napkin. "You could be very useful once you've been broken in."

"Yeh making a joke or tricking me again?"

"No, I'm quite serious," said Allwise. "Attending school would be a great change for you but the change will serve you well."

Jack clenched his teeth.

"If it's your mother you're worried about," said Allwise. "I'd like to speak to her personally."

"Stay away from Ma," said Jack, bolting to his feet. "She chucked yer stupid beans out the window. She don't care for yer tricks and neither do I."

"Have you seen her lately? Ask her again, she may surprise you."

"Yeh sneaky geezer. I been getting along fine."

"Careful, young man. That attitude makes you a danger to yourself and anyone who would count on you. I offer you a future but one that must be done on my terms."

"Yeh ain't breaking me. I got my own smarts to get by."

"Stubbornness is your enemy, Thief," said Allwise. "Let's see how far that gets you then." He walked away briskly, without another word.

On his wagon, the old man snapped the reins, glancing at Jack. "Come to your senses, and then come see me." His mules pulled him down the lane and out of sight.

"Beat it, old man," grumbled Jack.

The hero's feast was over. The Champions were ready to leave.

"We thank you for the hospitality," said Ardus, bidding Mister Vintner farewell.

The winemaker said in return, "My men have my leave to join you if the time comes."

"It may come," said Ardus, clasping his hand. "Let's hope not."

Jack was done waiting for an invitation. "Can't ride but I can keep up," he said to Ardus.

Ootan and Redvere looked at Jack as if bewildered.

The captain said firmly, "You are strong and courageous, Jack, but you cannot go with us."

"What'd yeh mean?"

"Allwise offered you a place at the Orchard. You should take it."

"There's a real fight waiting," said Jack.

Ardus pointed at the rangers. "These men are properly trained for the fight. We will gladly have you as a soldier when you are ready."

"I am ready. Yeh saw what I done. I shot the dragon's eye. I found Ella when yeh couldn't. Yeh said the killer weren't even a killer. Yeh need me!"

Ardus shook his head, "You are full of surprises, but still—"

"It ain't right!" Jack interrupted. "Yeh said yeh wouldn't doubt me."

"You're an honest hero, Jack, but you're scarcely more than a boy."

"No younger than we was, Arto," said Gwachmai.

Ardus turned in his saddle to face his brother, "We had no other choice. Our family was lost to an ogre slaughter." Then he addressed Jack. "Son, war is not for the untrained. Be patient. Let yourself learn, Jack."

Jack spit at the ground and ran away. After ducking into the trees, he glanced back at the Champions, sitting tall on their horses. Ardus watched with a troubled frown but Jack knew he would have no change of heart.

"The boy is like a mouthful of molasses," said Gwachmai. "Too hot to swallow, too sticky to spit out."

Jack Spriggins, hero for an hour, ran until he was surrounded by the lonely shadows of the woods he knew too well.

Chapter 15

VINES

" Dirty rotten luck," said Jack. "Allwise always brings rotten luck."

He jangled the hefty reward pouch, which was no longer satisfying as it should have been.

"Ain't coming home with beans this time. Maybe all this coin will brighten Ma's spirits." Jack put his hands to his head. "Why do I feel so empty?"

Like Ella, he had never been gone from home this long. When the little hovel at Thin Creek came into view, he did not recognize it.

"Where's the rickety wood shack that used to lean to one side?" he said.

The cabin looked new, with straight, repaired walls and fresh-varnished boards. A small garden had been planted beside the house. Bluebirds and robins bobbed up and down on a line strung with clean laundry. A fresh raked path with bright yellow daisies led to the doorway. There was an actual door, too.

Jack knocked. "Solid pine," he said. "Who lives here now?"

Behind him, Ma's voice honked like a goose. "Ooh, Blessed Green Lady," she said. "My wee Jacky-boy!"

Jack turned around and saw her shuffling towards him with a bucket of water. She walked from the creek upon a neatly laid rock path. "Ma?" he said. "What the devil's got into yeh?"

Her skirts were crisp, her bodice laced. The shoes were on the proper feet and her hair looked clean, put up with shiny ribbons. She wore something else that surprised Jack more – *a smile*. Ma dropped the sloshing bucket and engulfed him in a hug that squeezed the air right out.

"Ma?" grunted Jack. "What've yeh done to the place? To yerself?"

"I know, dearie, ain't it a wonder?" she said. "The beans done it, son. Twere the beans."

"What do yeh mean?"

"Come-n-see!" Ma kept her arms tightly around him, guiding Jack behind the cabin. "Them seeds from Allwise sprouted where they fell. Just look at em grow, well-nigh into the trees." She proudly clasped her hands together.

Dozens of beanstalks had lengthy vines hung down in coils. Black-green bean pods dangled from them. "They're growin strong," he said. "The ones in Allwise's glass house weren't tall like that." The vines were very flexible but would not yank free. "Can't break em."

"Oh, don't bother with the vines," said Ma. "It's the beans yeh want." She plucked one of the pods with little effort. "Yeh see? They snap off easy."

Jack squeezed it in his hand. A milky string of goop spurted out, along with several large, gray beans.

"Yuck!" he said, trying to flick the sticky mess.

"Don't yuck at em," said Ma. "The beans are lovely. I've been eating em. At first, 'cause there were nothing else but soon, I'm feeling rosy, stitching things and cleaning up. Even took to humming songs."

"I ain't so sure they did yeh good."

"They ain't stopped a'growing, prob'ly never will. I been selling em in Rivercross Square."

"Yeh go to the village now?"

"That's the good they done for yer dear ma!" she said. "Been making a humble living. Been making friends. I tell yeh, soon as I earn enough, I might just buy us a mule."

Jack placed the reward purse in her hands. "Buy the mule now."

When Ma opened it and saw the gleaming silver, she slapped her forehead. "Forget the mule. With this, we can afford a place in town." She lowered her hand and gazed at Jack. "But tell me, son. Did yeh come by this honestly?"

"Since when do yeh care how I get stuff?"

"About time I started, don't yeh think? Yeh earned it proper, did yeh?"

"Yeah, Ma, too proper. But doing things right ain't paying off so good for me."

"The hard things in life seldom do but yeh feel better about yerself after," she said, shaking the pouch.

Jack toted her water bucket beside the cabin and dumped it into the barrel. Ma turned the iron latch and opened the door. "Jacky, see inside our home."

"Door don't squeak?"

"Not no more," Ma grinned.

Inside the hut was cleaned up with a fresh pine smell like the Orchard school. The wood panels were whitewashed, the shelves dusted and lined with cloth. Straw mats had been shaken and placed over a swept floor.

"Yeh sure been busy."

"My aches and pains be gone and I got strength to do all the chores."

"Yeh got a table too," he said. It was small, placed in the middle of the room with benches on either side. Jack noticed his hammock in the corner of the room had turned green.

"What happened?" he said, inspecting it.

"Beanstalk vines. Restrung it myself." Ma took a bone knife off one of the shelves and snipped a straggling coil.

"How'd yeh know to use a bone knife?"

"A friendly young fella from the Orchard school paid a visit," said Ma. "Said his name was Perdur, sent by Master Allwise. Brought a basket of bright golden apples and this here bone knife. Showed me how to cut the vines and make good use of em."

The basket was resting on the table. "I know Perdur," said Jack. "Allwise prob'ly sent him to spy on us."

"Well, the boy fashioned a pine door and even hung it on the frame."

"He's good with things like that," said Jack, setting his crossbow by the door.

"I got a feeling Allwise ain't the marvel folks think he is," said Ma.

"He ain't."

Spindles of colorful thread rested in a wicker basket next to a wooden rocking chair.

"It's hard to get my head round yeh and this new place," said Jack. "It all's so different."

Dimples formed in Ma's proud, quivering cheeks. "Twere the beans, son."

Jack plopped onto his green hammock. It was firm, no longer sagging to the floor. The cabin was warmer than usual because the stove was lit. An iron pot steamed on top.

"Yeh want anything to eat?" said Ma.

"Naw." Jack was full with the Vintner's feast. "Yer cooking again?"

"Bean stew," she said, ladling some into a wooden bowl, which she handed to him. "Taste it."

"It's gray and lumpy. Looks like dwarf snot."

"Go on, boy."

"Jits!" exclaimed Jack, spitting it out. "Said I weren't hungry."

"How about some tea then?" she said, trading the bowl for a wooden cup.

"What's it got?"

"Brewed beans."

Jack pushed the cup away, "Naw, water's good." He sipped from his canteen to rinse out the bean taste. "Whatever good the beans done yeh might not be the same for me. I need to keep my head where it's at."

Ma shrugged and sat to chitchat, sipping from the cup. "Did yer little friend Ella find yeh?"

"I found her," said Jack.

"Such an angel, and pretty too. In a few years yeh should grab and wed her."

"That's crazy talk, Ma." He stretched out his arms and yawned. It felt right homey to be in his old hammock again.

"Rest easy, son. Yeh look tired." Ma patted his arm. "Sleep'll sort yeh out. I'll gather up some more beans."

"No more beans," said Jack, who easily drifted asleep.

When Jack awoke, the day hardly seemed to have changed. "Ain't evening yet?" he said, rubbing his eyes.

"Thought yeh was hibernating," said Ma. Jack's trousers were missing because she had been mending them along with his torn shirt. "Hung yer pants outside to dry," she went on, "But that ugly snake pin fell from yer pocket. Don't know why yeh didn't throw it away."

"It's just an ogre brooch, Ma."

"Well, pick it off the floor. Brings bad luck."

"Folks make their own luck," said Jack, taking the pin. "I'm gonna wander out by the creek to do some thinking."

"Yeh slept half the day, son, let me boil yeh some stew."

"Naw." Instead, he grabbed a golden apple from the basket and took a bite as he went out the door. "Got this."

"I'm making a bean pie for supper."

By the creek, Jack chucked the ogre brooch like Ma wished, watching it skip as it went downstream. "Ol Goatbeard wanted me to plant gardens instead of squashing ogres. I'm already as good in a fight as any ranger."

He chomped on the apple, looking at his reflection in the creek. *"Be patient*, Ardus says. He thinks I'm just an ig'runt kid cause yeh grew up in the wild woods." "Maybe book-learning ain't for me but I'm smarter than them rangers."

The wind rustled. Leaves swept off the bank into a funnel shape, blowing in circles around Jack. "What the heck?" He watched them fly in the turning wind and caught the whiff of a faint smoky scent that was strangely calming to him.

"Where did I smell this before?"

"Does being stubborn feel right, Jack?" said a mysterious voice. Whether it had spoken aloud or the words just popped into his head, Jack could not tell.

He spun round, looking. "Nobody there. Is my head playing tricks on me again? Sure do feel like somebody's watching me." Then he recognized the voice. "In my cave! Someone said my name when I was in there. I smelled the same smoky spice too."

"Are you stubborn, Jack?" the voice asked again.

Jack looked at the trees, the water and sky, the leaves at his feet. "I ain't stubborn. Yer stubborn."

There was no response.

Jack spit the apple out of his mouth. "This is from the Orchard. Prob'ly grown in too much horse crap," he said, pitching the core over his shoulder. "It's making me as nuts as Humfrey."

"Let yourself learn, Jack."

These new words came on the wind like a dwindling whisper as the spice smell grew stronger.

"Yeh got a face or yeh just talking?" said Jack, looking all around. "Are yeh hiding in the trees? Stupid elves, show yerselves."

Deep down, he sensed there was no elf. There was a deep, still silence but the words clung on.

"Let myself learn? Bunk. I ain't no good with books," Jack shot back. "Put me at a desk? Ain't gonna look like a blarn fool by doing that. I'm Jack Spriggins. Tracking, stealing, and running, that's what I know, and I know it better than most."

"You have mountains to climb, Jack Spriggins."

The floating leaves gently settled and the spice-smell fizzled. Jack knew the mysterious whisperer had gone. "Mountains," he repeated, feeling excited as a fresh idea came to him. "Broog's Range, where the giants live. That's where I'll go. I'm gonna trick the giants into fighting in the war."

The plan began to sprout like Ma's beans.

"I been running my whole life. Folks chase me and I never get caught. So, I'll bring the giants down to the woods. I'll steal something they got. Something they want real bad. Make em chase me for it. The Champs want the giants. Allwise too. Haha! But they couldn't get them. Ain't smart like me. I'll do it and I'll do it without reading a single book."

He scanned the creek bed for the brooch he had just thrown away. "I can make the giants think that ogres did the stealing. Give em cause to join the fight."

The bronze and blue snake pin was half-buried in the mud underwater. "They'll never know it was me, until I set em straight. Shoot, by that time, I'll be named king-o-the-rangers, they'll be so grateful."

Jack sat down in the creek bed and splashed water at the sky. "That's what I'll do, steal me some giant treasure. They'll see for themselves we Forestlanders ain't so far below em."

Of course, there was a small matter of getting up the mountains. "Broog's Range is high as the sky out east. Ain't ever climbed anything that big before."

He ran behind the cabin where the beanstalks grew and remembered Allwise's words, *"A lad of your talents might make use of them."*

"Just might at that," he reckoned, stretching the vines hard as he could. "Could these make good ropes?"

For an hour, he hacked, sliced, and burned them. Nothing except the bone knife cut through. When it did, the vines coiled into easy loops. "Good for lugging and good for climbing."

Jack freed a long vine and chucked it over a tree branch. Gripping the line, tiny leaves unfurled by his hands. "What do yeh know! Climbing grips." When he let go, they closed tightly against the vine. "Wizard beans, all right." Jack then remembered his grappler hook. "I'll use it to hook a ledge just like the Orchard boys did."

He cut several long ropes. By the time he was done, it was late afternoon. "No more smoky smell," he said, thinking about the creepy voice. "Redvere said there's a *Silent One*, the spirit who comes when yeh need to see inside yerself." He shrugged off a shudder and squared his shoulders. "Aw, jits, I sound just like Ella. Cut it out! I know where I'm going now – so I'm going. "

Ma came outside just as he was coiling up all the vines he could carry. "I stitched new sleeves on yer shirt," she said. Her cheery look quickly fell. "Aw me. Yer off again?"

"I got mountains to climb."

"Mountains?" Ma scratched her head. "Well, yer making use of them vines, so that's good. Yeh remember how to tie the knots I showed yeh?"

"See for yerself," said Jack, holding out the green ropes. "Yeh ain't mad I'm leaving, Ma?"

"Naw, used to it. Reckon I'm proud." She yanked his laundered trousers off the clothesline and tossed them over. "Yer pa was a hunter and trapper, best-o-the-lot. It's the Jodd Spriggins in yeh that put surviving in yer blood."

"I know, Ma."

"Come in fer supper. Can't let yeh go hungry."

"No beans."

"Finicky brat! I cooked yeh oat porridge it so happens."

That night, after a grueling meal made with a mother's love, Jack grabbed a few more winks of sleep and then got up while the stars were still in the sky. He dressed and armed himself for the climb. Ma snored peacefully in her hammock, a sweet smile on her face. For once, there was nothing for him to leave her that she did not already have. Jack turned and headed off to seek giants, treasure, and a place in the tales of lore.

Chapter **16**

MOUNTAINS

A cattle barge headed up the Green River in the dark before dawn ferrying a herd of sheep from Rivercross to Tarnvil. The father and son who ran it were oblivious that Jack was also onboard. The crossbow-armed thief stole a free ride through the night and, so far, nobody had noticed.

"Ain't feeling so good now," said Jack, who lay on the filthy, stinking deck. "Fed up with these bleeters and their dang hoofs stepping all over me." The reek of cud puke and sheep dung, along with the constant rocking of the boat, made him queasy but the wooly critters were good for keeping him hid.

A canvas sail cracked and then fell limp.

"Danny boy, you awake up there?" called the ferryman.

The mutton-headed son was dozing against the fore rail and twitched with a start. "Am now," he said rubbing his eyes.

A shepherd was also aboard but sleeping on a bench to one side of the boat.

"Wind has shifted. Mind the sail," said the ferryman. "Sun comes up any minute."

"Yes, pa." The boy went to the mast and got the sail to unfurl again. The barge kept apace against the current.

At first light, Jack peeked above the back end of a sheep and looked upriver where he saw mountains.

"Broog's Range," he said. "Sure looks taller than I reckoned."

The towering peaks jabbed the dawn with purple-white crowns, falling to black where it met the forest.

"I'm itching to jump overboard and make tracks for them mountains."

Unfortunately, Jack was not a good swimmer. "Buzzards luck. How'll I ever get off this grungy keel?"

Danny Boy walked along the side rail probing the river with a long oar, which did not sink very deep.

"River seems shallow," said Jack. "I bet my feet could touch bottom." The barge scraped to a jostling halt on a sand bar.

"Doggone sandbars!" cursed the ferryman, as the sheep stumbled and baaed in the commotion. Jack covered up to avoid being trampled by hoofs but Danny Boy fell too and landed smack on top of him.

"Hey!" he said to his pa, "This one ain't part of the herd."

"Who's that, son?"

"Stowaway, Pa."

The shepherd woke up and also glared at Jack.

"Nice meeting y'all," said Jack, who pushed Danny Boy out of the way and leapt over the side.

The icy splash was a shock and the current swept him along. "Brrr!" said Jack, floundering until his heels brushed the river bottom. Rib-deep, he dug in and steadied himself against the current.

"You there!" shouted the ferryman, "What the bunk do yeh think yer doing?"

"Thanks for the ride," said Jack, working his way towards the far bank.

"Don't bother to help us get unstuck?" said the ferryman, struggling to free his oar from the mire.

"Yeh got stuck without me, yeh can get out too," shouted Jack over his shoulder.

"Why, yeh river rat!"

Beneath Jack's feet it seemed as if a trapdoor had opened because the sand gave way and the water went over his head. Bubbles rushed past his wide eyes as he gulped out desperate gurgles, kicking his feet and thrashing his arms. The current carried him farther downriver before his boots touched again and Jack thrust into the air, gasping. "Ahah!"

The folks on the barge laughed as he splashed his way to the riverbank. "A snootful of water's what yeh deserve, freeloader," shouted the ferryman. "My wife's cat swims better."

Soaked and irritated, Jack pulled himself to dry land with all but his dignity. "I needed a bath after riding yer stinking boat, anyhoo," he shouted.

"Course yeh did, vagrant! That's what yeh get for laying in the muck instead of paying for a decent ride."

Jack had not considered bringing any of the reward money along. "Never thought o'that," he shrugged.

He squished through the tall, clinging grass. Soon, he was dry again, trekking in the morning sun through big tooth maple groves, fording streams, and making his way to the foothills of Broog's Range. He wore a belt of beanstalk vines, braided so that the arrows fit snugly between the crisscrossing plaits. The rest of his green ropes were coiled across his body like the strap of his deerskin canteen. "Got all I need," he said. "Right and proud a'venture."

In the late afternoon, he made camp on top of a knoll at the foot of the range. He made a fire and cooked trout for dinner. Afterwards, he looked up and studied the mountains. "Jits," he said, scratching his head. "Gotta find a good climbing path. Can only see where the mountains go up into the clouds. Giants got cities up there? Chee. Well, I got beanstalks."

* * * *

The next morning on a slope of scree that was steep as a log chute, Jack followed the line he had picked out from camp. "Keep my bearings," he said. "Stick to it. Ain't turning back."

He scrambled upslope until he was above the timberline where he met the first rock face. Jack patted the wall. "No wizard tricks here. Just climb-climb-climb," he said with a smirk, reciting the encouraging words of Humfrey.

Slinging the canteen around his back, Jack got a finger-hold in the rock and scaled upwards. There were rigid threads of stone to grip and notches to secure footholds, but the throb of his fingertips forced him to make strict choices for picking his route. "Fingers find the way, legs don't give away," he said. "Hee! Put that in yer songs, Redvere."

By mid-morning, the brawny sun beat at his back. "Can't suck enough air. Hah! Must've climbed a thousand feet." There were thousands more to go. He fought off a bout of dizziness. "Ain't lookin down."

Jack climbed and rested on one ledge after another, taking a bite of jerky or sip of water before pressing on. Past midday, the sun crested the peaks and left him climbing in the shade. The thin air made his throat burn. He picked his way to a ledge where a vaulted roof of stone offered shelter from the whipping gusts but saw no way of climbing past it.

"I'll hold up here until I figure what to do next." He turned around and took in the view of the Great Forest. "Whew, long ways up. Only me and the birds ever saw this."

Below, the Green River unraveled westerly across the landscape, twisting between the woods and golden fields that rose and fell on the farmlands of Havensbend. The river disappeared from view somewhere before Rivercross. Beyond that, green forest stretched out as far as he could see. In the midst of it laid a great black mass. "That's the Briar," said Jack.

To his left, he saw the vast prairies of the Horse Province, tucked in a great valley and framed by the blue of Majesty Bay. "Redvere comes from there. The horse land be high country but how puny it all looks up here."

Part of Big Pine Lake showed itself on his right, amid the reedy Swamplands where he had fought the dragon with the rangers. He had to squint to make out the far peaks of the rugged Iron Hills of the dwarfs. "Somewhere out there the Champs'll make fight with the ogres."

Taken on the whole, Jack felt a pang of pride. "Ain't the worst place to live, I reckon, and worth fighting ogres away to keep it. If only we got rid of the stinking elves, I'd say it's a right-decent home."

Jack popped dried apricots in his mouth with another swig of water. Thick clouds waited on the west pitch of the mountains. "Reckon I'd best move on."

It was impossible to see beyond the vaulted rock overhang. There was a ledge angled some hundred feet up. So, he slipped a metal rod from his belt and opened its iron prongs. "Gonna need this grappling hook," said Jack.

He took the beanstalk vines off his shoulder and threaded the hoop-end of the quarrel but he noticed something odd about the ropes. "These vines ain't dried out yet?" In fact, they were as green, fresh and rubbery as when they grew by the cabin at Thin Creek. "Tough greens," he said with a smirk. Once Jack loaded the crossbow, he aimed high and pulled the trigger.

Fwish! The quarrel shot out with the vine trailing behind it. The line arced over the ridge. It struck rock but ricocheted back down.

"Bunk!"

Handling the beanstalk line was awkward. The quarrel was heavier than arrows and the green vine added drag when shot out.

"Ain't getting stuck on this ledge," he said, trying again and again.

Fwing! Fwooz! Fwap!

"Jits! Jits! Jits!"

The green coil had to be rewound and stacked properly or else the arrow did not clear the overhang. Finally, it worked out as Jack's last shot flew in a magnificent arc. *Clink!* The grappler hooked against the cliff and the vine stretched tight in his hands.

"Yippee! Hooked."

A few hard yanks proved it was secure. He fastened the crossbow to his belt and harnessed the line at his waist. "Here goes!" With a hard gulp, he swung across the mountainside with his cheeks flapping in the wind.

"Whoa!" shouted Jack, as the line swung to its limit and swayed back until he steadied and planted both feet on the rock wall. His hands gripped the beanstalk and its small leaves splayed open from the vine, making it easy to grip as he climbed hand-over-hand to a higher ridge.

In the next hour, he fired and shinnied some thousands of feet. "Fwish! Swing! Climb! I, Jack Spriggins, claim this mountain mine." Up sheer faces and over wind-gusted rifts, he ascended into the mist.

"Fingers are going numb," he finally said through chattering teeth. He shot the quarrel into a gorge where it hooked amid a wreath of twigs on a higher ledge. The gaping rift was pocketed with drifting mist as he swung inside.

"Get a spooky feeling in here," said Jack. The hairs on the back of his neck straightened when a passing shadow put his senses on alert. Something hidden in the mist made a sound above him. "Sounds big."

A burst of wind roared in his ears and then he could hear nothing else.

"Shifty clouds, what're yeh hiding?" Jack put his feet on the cliff and gazed up at the drifting mist. "Ain't ever seen a giant before. S'pose they wait on the side of their mountains to club climbers back down?" With a sneer, Jack climbed his beanstalk vine. "Naw!"

The rock before him quickly darkened, accompanied by an angry screech. Jack whipped his head round as a dark shape swooped at him. "Eagle!" The bird was huge and had a wingspan of twelve feet. "I knew yeh was something big."

The eagle plunged at him from a gap in the clouds. Jack wrapped an arm around the vine and jiggled the crossbow off his belt. There was no time to load. "Aw, buzzard guts!"

The eagle attacked with pointed talons and drove him against the mountain. Jack swung his empty crossbow to fend it off. The giant bird screeched, nipped, and pitched him against the rock as it soared away through the mist.

"Dang bird, yeh tore my coat!" Jack could feel an icy rush of wind near his ribs. "Wanna rip me to pieces?"

A screech in the mist gave a new warning. This time, Jack plunged an arrow into the catch. "Where do I aim?" He searched the gray murk but there was no sound or shadow.

"Maybe yeh turned chicken."

The eagle emerged unexpectedly from below and attacked so swiftly Jack had no time to shoot. A vicious screech, sharp talons, and snaps from its razor-beak had Jack kicking and fighting. "Get away from me!" He batted the bird on its crown with the crossbow, which forced the eagle away.

In the melee, the strap of his water flask ripped free and fell into the mist. "Bunk!" Jack shouted, watching it disappear.

The eagle circled round for another attack. This time, there was a break in the clouds and Jack had a clear shot. Despite the wind, the cold, and a racing heart, his eyes met the eagle dead on. "That's it, birdie. Get in tight. It's yeh or me, right?"

He gritted his teeth and could feel the tension of the crossbow's trigger. Only, Jack smelled spice-smoke in the air. That fuzzy, quiet voice burned through his concentration.

"Just like the dragon?"

"Huh?" said Jack. He was keenly aware of the eagle bearing down on him, yet also that he had threatened its nest. "The wreath o'twigs where I shot my arrow! Ain't no demon bird, just a mother protecting her young. I'm the attacker."

Instead of firing, Jack dropped down the line. The eagle veered off and soared away. The pump and whoosh of its wings ceased as it glided over its nest and perched. Jack swung across to an opposite ledge and landed in a surprising patch of mountain heather where he discovered his water flask as well.

"Ain't that a stroke-o-luck?" He tied the broken strap together with a strong knot. Then he remembered *the voice,* which had warned him.

"Just like the dragon," Jack repeated. "S'posed to mean something to me?"

Whether owing to the toll of the climb or some other spell, Jack closed his eyes and listened. His breath was steady, his heart pounding, but he was surprised by how controlled he had been in the fight. "How'd I know better than to kill that eagle?"

Tiny chirps came from the nest up higher. Jack opened his eyes. The mother sat perched, watching him. Little eagle beaks nipped beneath her wings.

"Keep away then, birdie. I ain't no danger to yeh." But Jack's anger, like venom, rose in his blood. "Where's that spice-smell come from!" he shouted to the air. "Whose voice are yeh, and why're yeh saying, *Just like the dragon*'? Killing the dragon weren't my fault."

The voice replied, *"Did you feel the dragon was wrongfully killed?"*

Jack quickly traded his anger with fear. "Ain't gonna go nuts," he said to the silence within. Closing his eyes, a sense of calm returned." Don't know why yeh talk to me but I don't like it one bit."

"What are you doing, Jack?" The voice was barely a whisper.

"Climbing this mountain."

"Why?"

"Gonna make the giants come down to the Forest."

"Is that your only reason?"

"Reckon not. I wanna show the Champs and ol' Goatbeard I'm ready to fight."

"How will you do this?"

"Make giants care about fighting ogres."

"Will anyone be harmed?"

"Dunno. Prob'ly can't be helped."

"Perhaps if you think before you act?"

"If yeh think too much, nothin ever gets done."

"Many heroes fall from great heights."

"Well, I've come too far to turn back now."

"Unless you turn within."

Jack frowned. "Yeh're the Silent Spirit that Redvere talked of, ain't yeh?"

"I am your Silent One, Jack."

No more words came but if Jack could have put a face to the silence, he would swear it was smiling. The spice-smell faded into the shifting wind. Jack stood up on chilled, aching legs. The peaks above were twisted and snow-covered. "Oof, it's cold! How can any folks live up there?"

He pulled on leather gloves from his coat pockets and scanned the ravine. Jutted out some fifty feet across was a neighboring ledge. "Shouldn't ruffle any feathers if I go over there."

With a running start he swung over to the next ridge. From this new vantage he shook his line and the grappler hook came free of the eagle's nest. The mother bird did not attack.

The next climb went along a thin vertical crack that ran up the rock face. Twisting his hands and feet into its jagged groove, Jack worked his way higher where he met harsher weather. After cresting the crag, he crawled across the rocky tier. The sleet cut sideways with bitter force. "Why're yeh fighting me, crazy wind? Yeh ain't getting me off this mountain."

Jack hunched down to hold on but his fingers and knees kept slipping on the icy rock. The ends of his hair whipped his eyes and he had to squint, searching out notches to pull his body along the ridge line. "Ain't me falling from high places!" he shouted. His ice-caked ears and cheeks ached, and his lips burned from the cutting blasts of sleet.

There was a crack in the mountain wall, wide enough to crawl inside. "Other folks fall, but I'm turning inside." shouted Jack, through stiff, frozen lips. With numb fingers he wriggled in.

The wind bullied and wailed loudly inside the rift. "Brrr!" said Jack, through chattering teeth. The little tunnel led him to an upward crevice. Some hundred feet above, a trickle of light bled down. "C'mon, stiff fingers, wake up," he moaned, clapping and rubbing them to get a little feeling back. Pushing on to his feet, Jack pawed the sidewalls. With his back braced against one side, he pressed his feet against the other and worked his way up the skinny rift. Narrow and jagged, it provided an occasional rocky shelf to rest his rump on.

"Scrunch and step," chanted Jack. Slowly, steadily, the light at the top grew brighter.

His gloves grew squishy, no longer stiffened by ice, and the feeling in his fingers slowly returned. Water began to trickle down the chasm. "Don't figure. Ain't so cold now. What's melting the ice?"

Nearly everywhere he reached was slippery but he kept his feet carefully braced and maneuvered up the chasm.

"What sound was that?" A gong like a distant bell rang and birds chirped outside the rift above. "Why does the air blow sweet and fresh up there?" Jack got hold of the opening and stuck his head out the top.

Two glassy, black eyes and a pair of curled horns greeted him. He was face to face with a mountain goat. It was large as a bull with silky hair and it looked just as surprised to see him. The goat cocked its head and reared into a ramming posture.

"Aw, bunk!" Jack was sure he was about to be butted back down but instead the huge nanny turned and leapt away with a "*N-N-NEAH!*"

With one strenuous heave, Jack was out of the gap, standing on a slope beneath sunny skies, overlooking a long green valley. "What the blarn?"

Majestic peaks on all sides concealed a hidden land. Magnificent falls gushed with rainbow-circles in their spray, joining a river that cut through the lush valley. More gongs resounded from the valley center.

"Bells," exclaimed Jack. "I was hearing right."

They tolled from the direction of two cities, which faced each other on opposing sides of the river. The far city had green buildings. The closer had shiny white ones. Drawn buggies moved on carriage roads while a barge drifted on the river between them. Folks were moving at a busy dock where a large wheel churned the river. From Jack's vantage they did not seem big at all.

"Up here, I feel like a giant," he said. "They look like ants moving round an anthill."

There were herds of sheep grazing in the meadows. With a gulp of water from his flask and gnaws of hunger in his belly, Jack followed a goat's path downslope. "Giants just ahead."

* * * *

The memory of Giant Valley was fresh and clear, like the taste of blood was in Jack's mouth now. He felt a world apart laying on a lonely ridge on the other side of their mountains.

"So, that was the climb," he said to the Silent One. "The climb that started this whole mess."

"*Every step forward was a new lesson,*" replied the spirit.

"Why don't I feel I learned anything?"

"*Perhaps you prefer running.*"

"Running away, yeh mean." Jack glanced over the ledge at the forest floor, which was dotted with distant trees where Roidaroy and the other giants had fallen. "I doubt the giants ever saw me coming."

"*I know one giant who was looking for a change. And a friend.*"

"Beirboor," said Jack with a sigh. "Reckon he was."

"*The day you arrived was one he will never forget.*"

Jack asked a question he had been wondering. "Why me?"

"*You were the one who climbed; the spur of change the giants were waiting for.*"

"I was? Bunk, I sure don't see it that way."

"*Take a closer look.*"

A misty cloud enveloped him and transformed the cold mountain ledge into the warm glow of an alcove within the Gogmagogg Manor where Jack's adventure in Giantdom had really begun.

Chapter **17**

GIANTDOM

The Constitution of Greater Giantdom stated in plain terms, "All Giants are created equal, yet, superior to all other races of life." This perplexed Beirboor as he read his history book. He was a thirteen-year-old, six and one-quarter foot giant, who found the other races of life to be captivating.

"None of our books ever talk about the Great Forest and the people who live down there," he sighed, trying to ignore the laughter of the arriving guests.

The cozy alcove where he had taken refuge had a considerable view of the reception hall of Gogmagogg Manor, Beirboor's family home. The vaulted ceilings and wide marble columns were hung with tasseled, purple drapery, his favorite color. In the center, on a pedestal, was the family's famous golden harp. The entering guests stopped to marvel at it.

"Perhaps Nollokirk will play a birthday song for me tonight."

He plopped down on the plush pillows in front of the hearth, far enough from the front door so he would not have to socialize but could still be seen.

"You're not fooling anyone," said his nasally tutor, Vikuvis, who hovered by the fireplace. "Your father expects you to be sociable."

"Can't you just pretend I have homework to do?" said Beirboor.

"We Jadins don't pretend anything," said Vikuvis, "We leave that to you Chelebs."

Defeated, Beirboor tossed the history book aside. He picked another honeybun off a platter on the floor. "The lesson on the Constitution didn't make sense," he said between bites, "Nothing's equal around here. Even I can see that."

"Then I shall have you read it again," said Vikuvis, "But not tonight. After all, this banquet is in your honor."

"None of the guests seem to notice me," said Beirboor, as he watched them rinse their hands in the rose-water fountain before entering the banquet hall.

"They are hardly to blame for that if you're going to lay there instead of greeting them with dignity."

"I don't like shindigs. Look at how phony they greet one another, kissing the air instead of each other's cheeks. Besides, they're father's friends. I hardly know them. They never even get my name right. Baron Skootafrey called me 'Breeboor 'last time he was here."

"If Baron Skootafrey did not have his own name inscribed on his sandals, he'd forget that too," said Vikuvis. "You can keep that between just the two of us."

With a smile, Beirboor rolled over on his back and sank deeper into the pillows, rubbing his hands across his bald head, which still felt itchy. Today, on his thirteenth birthday, he had undergone the rite of *Capillus Eximo*, a coming of age ceremony where every last folic of his hair was shaved. It was generally a proud affair for a young Cheleb, but not so much for Beirboor.

"Why don't Jadin giants shave their heads like we do?"

"Because it is a ridiculous practice," said Vikuvis. "Such a garish display of immodesty would never suit a Jadin." The tutor wiped his fingertips along the precise line of his matted black bangs.

Vikuvis was a tall Jadin (seven-foot, seven inches); lean and tense. He had a pointed chin and nose, with prominent cheekbones and dark, rigid eyes under an angular brow. His lips were thin, held tight, as if to lock up sniffy comments that he might otherwise let slip. Like all Jadins, he wore a green tunic with quarter-length sleeves and black leather sandals. Beirboor found it difficult to relax whenever he was nearby.

"Why do you stay then, Master Vikuvis? You despise these parties even more than I do."

"Because your father has requested it. As your tutor, not to mention Senate Minority Leader, I am obligated, out of courtesy."

"Gee, thanks."

At that moment, Lord Gogmagogg, Beirboor's father, entered the reception. He was not simply the lord of the manor, he was the most powerful, influential giant in all of Giantdom. A full seven foot, ten inches tall, he wore an ivory toga belted with a golden cincture. A royal purple sash hung across his body from one shoulder.

"Fe, Fi, Fo, Fum!" he shouted, with a powerful, jovial voice.

Loud barks and heavy, excited breathing announced the entrance of his four great mastiffs as they came skittering over the glossy marble floor to greet him. Gogmagogg opened his arms for the largest two, Fe and Fi, to set their huge forepaws on his chest and lick his face. After a few sloppy exchanges, all four dogs ran into the alcove and pounced on Beirboor, who hunched to protect himself from the wet greetings. Fo and Fum quickly discovered the honey cakes.

"Hey!" shouted Beirboor, as they made off with a bounty.

Gogmagogg bellowed to his guests, "Behold the harp, my fellow Chelebs!" He pointed to its golden frame and glistening strings. "The most beautiful and euphonious, honey-toned instrument in the world. Let it be taken to the courtyard. Tonight Nollokirk, our most celebrated harpist, will favor us with a selection."

The guests erupted into cheers as Nollokirk bounded in wearing a red-glittered toga with matching sandals, kissing and waving his hands to one and all. Trumpeters blew a pompous welcome. Two Jadin attendants, dressed in green tunics like Vikuvis, lifted the great harp from its pedestal and carried it out.

"Perhaps Father has commissioned a new song for my birthday," said Beirboor eagerly.

"A most impractical gift," said Vikuvis.

"My son," pronounced Lord Gogmagogg, as he descended the steps and patted Beirboor on top of the skull. "Look at that glorious shine; a proud day for the Gogmagoggs."

Beirboor winced. "I don't feel any different than I did yesterday."

"Nonsense. Look at you, nearly grown," insisted his father, while adding under his breath, "I do want you to trim down a bit before your official portrait is painted." Gogmagogg pointed to the painting of Beirboor's older brother, who always looked fit, robust, and beefy. "You should spend more time on your physique, like Roidaroy does, and earn an appetite for our many feasts."

Beirboor tried to suck in his belly, which was flabby and filled with too many honey buns. "But I already have a good appetite."

"Start an exercise regime tomorrow," said his father, strolling off to kiss the hands of a Cheleb baroness.

"Happy birthday," said Beirboor to himself, sarcastically. "My party will be no different from any other Cheleb banquet."

"No surprise," said Vikuvis. "Frivolous engagements of this sort occur almost nightly in your home. When Chelebs earn a million gold pieces, they spend two million celebrating it. Extravagant food, wine and flattery go around, simply for being the giants of Chelebraxia. It's ridiculous."

Beirboor picked up his sketchpad and with a couple of pieces of colored chalk, added new strokes to his latest drawing.

"What, may I ask, are you scrawling?" said Vikuvis.

"Forestland Elves and Faeries, Dancing with a Huge Brown Bear," said Beirboor, admiring his artwork. "It's my latest sketch. I wonder if bears of the forests really can be as large as we are?"

Vikuvis sneered, "The particulars of the Forestland are of no consequence to we of Giantdom."

"I've never met a Forestlander but I sometimes dream of their world."

"Why you fritter the hours sketching woodsy nonsense exceeds my comprehension," said Vikuvis.

"I can't help my dreams," said Beirboor. "I think the forest is interesting."

"Not another word," Vikuvis scolded. "It is one of the few issues on which Jadins and Chelebs wholly agree. The lowly forest is beneath us."

"Why is that?"

"Because the under-sized races who dwell there are ignorant, greedy and violent."

"Couldn't we giants teach them to be otherwise?"

Vikuvis sniffed. "No."

"Ooh me!" said Beirboor's sister, Lawrenlawra, who entered. "I can't imagine where the time went." She was prettied-up in a tightly pinned, peacock blue toga that reached her ankles. Her bald head was freshly polished, smooth and shiny. "Why, look at you, Boorie. The top of your head is pasty-white."

"I miss my hair," he said.

"Not to worry, brotherkins. You need to get some sun, then the color will even out and you will look magnificent just like me."

"Is mother coming to the banquet?" said Beirboor.

"No, Mummie is still rehearsing for her new play at the Opera House but word came that she hopes to be here for the concerto."

Beirboor's heart sank and it must have shown.

Lawrenlawra kneeled and fussed with his sash. "Please don't pout in front of my friends, brotherkins. Both Droositti sisters are coming and they already think you're strange."

"What's Mother's play called?"

"*A Giant Beauty Awakes,*" said Lawrenlawra. "It's going to be a smash. Ooh, that reminds me, Nollokirk is coming tonight."

"You missed his arrival," said Vikuvis. "But I am not surprised. You are never on time."

"Ooh me, I must go and bid welcome." Her face flushed as she rose. With a flurry of perfume, she was gone.

"Gosh, some birthday," pouted Beirboor.

"Put that scribbling aside," said Vikuvis, "And follow me to the portico."

Beirboor rose from the cushions and followed the Jadin outside. The rich yellow glow of late afternoon caught in the arches of the terrace that framed a lovely view of Giantdom. Jadinobblis, the green Jadin city, lay across the Windississi River and could not be more different than Chelebraxia. It was where Vikuvis lived. The buildings and monuments were crammed together like a jar full of pencils, tall and pointy.

Chelebraxia, on the other hand, was a city of colorful waving banners and white buildings situated on a hilltop overlooking Jadinobblis.

Vikuvis said, "So, you say Jadins and Chelebs are not equals?"

"Why, our attendants are Jadins, Master Vikuvis," said Beirboor. "They do our cooking and dishes, lay out our clothes, clean and fix the furniture."

"For a substantial fee, mind you."

"Yes, but that's just it," said Beirboor, hesitating. "I don't mean to sound snobby."

Vikuvis finished his thought, "A Cheleb would not be caught dead doing such menial work. Is that it?"

Beirboor nodded. "Well gosh, I just don't understand it."

"It is the obligatory mission, dare I say, privilege, of every Jadin to serve Giantdom with civic toil before retiring to a life of intellectual pursuits."

"I don't know if I could do that," said Beirboor, folding his arms over his soft belly.

"You're a bright Cheleb. Like your father, you may prove to be gifted at trade and negotiation."

"I doubt it. I'm only good at dreaming. There's nowhere I fit in Giantdom.

"You're a tad young to be pronouncing such judgment on yourself," said Vikuvis.

"Father wants me to be like Roidaroy and his friends, who spend their time lifting weights in the spa, but they make fun of me because I'm not any good at it. I hate attending parties and carriage races like they do. Honestly, Roidaroy is the last person in the world I want to be like.""That shows promise. Your brother's intellect is as numbing as an ice chip. Whereas you have applied yourself to study and shown insight, however misdirected it may be."

"What do you mean?"

"There is inequality in Giantdom," continued Vikuvis, "But it's not we Jadins who are underprivileged."

Beirboor rubbed his itchy head, "I see Jadins working the fields, operating the tram, and mining the hills."

"And teaching you to read and write."

"Yes, that too," said Beirboor, lowering his eyes. "But you never have any fun."

A swell of laughter flared from inside the banquet hall. The guests were having a terrific time celebrating Beirboor's birthday without him.

"Then I shall assign you an essay tomorrow defining the term *fun*," said Vikuvis, who took a step closer. "Beirboor, if those who attend the party cannot prepare the feast, then who do you think has the true power?"

"Are you saying I should make my own dinner?"

"No, but do not look down on those who do. After all, toil is the laboratory of knowledge and Jadins know how to apply it. It is science."

"Science isn't fun."

"You enjoy eating, don't you?"

"Gosh, yes," said Beirboor, "But I never thought about it as science."

"It is just food for thought. Your first taste of politics. Consider that your birthday present from me. Now, we should go inside where you can join *the fun*."

Beirboor moped to the rose-water fountain to wash his hands before entering the noisy banquet hall. "I have more fun dreaming of the Great Forest."

* * * *

"Battles!" said Lord Gogmagogg, setting his goblet down at the head dining table. "Borders, broadswords, and bloodshed. What gall men have to ask giants to give them aid in war. Just another example of how primitive the Forestlanders remain."

Beirboor took his seat in the banquet hall when this spirited remark by his father produced rounds of haughty laughter. The golden tableware glimmered in the light of the crystal candelabras set out for the banquet, but already the table talk sounded like any other party.

"Hail! Well-met," said Baron Krusedekulk, calling for a cheer.

Gogmagogg reigned over the social affair from a high-backed marble chair, its arms carved like gilded ram's horns. The hounds, Fe, Fi, Fo, and Fum, lay at the master's feet. To his right was an empty chair where Lady Elivalizz (Beirboor's mother) should have been seated."Let us now toast Beirboor," said Gogmagogg. "Our youngest son is shorn and officially a giant of Greater Chelebraxia."

"Hail Giantdom!" shouted the gathering, as one. Goblets were lifted, clanked together, and the revelers drank.

When Beirboor reached for his chalice, it was knocked so violently that the beat mead was sloshed all over his arm. He turned, knowing his tormentor well.

"You're going to need a stronger grip than that, Plumpy," goaded Roidaroy, his brother. "I guess being the Shaven One hasn't changed you much. Better go wash again." He was eighteen years old, seven-foot, eight inches, and pumped full of muscle, which was no surprise as he ate twelve ostrich-eggs every morning and spent most of the day in the gymnasium. His head was jar shaped, as if molded from a clay jug, and his wide nostrils flared when he spoke.

Beirboor ignored the taunts. "I already washed," he said, wiping his red-stained arm with a napkin.

"Better not touch me with that sticky arm," said Roidaroy, elbowing him.

"Roidaroy, leave our little brotherkins alone," said Lawrenlawra, fluffing her napkin at him. "Big fooly-bully."

"Let's eat!" ordered Gogmagogg.

Doors from the kitchen burst open. Jadin attendants served halved jenga fruits on beds of leafy salad. Jenga was Giantdom's proudest export. Its blossomy ambrosia now filled the air, causing Beirboor's mouth to water. Giants dug into the amber shells with their golden spoons.

"Juicy and ripe," smiled Beirboor. "Succulent red pulp and tangy seeds. Mmm, perfect."

A loud stomach rumbled. The sound came from near the curtains. Beirboor noticed a strange odor in the air too but gave it no further thought as his appetite won him over.

When the jengas were pushed aside, Jadins brought more courses of steamed squash soufflés, mashed sweet potatoes smothered with creamed pecans, hearty cauliflower walnut pies and caramel pudding.

"What a roaring appetite we share this evening," said Lord Gogmagogg, dabbing his chin with a fine linen napkin. "Baron Skootafrey!" he called out to a fellow Cheleb who presided over the second table. "You met the rangers of the forest realm. How did they strike you?"

Skootafrey was an eight-foot tall Cheleb who never had enough space around him. "Say what?" he blustered, knocking a tall decanter across his neighbor's dinner setting. He snapped his fingers at the Jadin attendants in the room. "Attend to that."

"Ardus Camlann of the forest realm," reiterated Gogmagogg.

"Oh, Camlann. Yes. We sent him away. Along with the other tree choppers."

"What kind of man was he?"

"Oh, hmm," said Skootafrey, "Well spoken, polite, with a mild semblance of intellect. Not as bad as you'd expect. His clothes, of course, were crude and badly tailored but he is a man of the woods, after all."

Chuckles went around the hall.

"His thickset companion, Gwachmai, on the other hand," continued Skootafrey, "I declare!" The Giant snorted uproariously and inadvertently upended his plate as he struck the table with his elbow, spattering sauce on his other neighbor. "Absolutely primitive. Our goats have more class."

"Fellow giants, I ask you all," said Gogmagogg, rubbing his shiny head. "What kind of low minds fight over anything these days?"

"Perhaps," interjected Vikuvis, "Those who face opponents with even lower minds." He sat in a chair at the far end of the host's table, with hands folded.

Gogmagogg's face lit with a smile of challenge, "So, Vikuvis, you would argue our senate was wrong to turn away Ardus Camlann and his so-called 'Champions? 'Would you recommend we also join their fight against the ogres?"

"No, not at all," said the Jadin. "Combat will always be the lowest form of expression. We stand to gain nothing by getting involved. But it was suggested to me just this evening that we might have other means to offer the man's cause."

Giants stirred in their seats. Beirboor slumped in dread. "Please don't say my name. Please don't say my name," he prayed.

"What other means, Jadin?" said Gogmagogg. "As in gold? Comestibles? That would be hypocrisy."

"No," said Vikuvis. "By educating them. Even dogs must learn to be housebroken. Perhaps Forestlanders can be properly civilized."

"Go on," said Gogmagogg.

"With all those woods surrounding them, their resources could be used productively to fortify their lands and keep the ogre intruders out. If we introduced them to proper industry, they might evolve. Mind you, I would be first to admit the slim hope of their improvement."

Jadin attendants applauded and a few Chelebs struck spoons against the table. "Cleanliness," he went on, "Would be a first step in reforming their crudeness."

"Good!" said Baron Krusedekulk, waving his hand. "The mere thought of them seems to have produced something of their odor."

"Indeed," enjoined others, exchanging looks. "We smell it too."

Beirboor looked at the curtains again but feared the odd scent might be coming from the kitchen.

"What curious aromas," said Lawrenlawra. "Is it nearly time to go outside for the evening's entertainment?"

"And skip my birthday dessert?" said Beirboor.

"Daughter," scolded Gogmagogg." You're changing the subject from a compelling point made by your learned tutor. Please go on, Vikuvis."

"I've little to add," said the Jadin. "It's just a pity that forest men expected us to bear arms with them. Giants could never contribute much in the way of battles."

Roidaroy stood up in anger. "Father! Did you hear that? Teacher said we giants have lost our might." He flexed his arms and stretched his purple toga to its seams.

"That is not what I said," Vikuvis defended.

Beirboor chimed in, "I've never known any giant who thinks of using might against others."

"Of course you haven't, Wimpy," said Roidaroy, with a shove. "All you can lift are honey buns."

"Father, tell him to stop hitting me," said Beirboor, rubbing his shoulder.

"Enough!" boomed Gogmagogg.

"I was not suggesting that giants are inferior," said Vikuvis. "Far from it. We set our weapons aside centuries ago and have nothing to contribute to the barbaric condition of the forest realm."

"A clever idea, to consider proliferating their resources," said Gogmagogg, "But not to our benefit?"

"The Forestland has nothing we giants need."

"Very true. So, I believe we stay the course laid down by our glorious benefactor," said Gogmagogg, pointing at a bust that rested on a pillar by the back wall. "My ancestor, Lord Broogmagoog, declared long ago, the Forestlanders are unworthy of our attention."

"Hear, hear!" agreed many Giants.

"Enough talk of them," said Baron Krusedekulk. "How about dessert. And Lawrenlawra was right; a bitter smell has wafted in. Incense, please!"

Gogmagogg stood, covering his nose with the sleeve of his toga. "I think we should have dessert on the veranda with some harp music."

With much clamor, giants and giantesses rustled outside to the portico. Beirboor fluttered his lips with frustration and moped out for the show.

Night had fallen and dusk produced a magical backdrop of starry blue. Seats had been arranged on the veranda, with foot-candles lighting the aisles. On the dais rested the harp, looking grand as ever, its strings sparkling in the candlelight. Beirboor took a seat in the back row, sulking, until a Jadin handed him a plate with birthday cake. "Gee, thanks."

Nollokirk stepped to the platform, pulling up a stool. He whipped his hands forth and slowly brought them back, closing his eyes as if to summon his talents. He leaned the harp against his shoulder. A giantess in the front row swooned. Lawrenlawra glanced back at the Droositti sisters with tears in her eyes. Beirboor rolled his.

Then the music began. The harp was like a symphony unto itself, as if bells and strings from the spheres invisibly accompanied it. The new notes met and danced with wonderful sensations that caused Beirboor to forget the taste of cake and follow the sounds. A tapestry of color was weaved upon his mind by the harmonious symphonic rhythms. Nollokirk thumped his leg on the platform for cadence. Next, his voice boomed out the chorus to a Cheleb favorite:

"Fe, Fi, Fo, Fum!
Fashions go and fashions come,
More for Giants, less for some,

Fe, Fi, Fo, Fum!"

"Fe, Fi, Fo, Fum!

Giants hail to Giantdom!

More for us, less for them,

Fe, Fi, Fo, Fum!"

Yet, the mystery odor again intruded upon the evening, making it difficult to enjoy the music. The mountain breeze and flowers had no power to obscure it. Baron Skootafrey violently fidgeted in his chair and Beirboor watched him leap up, turning his head as if to search for the stink. Waving his arms, Skootafrey sung at the top of his lungs over everybody else, "Fe, Fi, Fo, Fum, I smell the blood of a Forest Son!"

A sour chord twanged from Nollokirk's harp and the stars nearly fell from the sky. Bald heads whipped around at Skootafrey, who pointed his finger to the dining hall.

Lord Gogmagogg rose, shushing the music.

Beirboor's jaw fell open. "I don't believe it."

A small human boy with yellow eyes was at the vacated banquet tables, gobbling the scraps of food.

This is the best birthday gift ever," said Beirboor. "A Forestlander has come to Giantdom."

Chapter 18

CAUGHT

If Jack had known that giants possessed a sense of smell better than his own, he would not have hidden behind the curtains with an empty stomach watching them scoop, spoon, and relish their feast, while his own hunger grew unbearable. Moreover, he lost all concern about being discovered after they referred to forest-folk as dogs who needed to be trained. Soon as the giants left their tables, Jack stopped hiding like a mouse and started thinking like a fox.

A hungry fox.

Now, as Lord Gogmagogg returned to the banquet hall, the others followed him covering their noses. The throng took cautious steps toward Jack as if he were rabid. "You are a forest son?" said Gogmagogg, loud and slow, like one speaking to an idiot.

"Yep," said Jack, chewing.

"How did you get here? "

"Climbed."

"Faa-ther!" protested Roidaroy. "That's a lie. It's impossible to enter Giantdom by climbing."

"Silence," said Gogmagogg, raising his hand. "Baron Skootafrey, what say you?"

"No Forestlander was admitted through the border gate."

"You climbed?" said Gogmagogg, turning to Jack. "Which side of the mountains did you climb?"

Jack pointed southwest.

"Butterballs!" exclaimed Skootafrey. "The south face is utterly impassable."

"I told you, Faa-ther, the little whelp is a liar," said Roidaroy.

Gogmagogg stared at Jack for a moment, rubbing his chin.

"Yeh gonna eat me?" said Jack, fidgeting.

A smile cracked on Gogmagogg's face and he began to laugh. "Giants do not eat meat. We have no taste for blood whatsoever. You are safe in that regard." Lowering to the bench, he sat beside Jack, "Please continue. Eat and entertain us some more. Do you have a name, Little Climber?"

"Jack Spriggins."

"Wonderful," said Gogmagogg, who motioned to the giants in green tunics. Like servants, they brought over a crock that was big as a washbasin.

"Caramel pudding!" said the plump young giant, who squeezed through the guests. Freckle-faced and only a foot taller than Jack, he held two empty bowls in his hands offering one. "My name's Beirboor. And today's my birthday."

Ignoring the bowl, Jack stuffed a hand inside the crock and then into his mouth, spattering in response: "Happy bir-f-thday!"

"Ooh," said Lawrenlawra, as she tiptoed behind her father, "Daddykins, look how he eats with his dirty hands."

"Yer spoons are too big," Jack slobbered out.

"So they are," said Gogmagogg. "Forgive us, Jack Spriggins, and we'll forgive your manners." He grabbed a large serving spoon and heaped globs of caramel into Jack's bowl.

"Yeh the king here?" said Jack.

"King?" said Gogmagogg. "How Forestlandish of you. Of course not, Jack Spriggins. There are no kings in Giantdom. All giants are equal to each other."

"What is your age, interloper?" said Vikuvis, who had been staring at Jack with a sour face.

"Thirteen," said Jack.

"Thirteen years," said Gogmagogg, who rose to put his hands on Beirboor's shoulders. "Why today, my son, Beirboor, is also thirteen. He takes a keen interest in your kind. By drawing, not climbing mountains or *spying*."

"Really, Father," blushed Beirboor.

"I ain't a spy," said Jack.

"So, tell us what brings you to our happy home?"

"Ain't nothing but ogres and war down in the forest anymore," said Jack. "Guess I wanted to see what peaceful living was like."

"How interesting," said Gogmagogg. "Did you hear that, Master Vikuvis? This tiny boy has risked his life to join us in our glorious mountain haven. What do you make of it?"

"I'd say there's more to Jack Spriggins than meets the eye," stated Vikuvis.

"Seems to be the question of the evening," said Gogmagogg to the gathering. "With the likes of Jack Spriggins here, one Forestlander who seeks a loftier way of life, is it possible the Great Forest is changing? Or, is this brave little climber a diamond in the rough?"

A hubbub came over the hall as giants turned to each other with varying opinions:

"Changed for the worse, I'd say."

"Well met."

"At least the little one's avoiding violence, not entreating it."

"It can't hurt to understand them better."

"Never!"

Roidaroy stamped his foot. "Faa-ther! This yellow-eyed forest creature has stolen enough of our evening. Toss him out, like the puny Champions."

"No, Father, don't!" pleaded Beirboor. "Roidaroy is a bully. He doesn't care to learn about others. Please let Jack Spriggins stay, just for a while. He's so interesting. I'll take care of him myself."

"Daddykins," said Lawrenlawra, "This is more interest than Boorie has shown in anything but a sketchpad for months. Let the woodsy boy be his birthday present. We could wash and dress him up. My old doll clothes might fit."

Jack sprang to his feet. "Ain't no way! Forget it."

"Sit, little climber," chuckled Gogmagogg, patting him with an enormous hand.

"I ain't nobody's pet," said Jack.

"Of course not. Have some more pudding."

The giant named Krusedekulk stepped forward. "Surely, Gog, the idea of allowing a Forestlander to live in Giantdom must be forbidden," he said. "Who knows if he might carry disease?"

"Oh, I doubt that," said Gogmagogg. "He certainly has a healthy, giant-like appetite."

"Father, what if Vikuvis could teach him?" said Beirboor, "He suggested that possibility himself at dinner."

"No, Beirboor," said Vikuvis clearing his throat, "Absolutely not, that was a hypothetical postulation."

Gogmagogg turned. "Well, tutor, it is a chance to test your ideas. Could you civilize this small, woodsy, under-privileged head?"

"Yes!" said Beirboor. "Master Vikuvis, if anyone could, it's you."

"I could keep watch over it," said Vikuvis. "Perhaps Master Beirboor would benefit from the experiment."

Jack did not like the look the tutor gave him. Of all things, why did Beirboor have to mention school?

"Then it's settled," boomed Gogmagogg. "Our house will play host to Jack Spriggins."

Applause echoed throughout the hall.

"Chee," muttered Jack, rolling his eyes. "Always, it's gotta be school, school, school."

"Of course, Jack Spriggins, you don't have to accept my generosity, if you wish to remain as you are," said Gogmagogg.

Jack had just gotten further with the giants than any ranger ever had. "Sounds okay to me."

The guests gave a hurrah and then returned to their seats on the portico for more harp music.

"I'll make sure you get the best of everything, Jack Spriggins," said Beirboor. "We'll do everything together. You must tell me about the forest, the elves, the dwarfs, and the bears too!"

"Well, they all burp and sneeze like anyone else."

Outside, the harp song resumed.

"Fe, Fi, Fo, Fum!
Smell the blood of a Forest-son,
Make us laugh, bring us fun,
Fe, Fi, Fo, Fum!"

Chapter **19**

LESSONS

The giants 'experiment to "civilize" Jack began immediately. Jadin attendants promptly escorted him downstairs to an enormous room with a pool of warm water, where he was instructed to bathe. Poolside torches flared and goat-shaped fountainheads sprayed water over Jack's head.

"This rosy water is waa-arm," he said, enjoying how his voice echoed off the smooth, blue tiles.

"It's heated beneath the city and runs through all our houses," explained Beirboor, who had tagged along. "Why, where does the water in your home come from?"

"A bucket from Thin Creek," said Jack. "It ain't clean and it ain't warm."

"Gosh."

A Jadin steward named Veedivee showed Jack how to scrub using a squishy, springy clump called *a sponge.* After the bath, Jack was engulfed in soft cotton towels. It was strange to have servants doing what any halfwit could do for himself.

"Don't yeh even put on yer own clothes?" said Jack.

"Why should we?" said Beirboor. "We're Chelebs. The Jadins take care of us."

Jack's Forestland clothes were exchanged for a Cheleb tunic and soft leather sandals that fit his smaller feet (Beirboor had worn them as a child). Then began a debate over his straggly hair, which lasted some days because Jack refused to be shaved.

"The matter has been taken up by the Senate," said Beirboor.

"I don't get what all the fuss is about," replied Jack.

"Father asserts that *the experiment* should represent a Cheleb enterprise, while Master Vikuvis argues if he is the one to teach you, then you should wear a Jadin bowl cut."

"Don't I get a say?" said Jack.

"Well, it is your head, Jack Spriggins, but isn't all the attention fun?"

"Yeh're sorta sappy."

When the issue was settled, Jack agreed to have his hair washed and combed, not trimmed. Giantdom was satisfied that an improvement had been achieved.

Beirboor had a daily routine, and now, Jack did too. They lived and ate like princes but, as soon as breakfast was over, Jack was sent with Vikuvis to sit for reading lessons in the conservatory.

Jack did not take to the reading of words with pleasure. In fact, he was stubborn as a mule. There were writing desks with inkwells to sit at, which he could barely see over. Stone heads called "busts" rested on pillars in the corners and under their stares, he felt judged for what he did not know. Jack wished for a window to jump out of, or a doorway to slip through, to escape the towering figure of Master Vikuvis. "Don't dally," said the tutor, tapping the leather book. "Your reading primer. Open it."

The book was thick, not terribly heavy, just daunting. Jack's hands were sweating as he flipped the book cover. One glance inside and he quickly shut it and shoved the book away.

"I had almost expected this, Forestling," said Vikuvis. "You're as hopeless as I feared you would be."

"What if I can't figure out what all them squiggles mean and I really am a lunkhead, after all?"

The tutor slid the book closer. "Then I will thank you for proving me right," he said. "*Teaching you* was always a doubtful proposition. I will inform the other giants the experiment is over and you will be sent back to the woods where you belong."

Vikuvis turned away.

"Yeh got any books that ain't so big?" said Jack.

Vikuvis looked back, his lips tightened for a moment then he gave a faint sigh before opening the book. "This page has written on it an alphabet even an animal could learn. First, sound the letters out aloud. Beginning with 'A'."

Jack took a gulp of air and began.

Each morning, he sat alone with the Jadin tutor. Each morning, the routine continued. Jack was steamed that Vikuvis always got him mad enough to get started.

"Next page," Vikuvis insisted.

"The f-fox ran unn-der the f-f-f—"

"Fence!" snapped Vikuvis. "Read the next sentence, and sound it out."

"The hun-hunnn—"

"Keep going."

"The hun-ter cha-chased the fox?"

"Yes, yes, yes. The hunter chased the fox," repeated Vikuvis.

"All that scribbling makes some sense now," said Jack.

"I purposely chose a text you could follow."

"Do yeh giants hunt foxes?"

"Of course not. Next sentence."

Jack took to standing on his chair to see better what he was reading. The Jadin still towered over him, clapping his hands at the slightest mistake. Yet, within a week, Jack was reading passages aloud without trouble.

After the morning lesson, Beirboor, Roidaroy, and Lawrenlawra joined the class. Vikuvis quizzed them all but his eyes always watched Jack, who surprised even himself by remembering facts quickly.

"Name the poet who Broogmagoog took on his expedition to settle Giant Valley."

"Jado the Small," answered Jack.

Vikuvis seemed impatient with the others. "Roidaroy, please tell us, what was significant about Jado? Roidaroy?"

The beefy giant had fallen asleep at this desk.

Jack spoke up. "Jado was a shorty who made up rhymes and Broog liked him so much he named yer green city after him."

"Jack Spriggins is improving fast, don't you think, Master Vikuvis?" said Beirboor.

Vikuvis winced a lot during these lessons. "He is unruly as a wild ferret, answering out of turn."

"I reckon I never want my smarts to stop growing," said Jack.

"Daddykins has been impressed with the Spriggy one," said Lawrenlawra, "The experiment is working."

In the evenings, Lord Gogmagogg invited Jack to join them in the alcove, where Lawrenlawra played the family harp before bedtime. "Now daughter," said Gogmagogg, "Play for us, a sweet lullaby for sweet dreams."

Lawrenlawra played decent enough but, no matter who strummed it, the harp made listening a magical experience.

"I ain't heard nothing as fetching as that music, ever," said Jack, honestly.

Gogmagogg chuckled merrily. "Ah, Jack Spriggins. It pleases me to see you gain so much culture living here among the giants."

Each night, Jack shared Beirboor's chamber where he slept on a daybed outfitted with plush pillows and soft blankets. There was a

window overhead, with openable glass panes, through which Jack
watched the stars.

Unfortunately, Beirboor peppered him with annoying
questions:

"Is the Great Forest really dangerous?"

"Is it true people practice magic there?"

"Are dwarfs smaller than you?"

"Are elves even smaller?"

Flatly, Jack answered "yeah" and "naw", but Beirboor was
tireless with his sketchpad. Even by candlelight, he held up pictures
of Forestland rangers, adorned like knights doing battle. "Like this?"

"Less shine, more blood," yawned Jack.

Jack's personal belongings – his forestland clothes, boots and
coat (with the ogre brooch fastened inside), the beanstalk vines, bone
knife, and the crossbow – were kept stashed under the daybed. He
did not want others to touch them. However, one morning after
returning from breakfast, he discovered everything was missing.

"Hey Boor, where's my stuff?"

"Vedivee, put it the wardrobe," said Beirboor, who took the
crossbow off the highest shelf, staring at it with annoying curiosity.
"What is this thing?"

"Crossbow," said Jack. "It's mine."

"I know it's yours," said Beirboor, holding it out of reach. "I
just wanna look at it."

Jack jumped to snatch the weapon but Beirboor was much
too tall.

"What's this button do?" He released the lever, which popped
the cross arms open. "Gosh."

"Give it," said Jack.

"Tell me what it's used for."

"Hunting."

"Have you killed anything?"

"A wolf or two, and a spoiled giant brat if yeh don't hand it over."

"No bears?" asked Beirboor.

"Got a dragon in the eye once," bragged Jack.

"Really? A fire-breathing dragon?"

"Naw. Orange spit, no fire."

Beirboor looked disappointed.

"It weren't easy, y'know," said Jack.

"Show me how to shoot, will you?"

"Yeh can forget it," said Jack. "If one of them Jads sees, they'll take it away."

"No, Veedivee won't ever know, I promise," said Beirboor, who turned, running off with Jack's crossbow.

"Hey!"

Jack chased Beirboor beyond the parlor, through the alcove, until they stopped in the conservatory.

"Give it back, I ain't kidding around."

"No," said Beirboor. "Unless you promise to show me how to shoot, I won't."

"Jits," said Jack. "Ain't anything yeh can shoot in here."

"Sure can! That bust in the corner could be our target."

"Yeh mean the one with the chubby cheeks?"

"That's Spiroshakes, Chelebraxia's most famous bard," said Beirboor, steadying himself. "I hate memorizing his lousy sonnets."

Jack thought about this and could not help his smile. "Ha, well, now yeh're talking."

Beirboor pointed the weapon.

"Hold up a sec," said Jack. "Yer pitiful. Don't hold it by the cross arms. That's aiming backwards. If it were loaded, yeh'd shoot an arrow straight up yer nose."

"Well gosh, can we use a piece of chalk instead?"

"S'pose so," said Jack, picking an orange-colored stick from the blackboard.

He climbed onto a stool to meet Beirboor's eye-line and loaded the chalk. "First, line up yer sights by yer arm, straight-like."

"I'll bet I'm the first giant to ever do this," said Beirboor.

"Don't talk, just shoot," said Jack, who was antsy someone might come through the doorway. "Let's get this over with."

"Like this?"

"Yep," said Jack. "But squint yer eyes to fix on the spot. Tilt the bow to meet it, yep."

"Then what?"

"Pull the trigger." Jack pinched Beirboor's large, pudgy finger. "Squeeze."

Fwap!

The chalk launched across the conservatory. It struck Spiroshakes and exploded into a dozen pieces. The bard's bust now wore an orange blotch above the left brow.

"Hoowee!" cried Beirboor. "Thank you, Jack Spriggins." He grabbed another piece of chalk. "I want to try a shot by myself."

"That weren't the deal," said Jack. "I let yeh shoot, now hand it over."

"Once more, just for fun," said Beirboor, twisting out of reach. "I'll go for Tottlestots, Master of Philosophy." Beirboor fired hastily. The chalk flew wide and ricocheted off the blackboard, the floor, and finally, Roidaroy, who just happened to stick his head inside the conservatory.

"Ouch!" he yelled, rubbing his jaw. "That hurt. You're in for it."

"Are not!" shouted Beirboor. "If you didn't have muscles for brains, you might have ducked."

"You won't duck before I thump you, Blubberbutt!"

Beirboor ran for cover under the desks. Roidaroy chased, stumbling over them to reach him. Jack pursued as well, going for his crossbow.

Vikuvis entered the room. "What is this disturbance?"

The boys stood at attention, Beirboor hiding the crossbow behind his back. "It's nothing."

"Nothing," echoed Jack.

"Liars," said Roidaroy, fuming. "Plumpy shot me with that crude weapon he's hiding behind his back."

"Let me see it," said Vikuvis, snapping his fingers.

Beirboor looked apologetically at Jack and handed the crossbow over.

"I'm confiscating this," said Vikuvis. "Having a Forestlander on the premises is as disruptive as letting wild goats wander about the desks."

"Buzzard's luck," said Jack, through clenched teeth.

"I'm sorry, Jack Spriggins," said the young giant.

"It's hard to believe such barbaric weapons still exist," said Vikuvis, who went to the podium and rang a hand bell.

Veedivee entered. "You rang?"

"Dispose of this weapon."

"Yeh can't destroy that, it belongs to me."

"Jack Spriggins, take your seat. We of Giantdom conduct our lessons in an orderly manner. We do not tramp about like elves in the oaks. You will learn to do the same."

Jack slumped in his chair. Veedivee walked away holding the crossbow like he had a dead rat by the tail.

"Eyes front," said Vikuvis. The tutor pulled a string above the chalkboard and unfurled an enormous map. "Today we will discuss the semi-impressive history of the Dragonlands of the eastern seas."

Late as usual, Lawrenlawra fluttered in. "Have I missed anything?"

"The concept of *punctuality*, once again," said Vikuvis, "Which means to arrive at the agreed time. Now, let us continue with lessons."

After class ended, Jack stood with Beirboor gazing through the windows of a hallway, where the Gogmagogg residence viewed the Avenue of Prosperity, the main roadway in Chelebraxia.

"There's only one street in the world paved with real gold bricks, Jack Spriggins, and we live on it," said Beirboor. "Ours is Chelebraxia's most prominent house. "You see the wonderful view of the opera house? My mother is there, rehearsing as we speak."

"What's '*rehearsing*'?" said Jack.

"Practice for the opera. Or in this case, an operetta, because the show is only six hours long."

"An opry for six hours?"

"Yes, isn't that wonderful?" Beirboor clasped his hands together.

"Will we hear harp music there?"

"I guess I should have mentioned that," said Beirboor. "Jack Spriggins, you cannot attend."

"What d'yeh mean?"

"In Giantdom theatre is high art and you're a Forestlander. You'll never be admitted."

"Huh?" said Jack. "What's the fuss over a play? In Rivercross Square anyone can watch. Yeh can even yell 'boo 'if yeh hate it."

"Well, nobody boos our shows."

"Chee," said Jack, folding his arms. "Who cares?"

"Please don't be upset. I didn't make the rules."

A carriage rattled past outside the window.

"Look," said Beirboor. "That's Baroness Droositti's coach."

A pair of white rams pulled the carriage to a stop in front of the manor. Two Cheleb ladies in red togas got out and went up the steps.

"The Droositti sisters," exclaimed Beirboor. "They're such dilettantes."

"I invited them," said Lawrenlawra, who was passing by. "To attend your portrait-sitting."

"No! Why did you do that?"

"It's no small affair, brotherkins. The whole family will be there. I'm going to play the harp to help you relax. Come now, you must leave the Forestlander behind."

"I have somewhere to be, Jack Spriggins."

"Suits me," said Jack. "We don't gotta do *everything* together. I'll mosey out for some fresh air."

"No," said Vikuvis. "Jack Spriggins, you will spend your time writing sentences into this ledger I've prepared." He handed him a paper tablet, a quill, and an ink bottle. "Take these with you to the conservatory. I'll join you this evening to correct your work."

With that, Vikuvis and the other giants went their way.

"What a hoot," said Jack, as he moped out to the conservatory. On the way he overheard Veedivee, the Jadin butler, speaking behind a door.

"This crude weapon of the young Forestlander," he said. "I must toss it out with the other disposables when the trash barge arrives."

Jack spied around the corner. The Jadins were lugging garbage in woven canvas bags. Veedivee had the crossbow tucked under one the arm as he went down a stairway.

"Jits!" Behind a large hallway plant, Jack set aside his writing materials and kicked off his sandals, silently padding downstairs after the Jadins. Veedivee led the others to an underground culvert, where a water canal reeked of garbage. On the platform, Jack snuck behind a mooring post and hid beyond the torchlights in the tunnel.

A bell echoed and a flat-bottomed boat emerged. The Jadins hefted the garbage aboard, and Veedivee tossed Jack's bow on top. Covering their noses with handkerchiefs, they returned upstairs.

The drifting barge was only a few feet from the landing. Jack leapt aboard. A Jadin masked with a green handkerchief was steering the boat and did not see him. Jack retrieved his crossbow and then rolled off the muck, leaping back to the landing where he watched the barge drift out of sight.

"I'll remember this place," he said. Bobbing skiffs were tied off at some of the mooring posts. "This canal goes out to the river, I reckon."

He flicked the lever of his crossbow. The arms popped open and a glob of rotten gunk spattered on his face. "Yuck!" gasped Jack. "Still works. No Jadin's gonna chuck my bow now." After rinsing the weapon in the channel, he returned upstairs.

"Are you still awake, Jack Spriggins?" Beirboor called out later that night from his bed across the room.

Jack had climbed up to the windowsill for some air, where he watched the midsummer night sky. "Yep, just counting stars."

"You forest folk don't sleep much, do you?" Beirboor kicked the covers off his bed.

"Not as much as y'all." Jack had grown restless. Sitting all cozy with no plan was gnawing at him.

"You must be glad living here, where no danger is lurking," said Beirboor. "It must seem peaceful compared to the wild forest, but I admit your world is fascinating. I would have a hard time sleeping if bears and wolves were trying to eat me or ogre warriors were attacking my home."

"Did yeh hear news about that or something?"

"No. I can only imagine. Is that what keeps you up late?"

"Naw. I stay up 'cause it's the only time I git left alone."

"You don't like having others taking care of you?"

"Nope."

"Well, you should," yawned Beirboor. "You've never had it this good."

"Never had anything."

"It's funny. You wanted to know what life was like up here, and I always wondered what yours was like. Now, here we are, friends."

"Reckon so. Don't suppose yeh'd ever go down and see the woods yerself?"

"Gosh no." Beirboor shook his head. "It's forbidden. I'm a giant and we don't mingle with other races."

"Too low for yeh?"

"Giants detest fighting and there's a war where you live. I can dream about the forest, but that's it."

"The ogres made the fight. It weren't our fault."

"Still, Giantdom is above all that. Isn't that why you left?"

Jack shrugged. "I get sort of curious about what's happening down there."

"You're safe here. You can forget all about fighting now."

"Jits, Boor. Ain't so easy."

"It is. Just change the subject. Do faeries really come out at night? Is it true they glow like the moon?"

Jack rolled his eyes. "They're just a flock of girls who live in the woods."

"Are they beautiful?"

"Reckon so."

"You ever see them?"

"The Fae? I seen them. It's real tough to look away. But yeh can forget it cause yer a giant and they live in the woods. So shut up, will yeh?"

"Gosh." Beirboor fluffed his pillow and turned over. "You're angry because you can't come with me to the opera?"

"Chee."

"I'm sorry you won't see that, Jack Spriggins."

Jack stared at the sky for a long while until he dozed.

A breeze awoke him, carrying a song of the Gogmagogg harp through the manor. "There it goes," murmured Jack. "Playing by itself again."

He kept his eyes shut, listening and weaving to the flow of the harp song, which pulled as if calling out to him. The bewitching notes trilled up and down in such a manner that only fingers could have made such sound.

"Hey Boor," Jack whispered, "Who do yeh reckon's playing the harp?"

Beirboor was asleep, snoring gently.

Jack climbed down to do some snooping. The marble in the grand entryway was cold against his bare feet, which was odd considering how warm the evening was a moment before. Stranger yet, fog drifted around the harp pedestal and he could not see who was playing. With a jealous pang, he waved his hands to clear the mist. There was a mysterious woman seated at the harp. Her face was turned away and she wore a black dress and veil. The coldness in the chamber seemed to come from her presence, which filled Jack with an awful need for her music.

"Play on, lady," he said.

She plucked the strings with pale, thin fingers and began a tune that drew Jack nearer to danger than he had ever felt. An urge to reach out and touch the strings caused the music to change. Sour notes trembled and the idea that Jack was falling overtook him. His knees felt wobbly. He knelt down to steady himself. Iciness coursed through his veins. "My blood's gone cold," he uttered. "Is that song for me, lady?"

The woman did not look at him and said nothing. She only played on.

"Yer Lell, ain't yeh? The Dark Spirit?"

She turned her veiled face so that all Jack could see was the curl of her black lips forming a smile. Her song carried a clear message: *The harp is mine.*

"Are yeh offering me this harp?" he said, as he ran his hand along the instrument's shimmering, gold inlaid base. He pressed his cheek to the wood and basked amid the icy vibrations that ran all through him, and hummed with the tune, reciting words in his head:

"The harp is mine; mine all mine.

Mine to the end of time.

Dark Lady Lell, play it well,

Play this song of mine."

A sudden snort from Beirboor caused Jack to jolt awake. It was morning and the air was warm. He had slept all night on the window's ledge. He frowned at the door of the bedroom, which was closed. Dark Lady Lell, the cold mist, and the haunting harp song had all been a dream.

Jack leapt down and padded silently out to the hall. This time, there was no cold fog and no lady in black. Only the treasured harp, which stood alone. A soft breeze from the portico caused music to play on its strings.

"It's that song again," said Jack. "My song."

He shut eyes to the music and knew the message was true.

"Dream or not." Jack was now aware of what he had to do. "The Dark Spirit wants me to steal this harp, so I will. I'll take it down to the woods and hide it from these stupid giants so they'll never find it. The Cheleb's ain't deserving of it. The harp's mine."

The strings continued lulling him into a sanguine trance until a clocktower struck seven times across the river, breaking the spell.

Veedivee, the Jadin butler, was standing on the portico with a stack of linens in his hands, staring over at the city of Jadinobblis and listening to the gongs. Jack walked out to meet him, yawning.

"Mind if I have a gander?" said Jack.

Veedivee spoke with a thin voice. "Impressive, isn't it?"

"Yer green Jadin city?" Jack squinted. "Reckon, maybe. Never been there."

"It is an entire metropolis dedicated to giant academia and the severity of existence."

"Sounds stuffy."

Veedivee smiled, revealing his crooked white teeth. "On the contrary, it is the pinnacle of Giantdom, where all our great ideas are born. Remove Jadin culture and the very structure of giant society would collapse."

"What do the Chelebs think?"

"I doubt their frivolous, shaved heads think anymore at all. But that's fine, we think for them. Now, Jack Spriggins, I have chores to finish." He went on his way.

"Cold fish," said Jack, after the servant had gone.

"Good morning, Jack Spriggins," said Beirboor. "Did you sleep well?"

"Hey Boor, you ever been to the green city?" said Jack.

"I hate it there. All they do is read books all day. It's like one big, stale library."

"They got harps?"

"None. No music, no art, or fun of any kind."

"I gotta say, it don't seem like they get along with y'all so good."

"They're nice to me." Beirboor looked about, as if expecting breakfast to be served." I like having them around."

"Chee, I'll bet."

Roidaroy was also outside near the portico, rasping his breath and lifting shiny gold weights. Seven and a half feet tall, he was huge with popping round muscles in his arms. He had a small bandage on his chin where the chalk had struck him. "What are you looking at, Jack Spriggins, you earth worm. What did you come here for?"

"To get some air." Jack turned to leave.

"Not so fast, maggot breath," said Roidaroy, shoving him. "You know what I meant. You don't belong here and you know it."

"Stop it, Roidaroy, don't bully," said Beirboor. "He is my guest. Come Jack Spriggins, let's go wash for breakfast."

"He comes from a dirty forest hole," said Roidaroy.

"Yes, but Father said he could stay. So, leave us alone and stop pretending to be so rough and violent."

"I'm not pretending." Roidaroy got up and grabbed Jack by the nape of his toga. "Nobody would care if I throw this trash over the hillside."

"Yeh'll – regret – it!" said Jack, as he dangled off the ground, gasping for air. "They'll hear yeh screaming like a girl, cause yer going with me."

He reached out and gripped Roidaroy's ears so hard that the giant's face turned red.

The Jadin servants rushed to pull them apart. Roidaroy hollered like an angry bull and finally let go. Jack fell to the ground.

"Don't interfere, Jadins," said Roidaroy. "I hate you, Jack Spriggins."

"Is there commotion in my house?" said Gogmagogg, who stood at the doorway with a surprised look.

"Faa-ther! This forest creature attacked me and boxed my ears," said Roidaroy, rubbing them.

"That's not true, father," said Beirboor. "Roidaroy was going to throw Jack Spriggins off the hill."

"Enough!" boomed Gogmagogg. "This is most un-giant-like behavior and talk."

"Blame the Forestlander," said Roidaroy, pointing at his chin bandage. "See this? He brought a crude weapon to our home and all this trouble too. Send him away!"

"Our home is a peaceful one, Roidaroy. That you should be so bothered by him is an embarrassment to me," said Gogmagogg. "Forgive us, Jack Spriggins, and please join breakfast."

Roidaroy stormed off in a huff as Gogmagogg returned to the manor.

"Let's go, Jack Spriggins," said Beirboor.

Jack's pulse still throbbed. In a half-daze, he rubbed his sore neck. "I sure hope I get Roidaroy to hate ogres as much as he hates me."

For afternoon lessons on the garden lawn, a kooky Cheleb giantess named Madame Yurlagurla gave dance instruction. Jack and Beirboor were reduced to spinning and somersaulting. This was Beirboor's exercise choice after Gogmagogg insisted he get into shape. Jack tried to keep up. He flung his arms like the others, wallowing in the grass.

"Whiffle as the fluff of the dandelion," said Madame Yurlagurla. "Glide like a crane, skimming the crests of the Windississi. Plunge like diving fish!"

Jack was embarrassed to see Vikuvis approach. "Wish I could dig like a gopher and hide."

"Madame, I require Beirboor to come with me," said the tutor.

"Master Vikuvis," she said, circling her flabby arms. "Your interruption is harming the harmonizing of my class."

"Your vapid discourse may continue after we leave."

"How dare you, sir! Look how inspired they are."

"You have no authority to object," said Vikuvis. "Come, Beirboor. And bring Jack Spriggins with you."

Relieved to no longer *"bend like the wheat,"* Jack was actually grateful Vikuvis had arrived. The tutor led them through an orchid garden and stopped beside a reflecting pool.

"So, Beirboor," said Vikuvis. "What did you learn from the book I assigned you the other day, *A Giant Beauty Awakes?*"

"Was I supposed to read that already?"

Vikuvis hissed. "Your mother's play is opening this evening. I wanted you to review the history on which it is based."

"Everybody knows the tale of the Awakened Beauty," said Beirboor.

"Not everybody," said Vikuvis, whose eyes fixed on Jack. "Jack Spriggins, observe the mosaic on the bottom of that pool. What does it depict to you?"

Beneath the shallow water the tiles wavered with an image of a baldheaded giantess rising from sleep on a rose-covered bed.

"I'd say it were the Sleeping Beauty," said Jack. "Except she's waking up."

"Well, of course she's not sleeping," said Beirboor. "She *is* awake."

"No, Beirboor," said Vikuvis. "To him, she is not. The Forestlanders do not believe she is awake. Did you hear how Jack Spriggins even called her the *Sleeping* Beauty?"

"I ain't ever heard she woke up," said Jack.

"Naturally," said the tutor, who grinned as if he had snapped a trap shut on him.

"Why, Jack Spriggins," said Beirboor, "Any giant can tell you that she awoke and blessed the giants. That lore is centuries old."

"I dunno," said Jack, scratching his head. "If yeh say so. But Ma used to sing a rhyme that always ended, *'And still the Beauty sleeps.'* That's common learning where I come from."

"Close your mouth, Beirboor," said Vikuvis, "Don't look so surprised by how little Jack Spriggins knows. Now you see, Forestlanders are completely ignorant."

"I couldn't care less about sleeping beauties," said Jack. "Folks ain't got it in them to see real beauty. Except, maybe for the harp."

~ 221 ~

"I feel the same way sometimes," said Beirboor. "And you're so right about father's harp, Jack Spriggins. It's the only object of pure beauty that I know of."

Jack had an itch under his skin for the harp that was growing stronger. The song of Dark Lell haunted him now.

"The harp is mine; mine all mine.

Mine to the end of time."

"Master Vikuvis," said Beirboor. "Do I still have to read that history for tonight?"

"Yes," said the tutor, "But come with me for now."

Vikuvis led them to a carriage house in the gardens. "I fetched you to join me on a field trip."

"I don't feel like going anywhere," said Beirboor. "I'd rather sit by the harp and do some sketch work."

"Are yeh kidding!" exclaimed Jack, who did not want Beirboor going anywhere near the harp. "A field trip sure beats scribbling, grass-dancing, or waiting around to eat, don't it?"

A wicker buggy pulled by a very large, ugly bird rolled towards them on a golden cobblestone path, ushered by a Jadin attendant. The bird was eight-feet tall with legs that looked powerful enough to kick through stone.

"Jits, what's that?" said Jack.

"It's called an ostrich," said Vikuvis. "Imported from the east."

"Don't it fly?"

"Jack Spriggins, even you can deduce that not all fowl can fly." Vikuvis took the reins from the attendant. "Get in."

Beirboor pouted. "If Roidaroy and Lawrenlawra get to stay behind, then why do we have to go?"

"Because you showed interest during my science instruction," said Vikuvis. "As a reward, a glimpse of the mechanical marvels of Giantdom outside this city may further stimulate your appreciation of Jadin achievements."

"Sounds good," said Jack, who climbed aboard the buggy. "I'm all set."

The carriage basket jiggled as if on springs.

"Well, as long as Jack Spriggins is going, I'm going too," said Beirboor.

The boys began bouncing on the springs for fun.

"Stop acting like children," said Vikuvis. "This is a science expedition."

He snapped the reins and the buggy lurched forward.

Jack's head whipped back. "Whoa! Ostrigees are strong."

"*Ostriches*," corrected Vikuvis. "They are fast runners indeed."

The enormous bird plodded forward with swift kicks that went *thum-thump!* The chariot followed the bridleway out of the white city and crossed over the Windississi Bridge.

Halfway across, the gold stones of Chelebraxia gave way to the green ones of Jadinobblis. Vikuvis steered away from the Jadin city and followed a frontage road along the river.

"We're not going to Jadinobblis?" said Beirboor.

"Certainly not with a tree-chopper in our company."

~ 223 ~

Jack was accustomed to common put-downs. "I ain't ever chopped a tree but I get it – your green city is like the opry. I ain't welcome there."

"I have an errand at the Summit Barrow Station," said Vikuvis. "My exclusive shade of actuary green ink is due to arrive at the tram today."

"Father already went to the tram today," said Beirboor. "The Dragonland Ambassadors arrived and he is giving them a tour."

"Dragons?" said Jack. "Yeh got dragons?"

"Of course not," said Vikuvis. "The Dragonlands are a very wealthy country to the east. They have sent emissaries here to discuss business with Giantdom. They are people, Jack Spriggins, not lizards."

Beirboor leaned over, "They're even shorter than you are."

"Real funny," said Jack.

The ostrich-buggy approached a towering structure with moving ropes attached to it. There was commotion upriver as a barge was mooring at a wooden dock and a Cheleb transport blocked the roadway. Jadin dockworkers shouted directions to the driver of the stalled cart as it rolled to the landing.

"How inconvenient," said Vikuvis, "Traffic in Giantdom is getting beyond control."

"Gosh, I hope we don't have to be out in the sun too long," said Beirboor, rubbing his bald head, "My scalp burns easily after my Capillus Eximo. I wish your carriage had umbrellas to protect me like Father's does."

Vikuvis sighed. "I brought you along to observe and better understand the principles of applied leverage."

~ 224 ~

"Hey,look how that big tower moves," said Jack.

"Observe the crane," said Vikuvis.

A projecting arm from the tower reached over the wharf with ropes, lifting a cargo bulk from a barge on to the waiting Cheleb transport. Beside the dock, a barn-like building with an enormous waterwheel made rhythmic splashes that mixed with the creaks from the wheelhouse.

"My grandfather, Varkimedes, designed this system," said Vikuvis. "The river turns the wheel, the wheel moves the ropes, and the ropes do the heavy lifting."

"Jits," said Jack. "It'd take a whole village and all their horses to budge that where I come from."

"*Applied leverage*," said Vikuvis. "By which one giant handles the whole task with ease. My grandfather said: '*Give me a place to stand and I shall move the earth with a lever*'."

The roadway cleared. Vikuvis whipped the reins and the ostrich made towards a gap in the mountain peaks. At the end of the road, the Summit Barrow Station stood atop the ridge line.

" Behold the tram," said the tutor.

It was another towering structure with spinning parts. Massive cords were strung to a sideways-wheel passing baskets round its grooved rim into the station where they were unloaded and sent back down the mountain.

"What's in those?" said Jack.

"Shipments. One of which is my ink," said Vikuvis. "We freight them up the mountain from our seaside port. Go see for yourself."

Jack and Beirboor hopped down from the carriage and ran to the ridge. Several more towers strung with ropes and pulleys ushered the baskets down the mountainside.

"Gosh," said Beirboor. "The Sunrise Sea. It's so clear today, you can see forever."

"I ain't ever seen so much water before," said Jack. A blanket of blue stretched all the way to the horizon. From his vantage, several thousand feet above, Jack noticed that little specks were moving across the ocean. "What're them white flecks out there, Boor?"

"Sailing ships. "

"Where from? "

"Far-off lands."

The world was much bigger than Jack had imagined. "They look tiny up here."

"I know but they're really big up close," said Beirboor.

There was a loud *click-click-click!* as a basket of the tram swung into the station under the great sideways-wheel. It gently rocked to and fro as workers unloaded it. They were youthful Jadins, hardworking and engrossed with their duties. No Chelebs worked the tram but a handful remained parked comfortably in their carriages.

"Pampered puffs," muttered Jack.

Vikuvis was still in the ostrich buggy and a pair of Jadins went over and gave him a package. Jack took a good, long look before he could tell one of the Jadins was a giantess. Her tunic was tight and her voice womanly, otherwise she looked like the males. "Vikuvis," she said, smiling, "Your signature ink has arrived. Actuary green."

Vikuvis removed the string and opened the box. Several ink bottles were packaged inside. "Considerate of you to acquire it, Vyladalis."

The other Jadin glared unpleasantly. Strands of his black hair were plastered to his head. "Your parcel has a timely arrival, Vikuvis," he said.

"Velikoff," acknowledged Vikuvis, cordially.

Jack nudged Beirboor. "Hey, Boor. Do all Jads got the same name?"

"Yes, Jack Spriggins," giggled Beirboor. "That's Vikuvis, Vikuvis, and Vikuvis."

"I did not expect a meeting with you here, my fellow Jadins" said Vikuvis.

"A hasty decision on our part," said Vyladalis, avoiding his eyes. "We noted your schedule and came to meet you for an urgent matter."

"It is a terrible inconvenience," said Velikoff. "We always have to track you down."

"Your purpose?" said Vikuvis.

Velikoff thrust forward a ream of paper, thickly bound like a book. "Now that you have your ink, we Jadins who appointed you to the senate expect your signature on this document."

Vikuvis read the title aloud. "*The Rational Reform Referendum of Jadinobblis— Revised?*" His lips tightened and he gave a frown usually reserved for Jack. "You have tampered with my masterpiece?"

"Avoid our councils if you like," said Velikoff. "But when an urgent document lays untouched on your desk, many would view that as neglecting your post. I suggest you act as Secretary of Legislation and sign this immediately."

"I am used to such outbursts from you, Velikoff, but Vyladalis?"

The giantess bowed her head. "My betrothed, I am Minister of Transcription. By that duty alone I was obligated. It is a matter of record."

Jack nudged Beirboor in the ribs. "Old sourpuss has a sweetheart."

Velikoff's eyes met Jack. "We hear that you have taken this Forestlander under tutelage, Vikuvis."

"His name is Jack Spriggins," said Vikuvis. "Merely an experiment."

Velikoff Velikoff looked away as if disgusted. "And how is that developing?"

"With great patience," said Vikuvis, "A trait you and your cohorts could benefit from. I will consider reviewing your so-called revisions at a later time."

"No, Vikuvis," said Velikoff, "The Council of Jadin Solidarity meets tonight. We expect your attendance and your signature."

Velikoff handed the unsigned referendum to Vyladalis.

"I will keep this for you, my intended," she said, carrying it away to their buggy.

"Why did they behave that way, Master Vikuvis?" said Beirboor, once the two Jadins had gone.

"This was an unfortunate encounter, Beirboor. You are permitted to forget it altogether."

They climbed aboard the buggy and left the Summit Barrow Station. Vikuvis stared straight-ahead, tight-lipped, gripping the reins with white knuckles. Jack thought he looked like one of the busts in the conservatory, he was so rigid.

A spectacular open-air carriage pulled by a team of rams came bounding toward them on the road. Onboard was Lord Gogmagogg, with Barons Skootafrey, Krusedekulk, and three strangers.

"Father's transport," said Beirboor, waving at them, "And look, the Dragonlanders are with him."

Even from a distance, the three foreigners appeared to be smaller than Jack. Their faces were powdered white and their eyes were heavy-lidded shaded beneath square umbrellas. They gazed at Jack as curiously as he did them.

Lord Gogmagogg shouted as the coach rushed by." Greetings, my youngest son!" The wheels of the heavy cart rumbled like thunder on the dusty road, kicking up a cloud.

The ostrich panicked. Vikuvis fought the reins as the buggy slewed side-to-side. One wheel went off the road and Jack was jostled against Beirboor, knocking their heads together.

"Ouch!" cried Beirboor.

The box of Vikuvis's ink bottles flew out and the contents were scattered. The ostrich lurched and kicked, unable to move on because the buggy was half-resting in a ditch.

Gogmagogg's transport stopped. "Beirboor, you're at too great a risk in that Jadin buggy. Come, join us."

"Thank you, Father," said Beirboor, who climbed down and ran to him with his hands covering his head. "My scalp needs the shade of your umbrellas."

He got onboard the coach taking a seat next to Gogmagogg. "I'll see you back at the manor, Jack Spriggins."

The Cheleb's coachman whipped the reins and the team of rams whisked the royal coach away.

Vikuvis stepped away from the stranded buggy. The veins in his neck tensed as if ready to burst. Through a cloud of dust, Jack watched the raucous party of Chelebs roll away. Baron Skootafrey was laughing. Ink bottles were scattered all over the ground.

Jack began to pick up the mess. One bottle had shattered on a rock, spilling ink so dark it was almost black. "Yeh call that green?" he said.

"It is *Actuary Green*," said Vikuvis.

Jack gave the remaining bottles to the tutor.

"Come, Jack Spriggins," said Vikuvis. "Help me push this buggy from the ditch."

They hauled the rig back on the road then drove the ostrich in silence. Jack noticed how bright and magnificent Chelebraxia looked on the hill.

"Them Chelebs sure act high and mighty," he said. "Like they think yeh Jads should kneel to them like folks do to the Great Spirits."

"After all the lectures I've given, you are still empty-headed on this matter," said Vikuvis. "To compare the Chelebs to gods is as empty as the gods themselves. No such power exists."

On one hand, Vikuvis made sense but, on the other, Jack had seen Ella and the wolf pack, heard the voice of the Silent One, and dreamt of harp music of played by Dark Lell.

"Reckon I ain't so sure," he said. "Them that hear spirit-voices might tell yeh otherwise."

"*Spirit-voices?*" said Vikuvis, with more snark than usual. "We will take a different route back to Chelebraxia and I shall show you what becomes of gods and the fools that worship them."

Chapter 20

TEMPLE

Vikuvis and Jack crossed the Windississi bridge, riding in the ostrich buggy past Jadinobblis towards a mountain in the west valley. The river coursed by on their right. Pastures were on the left where Jadin goatherds used the huge billy goats to haul bushels of grain.

"Those billies sure make forest goats look puny," said Jack.

"Of course they do," said Vikuvis.

One goatherd was tugging the leash of an ornery straggler.

"Valdejin," Vikuvis greeted.

"Vikuvis," the goatherd returned.

"I am going up the hillside but just realized I brought no torch. Have you a flare?"

Valdejin squinted his eyes at the mountain. "The winds are blowing too strong for a flare. What you need is a lantern."

He produced a dried, hollow jenga fruit from his pack that was riddled with holes and bound together with twine. The goatherd lit the candle inside it and the beacon glowed green.

"Take that, Jack Spriggins," said Vikuvis.

"Sure is bright," said Jack, holding the Jadin lantern. "But why do we need it when the sun's still shining?"

"To light our way in the abandoned hillside temple. What it lights will enlighten you."

Vikuvis nodded to the herder and whipped the reins.

"Jenga is a very practical fruit," said Vikuvis. He parked at the foot of the hill next to a stone totem with etchings carved on it.

"Tem-ple path," Jack read aloud.

A trail of worn stone steps led upslope.

"Follow it." said Vikuvis, motioning him to take the lead.

The wind forced Jack to guard against the stinging green pebbles that swished off the hillside. Atop the steps, they reached a terrace where crumbling pillars upheld a tilted eaves over a doorway into the mountain.

"Carry the light into that chamber," said Vikuvis.

The flare hissed and flickered as Jack went in. Frightening moans of the wind lilted through the gloom. "Creepy place. Lonely and haunted."

"Give me the lantern." Vikuvis passed the light in front of them. A form of someone large – astoundingly large – perhaps fifty feet, was seated before them.

"Jits, who's that?"

"Don't you recognize your Wind Spirit?"

"Never saw anything like her."

The goddess was a bluish-green statue carved out of marble. She sat on a mountainous throne as tall as the stone spire at the Orchard. Her head nearly touched the cavern roof. Spiders had knit a webbed veil around her face. Moss grew out of the cracks in her sides. She was bald and rested her cheek on her right hand. The left was upturned but empty. A mischievous smile was fashioned on her lips.

"That's the Wind One?"

Vikuvis scoffed. "*That* was once worshipped by the giants a century ago when this place was enshrined. She does not speak. She does not hear. She is pure stone. As you can see, no one comes to see her now."

"Kinda looks like a Cheleb, being bald and tall," said Jack. "Is she s'posed to be holding something?"

"Aha!" said Vikuvis, "The missing object is one that you see every day. The Gogmagogg Harp. The family removed it from this temple long ago and claimed it as their own. It has remained in Chelebraxia ever since."

Jack's gut tightened with jealousy. "So, it ain't really theirs? The Gogs stole it?"

"Well, why not? The instrument was a useless here with this chunk of rock."

~ 234 ~

A low groan bellowed beneath the statue and shook the floor under their feet. Jack backed away. Vikuvis moved forward to cast light on the throne's base.

"A passage runs beneath her robes somewhere at the side. There!" the Jadin pointed.

"Where does it go to?"

"It is connected to an old network of mining tunnels from the days when we giants used them. Now, I want you to follow it, Jack Spriggins, and go back to the forest where you came from."

"Wait. Yeh dragged me here just to kick me out?"

"Unless you can prove to me that you are no spy," Vikuvis held the green lamp closer. "Beirboor tells me that down there you lived in Rivercross."

"Close enough."

"Do you know the Champion rangers?"

"Sure, everybody knows them."

"So Ardus Camlann sent you," accused Vikuvis, with a green glint in his penetrating eyes.

"Naw, he don't know I'm here."

"Are you claiming that you just wandered up the mountains into Giantdom because you had nothing better to do? Others have been taken in by your story but I was not. Somebody sent you. Who? The plotting botanist who fancies himself *All-wise*?"

"Yeh know ol' Goatbeard?" Jack spit in disgust. "I got nothing to do with him."

Vikuvis seemed to consider this for a moment. "Well, your contempt that pretender is respectable. He has tried to weasel his way across our borders more than once to see our Jadin libraries. Of course, he was denied."

"I don't blame yeh. But what do yeh got against Ardus Camlann? He ain't bad."

"I never said he was." The tutor's beady eyes came level with Jack's. "In fact, if I offered Giantdom's aid with that war of yours, would you leave and take word to Camlann?"

"Yeh can do that?"

"I can."

"What's the catch?"

"Do you want our help or don't you?"

"I thought yeh giants were above fighting."

"We may not be willing to exchange blows but we can tell you where to strike."

Jack bit his lip, figuring what to do. Only one thing was certain: he was not leaving Giantdom without the harp. "Naw," he said. "I ain't going back."

Vikuvis straightened. "I did not expect that answer." He held the lamp closer for a clearer look at Jack's face. "What did you really come here for?"

"I told yeh."

"Just a runaway, are you, Jack Spriggins? Not a liar or spy?"

"I ain't. What about yeh and yer 'Reform' ruckus?"

"You implied that we Jadins kneel to Chelebs. We do not. You'd be wise to notice who controls most everything in Giantdom. Make no mistake about it, Jadinobblis will have its day."

"So, yeh ain't trying to get me to leave anymore?"

"Stay in the Gogmagogg mansion for now but remember you are a Forestlander. The sooner this experiment with you ends, the better for everyone."

"Reckon yeh reminded me of that plenty."

Vikuvis passed back the lantern and walked from the statue. "Let us go now."

Jack held it up at the Wind One, admiring her smirk because he now wore one as well. A gust of wind passed through the chamber. "Stay put, Windy, old girl, yer gonna help me steal the harp."

"What did you say?" Vikuvis called back.

"I was just saying we ain't gonna need this lamp so I'll leave it here."

Jack snuffed out the candle and dropped the lantern on the floor as they left.

Chapter 21

HARP

The banquet for the opening night of the opera was even more highfalutin than Beirboor's birthday party. Shiny red banners were draped over the assembly. They were embroidered with two golden eyes, open wide and fire-lidded in honor of the awakened princess of giant lore. Trumpeters blew a fanfare announcing each dinner course. Platters were served on a golden divan fashioned to look like a bed of roses. The Dragonland ambassadors nodded appreciatively at the spectacle. All three wore fancy white headdresses.

"What're them hats made of?" said Jack.

"Ivory," said Beirboor, who had his face buried in a jenga fruit, licking its insides. "Elephant bone."

"Reckon that makes them boneheads, don't it?"

Beirboor spit jenga pulp back into its shell, erupting with a chuckle. "Good one, Jack Spriggins."

One of the Dragonlanders stood on his chair and adjusted his headdress as he gazed upon the gathering.

Lawrenlawra, who was in her mother's seat, jumped up, flagging with her napkin. "Daddykins, I think one of the ambassadors wishes to say something."

The conversations fell silent.

"Veedivee, translate," said Gogmagogg.

The Jadin butler set down a pitcher of mead and walked over to stand by the ambassador. The Dragonlander spoke with abrupt, choppy tones that had the rhythm of a cook's knife. Jack did not understand any of it.

Veedivee rendered the translation: "The Imperial embassy wishes to express concern about the ogre army that is advancing across the Forestland."

"What of it?" said Gogmagogg.

"The war's proximity to Giantdom suggests volatility in the region and they have reservations about conducting business here with us."

Several Chelebs gasped. Gogmagogg set his goblet down, staring at the foreigner.

The ambassador blinked uneasily and spoke again as Veedivee interpreted. "The Dragon Empire wonders why Giantdom offers no assistance to their Forestland neighbors?"

Jack put down his spoon, curious himself.

"Convey to the honorable emissaries," said Gogmagogg, "We giants would sooner deal with ogres than with men. That is, if their invasion prevails, because ogres have no history of making trouble for us like men have. If the Forestland cannot defend itself, then perhaps it's time we had better neighbors."

The giants laughed and applauded. The ambassadors huddled for Veedivee's translation.

"Jits," muttered Jack, putting his head on his hand. "Giants are rooting for the enemy."

Veedivee translated more. "Supposing the ogres may succeed and then attack Giantdom next?"

Gogmagogg shook his head, "Our high peaks are impenetrable. Giant Valley has never been breached by outsiders."

Jack stood up, thumbing at himself. "Except by me."

"Yes, little climber. By our generosity, you are the sole exception," said Gogmagogg, with a jovial bellow. "You came seeking peace and aren't you all the better to have left the lowly woods?"

Jack sat down. "Ain't smart to be mad now," he reckoned.

"Nevertheless, I'll be clear on this matter," Gogmagogg went on. "We giants are not interested in making alliance with the ogre warlords either. We have already denied their entreaties, to which extent they have recently failed to persuade. Isn't that so, Skootafrey?"

Baron Skootafrey jumped up, dragging his napkin and wine goblet off the table. "Pardon me. Yes! The ogres came knocking at our border gates, a pair of delegates covered in blue tattoos and armed to their teeth. Pointed teeth too. They tried to woo us with a gift."

He snapped his fingers at Veedivee, who produced a hand-harp. It had blue stones in a circular bronze frame that resembled a snake swallowing its own tail.

"That's the same snake on my brooch," realized Jack.

"This is an ogre harp," said Skootafrey with a laugh. He took it from Veedivee and plucked one of the strings. It made a flat, unimpressive note. "Doesn't exactly win a giant over, does it?"

Gogmagogg laughed. "No."

"We declined them an audience," said Skootafrey. "Sent the ogres away, just like we did Camlann's rangers."

The Dragonlanders convened. After a moment, the speaker bowed and then spoke.

"Giantdom is a strong and peaceable empire," translated Veedivee, "A trade accord with our Dragon Empire seems agreeable."

"Wonderful!" said Gogmagogg, raising his goblet. "To our wise guests."

Giants rose and cheered with self-congratulatory toasts.

A cold sweat broke out on Jack's head and arms. It was official: he hated giants.

Jack got up and left in a huff, but no giants seemed to care or notice. In the foyer, he kicked the harp pedestal. "I hate em all," he said. "Giants ain't got a right to be so snobby." Wind blew a murmur of music on the strings and a cold shiver went to his bones. Jack uttered the words of his song:

"The harp is mine; mine all mine.
Mine to the end of time."

"My harp," said Jack, gazing at the instrument. "Soon as I can, I'm gonna take this thing where no rich snob of a giant can ever find it. Make them think the ogres done it. Gogg might change his mind and make war to get it back."

Blasts from the trumpeters rang out in the banquet hall, which meant more dessert and wine was being served. The merrymaking grew louder.

"Those big, rich drunks," said Jack. "This harp thief is right under their noses but they'll never know it was me."

"Jack Spriggins?" Beirboor's voice echoed in the hall. "What are you doing by the harp?"

"Trying to be alone, what's it to yeh?"

"I figured their talk might have upset you," said Beirboor, joining him at the pedestal. "I spend time by it too when I feel that way. Have you ever noticed the harp plays by itself?" He plucked one of the strings and filled the alcove with a gentle, wondrous chime. "Dwarfs forged its golden post. The Fae strung it with strands of their lovely hair. Legend says Broogmagoog discovered its wood in the banks of the Green River. I don't know if that's a true tale but I wish we had stayed friends with the Forestland."

"Yeh mean the harp came from the woods?" said Jack. "So, why do giants hate us then?"

"I really can't say. Something happened long ago. Broogmagoog led the giants up here to get away. He closed off Giant Valley for good." Beirboor glanced at Jack, "I'd hate it if you left. A friend like you doesn't come along every day."

"Yeh mean, a pet like me."

"Why do you say that?"

"Cause, I'm done being trained."

"You're not going to leave, are you?" said Beirboor, clearly thrown off. "I'm sorry you can't attend the operetta tonight. I can ask father again to change his mind."

"Don't bother," said Jack. "Go to yer show. I'll be here when yeh get back."

Beirboor smiled and gave him a bear hug. "Best friends."

"Cut it out, will yeh," grunted Jack.

"I'm just happy you're staying, Jack Spriggins." Beirboor set him down. "I'll tell you all about mother's show when I get back, I promise."

"Chee, can't wait."

Chapter 22

BROOCH

After the Chelebs had left for the opera, a gathering of Jadins met outside the Gogmagogg Manor. Jack watched them from the hallway windows, holding a ledger and quill under one arm, given along with another writing assignment by Vikuvis. Jack was to be left alone for the evening.

The tutor descended the steps outside and joined the others. The angry legislator from Jadinobblis, Velikoff, was speaking with the Jadin servants. Several ostrich-hitched buggies stood by. Jack listened carefully.

"An assembly has been called," said Velikoff. "One that will shift the course of Giantdom's politics, as we have all wanted."

"No mere demonstration," Vikuvis added.

"Appointed Sir," said Velikoff, with a grin, "We are grateful, the time to act has come."

"So it has," said Vikuvis.

Vyladalis, who was also present and cast nervous glances at the opera house. "We only have five or six hours at most," she said.

"All of you who served in this household are summoned because you are useful to the cause," said Velikoff.

"Regrettably," said Veedivee. "Someone must stay behind to keep an eye on Jack Spriggins."

"No," insisted Vikuvis. "The Forestlander will remain here. He is housebroken and his writing assignment will take all evening. You will attend with us, as all Jadins must."

"This brings me great pleasure, sir," said Veedivee.

With that, the Jadins clambered aboard their ostrich buggies and rode away.

Jack lingered for a moment, listening to distant female singing, which could be heard belting from the opera house.

"That sure ain't harp music," he said as he turned." I'll show them housebroken. It's thievin' time."

The Gogmagogg harp sat unguarded in the main hall of the manor, looking grand, beautiful, and far too heavy for a Forestland boy to steal.

"Reckon they got a surprise coming."

The harp's frame reminded him of a grand longbow. Jack climbed onto the pedestal and ran his hand along the curvy neck of polished wood. It was inlaid with gold that made it shimmer. He pretended to line up his sights like an archer, drawing back the longest string with a musical *thrum!*

"The harp's mine. Ain't nobody gonna have it but me."

Using his legs, he pushed against the harp. "*Ugh!* Guess I know why it took two big Jadins to carry her. She could anchor a boat." He looked up at the ceiling. Arching crossbeams stretched from one end to the other. "Those'll be useful. Gonna need my beanstalk vines and a few other things."

He bolted outside, crossing the lawn to a garden shed. Inside, he shoved past all the shovels, rakes, and sheers, cursing the clutter until he spied what he needed. "Wheelbarrow." It was large and sturdy enough to hold the harp. He balanced the long wooden arms and wheeled it back to the manor. There was not a minute to waste.

Jack swiped several jenga fruits from the kitchen pantry and scurried through the manor snatching his beanstalk vines and bone knife from Beirboor's wardrobe. "Almost forgot the Ogre brooch." He unclipped it from his coat pocket as he sprinted back to the main hall.

The biggest challenge was lifting the harp. Jack tied a stopper (a big knot that Ma had taught him) around the neck of the instrument.

"A timber hitch oughta do it." He tossed the vine over the beam through its gap, then looped the line around the harp's post and slung it over the beam once more.

"Here goes!"

He yanked the vine and the harp came off its pedestal.

"Pried lev'rage," he said, harkening back to what Vikuvis said.

Jack gave himself a second to be proud. The strings hummed as he guided the lifted harp into the wheelbarrow. He muffled them with one of Beirboor's togas. Then, he pushed his musical cargo over the marble floors, out the back of the manor, and through the gardens.

"Windy, yeh ugly statue, get ready, 'cause I'm bringing my harp back to yeh."

The moon was gone from the sky by the time Jack returned from the temple of the Wind One. Thankfully, Gogmagogg Manor remained empty. He opened the window and heard a lady singer warbling like a plump sparrow all the way down from the opera house. Cheleb carriages idled on the streets beneath the lamp lights, waiting for her song to be over.

"Whoa, an opry goes on for a long spell. I prob'ly could've taken two harps."

The harp theft had taken three hours with the help of a large nanny goat, which toted the heavy instrument up the temple path for Jack. (The beast's reward was the stash of jenga fruits.) Jack had hitched the wheelbarrow to the nanny with the vines and coaxed her up the temple steps with the treat. The haul needed steadying, but the goat did her job well. Jack stored the harp neatly in the secret passage beneath the Wind One's statue. He pried himself away, hoping it would stay there.

Sleep would have been a great reward for pulling off his best robbery ever but there was more work to do. Jack quickly swept the Gogmagogg's floor around the harp pedestal with a tall Jadin broom. The singing from the opera house pushed his pace as he wiped away wheel marks and fallen grass. He needed to be rid of any proof on his person, so for once, he took a bath without being asked.

"Feel kinda jumpy that nothin went wrong."

He got dressed and mindfully placed the ogre brooch near the harp's empty pedestal where only a blind man could miss it.

"That ugly pin is a little message that'll go a long way."

Jack's legs ached. It was a clumsy yawning stagger back to Beirboor's room. He tied kitchen rags in his mouth and climbed into the daybed. He bound his own hands and kicked off the covers. Eyes heavy, completely drained, he let himself go to sleep.

Chapter 23

FLAGS

" The Harp! The Gogmagogg Harp is gone!" The cry jolted Jack awake. More alarmed voices went by outside the door of Beirboor's bedroom, accompanied by the heavy flip-flap of sandals running along the hallway.

"Aw c'mon, dumb giants. Hurry up and find me," grunted Jack with the gag in his mouth.

The bedroom door at last swung open.

"Jack Spriggins, look at you!" said Beirboor. "Tied up and left to starve by those black-hearted thieves."

"Mumps! Mogres!" mumbled Jack, "Mogres!" (Gagged, he could not manage to say *ogres*.)

"I'll free you." Beirboor yanked on the binds.

The simple slipknot should have been easy to untie but Beirboor pathetically wrenched Jack's arms, causing him to yelp with pain.

"Shhtp!"

"I wish Veedivee could help untie you," said Beirboor, "But the Jadins are long gone."

"Hmm?"

"Gosh, I should have undone the gag first. What was I thinking?" Beirboor unloosed it.

"Jits, yeh near yanked out my shoulder," said Jack, licking the chafed corners of his lips. "And what'd yeh mean, the Jads are gone?"

"They stole our harp and left."

"The *Jads?* Yeh sure about that?"

"Isn't it outrageous? So, who tied and gagged you? Was it Vikuvis?"

"Yeh think I got eyes in the back of my head?" Jack, nodded at the binds. "Just pull the loose end of the knot and get me out of this."

"Oh, is it that simple?" Beirboor looked triumphant, pulling off the ties.

Jack rolled off the bed and moved his achy shoulders. His legs tingled, still asleep. "Are yeh making a mistake guessing it was the Jads?"

"There is indisputable proof. Come, my father wants to see you."

The Gogmagogg family, Nollokirk, Barons Skootafrey and Krusedekulk, and other giants were gathered around the empty pedestal in the main hall, kneeling with clasped hands and sobbing as if it were a tombstone.

"Gone, gone, gone," bellowed Gogmagogg, with his head drooping heavily.

"Terrible shame," said Nollokirk, who gently held Lawrenlawra as she cried into a silk handkerchief.

"Do you think the harp is gone forever?" she sniffled.

"Don't even suggest it," said Gogmagogg, waving her off.

"What a scandal," said Krusedekulk.

"A betrayal," said Skootafrey.

"Father, we should just go take it back!" said Roidaroy.

There was no ogre brooch on the pedestal. Instead, the letter 'V' had been scrawled in its place in dark green ink and an ostrich quill lay beside it, dipped in the same color.

"Actuary Green," said Skootafrey, lifting the feather for a closer look. "We know who this belongs to."

"Vikuvis?" said Jack, stunned and confused. "Why did he do it?"

"Dear, simple Jack Spriggins," said Gogmagogg, setting his huge palms on Jack's shoulders. "I do not know if your little head will comprehend the importance of this matter."

"Try me."

"The harp means everything to us. You were here, what did you see? You must tell us what happened."

Jack's fake alibi had unraveled. With the brooch gone, his ogre story had to be dropped. "I saw nothing. Whoever suckered me tied me up and I never saw them."

"They bound and gagged Jack Spriggins while he slept, father," said Beirboor. "I untied him."

"Great Goblets!" exclaimed Krusedekulk, "And Vikuvis accused us of low behavior."

"The Jadins have overstepped the mores of giant civility," said Skootafrey.

"Gather our neighbors," said Gogmagogg. "We shall demand the harp be returned."

"Very good," said Skootafrey.

The big lummox bumped a side table as he left, sending a vase crashing to the floor. He clapped his hands twice but no Jadin servants came to clean up. The Chelebs exchanged pale glances at each other.

"What a mess these Jadins have created," said Skootafrey. "We'll nip it in the bud."

Gogmagogg rose from the pedestal, obviously shaken. "Skootafrey, escort the Dragonlanders to the tram. Send them home without a whiff of what has happened here. I'll alarm the Cheleb Senators after I set out a clean toga – *for myself.*" He nearly choked on the last words.

"I'll help you, Daddykins," said Lawrenlawra taking his arm.

"Funny," said Gogmagogg, taking a gander across the portico. "I cannot recall the last time I set foot in Jadinobblis."

"You're not one for slumming, Gogg" said Krusedekulk. "Let's gather on the Windississi Bridge. We'll march into Jadinobblis and take the harp."

Bitterly, Jack dipped a finger into the drops of actuary green. "I've been outfoxed. Vikuvis switched my ogre brooch for his own writing quill."

"Isn't this exciting?" said Beirboor, oblivious to the truth.

"Jits, Boor," said Jack, "It's a whole mess of trouble."

Word of the harp-robbery brought Chelebs by the hundreds out to the golden street. Like the Gogmagogg family, they also had returned to servant-less homes and now joined the march down the Avenue of Prosperity.

"Hurry, Jack Spriggins, we must keep up," called Beirboor. "What do you imagine Vikuvis will say when we call him out?"

"Ain't sure," said Jack.

Baron Krusedekulk, whose armbands swished with every step, passed by in a huff. "Look at us Chelebs, traveling by foot! Jadins will pay for this disgrace."

As the Cheleb mob reached the Windississi Bridge, Lord Gogmagogg raised a hand, halting them. The march would go no further. A crowd of Jadins was already assembled, prepared to meet the Chelebs. Vikuvis was out front with his beady, bird-like eyes fixed on Gogmagogg, waiting where the green bricks formed a borderline half way across.

"Yeh Chelebs are outnumbered," said Jack to Beirboor.

"My heart is beating fast, Jack Spriggins, isn't yours? What do you suppose they want?"

Jack scratched his head. "Jads are having their day, I reckon."

Lord Gogmagogg motioned forward and the citizens of Chelebraxia went out to meet their rivals. "My house is empty, tutor," he declared.

"And it shall remain so," said Vikuvis.

"Give back what has been stolen," said Gogmagogg, "Or else you will be permanently discharged."

"That offensive point of view is exactly why we Jadins have resigned," stated Vikuvis. "What a dire error you made mistaking us for property when we are, in fact, your equals."

Gogmagogg tittered, along with many of the Chelebs. "You resort to petty thievery and call yourselves equal?"

"There is nothing petty about this," countered Vikuvis. "Giantdom is now being restored to a rationalized balance of power."

"So, it's power you seek," said Gogmagogg. "Then why not handle this in a stately manner on the floor of our senate?"

"The senate is defunct," said Vikuvis. "You amend Jadin measures for your own needs and sit on those fat, lazy behinds while we run Giantdom."

"Giantdom flourishes!" boomed Gogmagogg, "Because we Chelebs excel at propagating the trade, while you Jadins stew and scheme behind those stagnant, green walls."

"Equality exists only when both sides respect it," said Vikuvis. "Chelebs no longer recognize that."

"You lack social skills, Vikuvis," said Gogmagogg. "Jadins are better suited for menial work."

"Chelebs are nothing more than spoiled children."

"I want my harp back!" shouted Gogmagogg.

"Let us see if this strikes a chord first," said Vikuvis, who thrust a massive document forward, the pages of which flapped in his hand. "The Rational Reform Referendum of Jadinobblis!"

The Jadins applauded. Gogmagogg took the reform and dropped it over the side of the bridge.

"My masterpiece!" Vikuvis exclaimed, rushing to see his document float downriver.

"All water under the bridge," said Gogmagogg, brushing his hands, "Just give back my harp."

"Harps?" said Vikuvis, turning to face him. "We are on the brink of revolution and you speak of harps?"

Baron Krusedekulk held up the writing quill that was stained with actuary green. "This belongs to you?"

"Indeed, that is mine," confessed Vikuvis.

"Criminal!" accused Gogmagogg. "What kind of an inferior culture do you lead?"

"You are delusional," said Vikuvis. "Without Jadin instruction, Chelebraxia would have no worth of any kind."

"Quit jabbering and hand over my instrument."

Vikuvis cast a sly glance at Jack. "If I had the harp, you can be certain it would never be returned to *you*."

Jack then realized, "Vikuvis ain't sure where the harp is."

"Which of you Jadins has it then?" said Gogmagogg.

Jack shrank. A smell of spice smoke rose in his nostrils and all sounds were shut to his ears as the voice of the Silent One spoke within. *"Jack, can you stop this?"*

A notion to raise his arms and proclaim to all of Giantdom that he, lone Jack Spriggins, had taken the harp, got stuck in his throat. Instead, he kept watching to see what the giants would do.

Gogmagogg stepped within inches of Vikuvis's pointy nose. "Tutor, we will not reconcile until the harp is returned."

"Jadinobblis will never negotiate with Chelebraxia unless our referendum is ratified," said Vikuvis. "After today, you will find life less comfortable." With that, he turned to walk away.

Roidaroy reddened with rage. He shoved his way past Jack and the others, tore the clasp off his own toga, and hurled it, shouting," Stupid Jadin!"

The flying brooch careened off Vikuvis's ear and went skidding along the bridge between the Jadin bystanders. The tutor touched his wounded ear, obviously in shock. A tiny trickle of blood fell from his earlobe onto the green bricks at his feet. Giants on both sides of the bridge froze.

"Brutes!" said Vikuvis, turning. "You are not the only ones who can throw stones." He cupped the wounded ear as several Jadins attended to him, and then led them away.

"You'll be back lacing our sandals within a week," said Roidaroy.

"That's enough, my eldest son," said Gogmagogg.

The Chelebs tramped back to Chelebraxia in a disordered frenzy, squabbling over what to do.

Beirboor stayed by Jack on the bridge with a bewildered frown. "You were right, Jack Spriggins. It is a mess. What do you suppose it all means?"

"It means the Jads are done taking care of yeh, Boor," said Jack. "They ain't gonna be any help now."

In the days after the confrontation on the Windississi Bridge, the Jadins raised a flag over Jadinobblis where it flew high on their clock tower. It was large and could be seen clearly from Chelebraxia.

The flag was actuary green, stitched with a likeness of Vikuvis's wounded ear: a single drop of blood falling from the earlobe.

Not to be outdone, Chelebraxia raised a flag over the dome of their Opera House. The ensign was purple, embroidered with a golden harp.

Beirboor flopped on cushions of the alcove with his sketchpad, scribbling. He had lost weight and stubble had grown on his head. "Stay where you are, Jack Spriggins," he said. "I'm going to draw you sitting at the scene of the Jadins 'crime."

Jack was dangling his legs from the empty harp pedestal, stewing in boredom. "Ain't yer pa going to do anything about the missing harp?" he asked. "It's almost been a week."

"Sure, Father is obsessed with getting the harp back," said Beirboor. "That, along with the Jadins 'portion of the treasury. The terms will be revealed as soon as the harp is returned."

"The Jads are gonna lick yeh," said Jack.

A jangling noise accompanied the approach of Roidaroy with Barons Skootafrey and Krusedekulk, who were toting large satchels on their shoulders.

"What do have there, Roidaroy?" said Beirboor.

"Bribe money. I'm not supposed to talk about it so don't ask, Blubberbut," said Roidaroy. "We're leaving. Father asked to see you alone. Not with the forest worm."

"Alright." Beirboor set down his sketchpad and left.

"This place stinks," said Jack, holding his nose. Without servants, food had rotted in the pantry, dishes were piled on the banquet tables, and garbage mounted by the canals. It had given him a headache that worsened by a hankering to get back to his harp. "This whole big house is nothing without it. I've had enough."

Jack went to Beirboor's room and got dressed in his old forestland clothes, slinging the beanstalks over his shoulder.

"Time to cut and run."

Beirboor stumbled into the bedroom, meek and pale. "I've been drafted into the Supreme Military of Chelebraxia. I'm going to make a terrible soldier." He fell onto the bed and buried his face in the pillow. "Just a week ago Giantdom was peaceful and Vikuvis was teaching me history. Now, I'm supposed to fight him?"

"At least yer part of their army," said Jack, "They didn't say yeh were just a kid."

"A real war." Beirboor sat and stared at Jack. "Why are you dressed in forest clothes?"

"It's time I be getting on."

"You were just going to leave without a goodbye?"

Jack reached for his coat. "Listen, Boor, y'all picked a fight yeh ain't gonna win."

"I hate fighting. Maybe I could go with you?"

"Chee, yeh'd never make it," said Jack, "Yeh ain't tough enough."

"Gosh, I wish I was fit like Roidaroy, then I could go along."

"Roidaroy ain't so tough."

"He will be, Jack Spriggins. He's becoming a warrior."

"A warrior in the gym-nazum, maybe."

"No, he's going to get real weapons," said Beirboor. "Roidaroy and the Barons are heading down to the Great Forest to buy them."

"What? For real?"

"They just left. Father gave them the Dragonlanders 'gold to bribe the ogres."

"The ogres!" Jack felt as if the ceiling had just caved in on his head.

"Those were my father's instructions."

"What about the Champs, huh? Giants could learn more about fighting from Ardus Camlann than from stinking ogres."

Beirboor lowered his head in shame. "I heard the ogres are winning."

"Yeh heard that?"

Beirboor nodded. "It's true."

"Tell me which way Roidaroy will go?"

"They're using the shortcut through the old temple."

"The temple of the Wind One?" Jack straightened up. "Yeh mean they know about that tunnel?"

"My family knows all the mountain tunnels. Our ancestors built it," Beirboor gave a curious look. "How come you know about it?"

Jack put his coat on and collected his remaining gear. "Ol' Vik took me there. Wanted to teach me a lesson."

Beirboor stepped in front of the door. "What's so special about the temple?"

"Nothing. Now git outta my way, will yeh?"

"Tell me why you're running off."

"Ain't got time for this," Jack clenched his fists. "Now move it."

"No." Beirboor used his large body to block the door. "Can't you be honest with me?"

"Yeh ain't gonna like it."

"Why ever not?"

"Aw jits," said Jack, throwing his arms up. "The harp. Vikuvis didn't take it. I did."

A confused furrow formed on Beirboor's brow. "You? You couldn't have, you're too small."

Jack gave his beanstalk vines a shake. "Wanna bet?"

Beirboor staggered over to the bed and sat. His face went pale. "I don't understand, Jack Spriggins."

"I wanted y'all to think the ogres stole it but the Jadins pulled a fast one on me. They tricked everybody."

"But you were tied up."

"I done it to myself."

Tears filled Beirboor's eyes.

"Don't sit there sobbing." Jack tried to use a nice tone. "Come with me, if yeh want."

"Father should never have trusted you," said Beirboor. "Roidaroy was right, so was Vikuvis and everybody. You were never my friend, Jack Spriggins. You're just a thief."

"Always have been."

Beirboor's face screwed up into a tight grimace and he let out a long, strained, and painful yell. "You're a rat, Jack Spriggins. An evil, yellow-eyed thief!"

The young giant lunged at him but fell when Jack dodged out of the way.

"Quit it, Boor. I don't wanna hurt yeh."

"You already have," said Beirboor, getting to his feet. "You've used my family's generosity, stolen what means most to us and destroyed our lives."

"Yeh always say yeh wanna see the woods." Jack stood in front of the open wardrobe. "So, come with me."

Beirboor rubbed his head. "Where I can get scalped by ogres?"

"Yeh don't have any hair."

"Or cheated by liars like you?" He started ripping the pages out of his sketchpad. "The forest was a dream, Rat Spriggins. That's all I ever do. Dream. You've stolen that from me too."

Beirboor's anger was frightening to see. Torn sketch papers went everywhere and then he charged at Jack. With a side step, Jack sent Beirboor crashing into the back of the wardrobe and quickly slammed the closet doors behind him, locking him inside.

"I told yeh to stop!" said Jack.

Beirboor pounded the doors, rocking the wardrobe on its stubby legs. "Rat Spriggins. Rat! Rat!" he cried, his voice hoarse and grating.

Jack ran. He followed the stairs to the underground past heaps of uncollected trash. Tears welled in his eyes. He felt as if he belonged there with the garbage. "Sorry, Boor."

He unhitched a skiff nearby and slipped into the reeking current, drifting outside Chelebraxia towards the Windississi River. Behind him, from the window of Beirboor's room he heard fists still pounding on the wardrobe door. "Rat Spriggins!" shouted Beirboor.

Jack turned forward and rowed into a mist on the river. He was grateful to lose sight of the giant cities as he paddled into it.

* * * *

~ 261 ~

When the cold fog cleared, time had slipped by again. Jack realized he was alone on the mountain ledge, continuing his conversation with the Silent One.

"Don't show me more," he said to the spirit. "It's godawful what Beirboor called me."

The Silent One's voice spoke beneath the thin and wispy air. *"Why do you think that?"*

"Because it's true. I ain't been a fox, I been a rat. Now I'm out of tricks, left to die here on this mountain, forgotten. I'll be a rotted skeleton on a cliff."

"And yet, you are not dead, not forgotten, and still very much on the minds of others."

"Like who?"

"Ella, Redvere, and the Crone, Hepkatee."

"Why would they waste their time on me?"

"They are having trials of their own, which you fit into, whether you were there or not. Would you like to see for yourself?"

"Show me."

Chapter 24

EMBERS

The heavy footfalls of Redvere's horse, clopping along the Timberock Road, lagged at the rear of the company while Ardus and the others rode out front.

"You are a Champion," said Leonel, who rode alongside Redvere. He was a veteran soldier only a few years older. "Why do you not ride with the others at the fore?"

"I don't deserve to," said Redvere, who could not bear the title of Champion. The very idea of it now seemed absurd. "Killing brings me no honor or glory, it only brings death."

"Be proud. You have fought bravely," Leonel said with a chuckle. "These battles are going badly."

"Only for now," said Leonel, "Ardus is a gifted leader. I can tell you – I was at Hedgewall where I saw many of our best soldiers fall. If he had been there, we would have fared better. His swift retreats have saved us and we live on, so we can fight again."

"Master Cai won't ever fight again," said Redvere. "He was the toughest, most respected instructor at the Orchard. Now he's dead."

The ogres had routed the Forestland militia at every clash so far and retreat was the general order of the day, but for Redvere, son of the mighty Bors Celot, not even victory would uplift his heart.

"War is savage, ghastly, and meaningless," he added.

"It is," said Leonel. "It takes a soldier to endure it but your friends do not fall in vain. Your swift arrows dropped many of our enemies. You are a hero."

"No, it's like the dragon."

"Sorry?"

"Jack Spriggins knew the difference, we did not."

"Who is Jack Spriggins?"

"Just a kid," said Redvere. "He knew the innocent from a real monster. He had the kind of courage that makes a hero. I'm not sure I can help win this war."

"If I may," said Leonel, "Don't lose hope. The Great Spirits watch over us. Our turn to strike will come."

"When is that?" said Redvere. "The ogres already control the northern forest. Now that Nethervil, Briarslate, and Delden have fallen, I fear all the villages along the Timberock will go next."

"We have Ardus," said Leonel, "Always out front bearing the standard. He is also a wise tactician. He knows when to cut and run. It is right to do so now."

Redvere's ears still rang with the clash of blades and screams of dying men from yesterday's battle when ogre fireballs had been hurtled upon the Forestlanders.

"Their method of warfare seems hardly fair," said Redvere. "No burials, no words to the Spirits were made for our dead friends," he said. "We joked and ate breakfast only yesterday. Now they lay mangled on the barren battlefield."

"Ogres are a vile race," said Leonel. "Giving no quarter, they cheer over the vanquished with shameless cruelty."

For a second time this morning, Redvere turned aside and vomited next to the trail.

Leonel reached for him, "Do you need assistance?"

Redvere waved him off. "I taste the acrid smoke of the battle still."

They passed by a village along the road. Folks were evacuating with loaded wagons, slowing the progress of the soldiers. Some villagers offered food and blessings as Redvere rode by.

"Terac and Rudd will fall next," he said to Leonel. "The tide of this war has not shifted in their favor."

"We will defend them."

Strangely, it was the enemies Redvere had killed who haunted him the most; the shocked faces of young ogre warriors whose lives were snatched away by his piercing arrows.

"Many of the ogre boys were younger than I," said Redvere. "I wonder if their last thoughts were of family and childhood homes."

"Don't pity them," said Leonel. "They picked the fight. They can lose it."

"I can hardly bear to take another life," said Redvere. "Jack Spriggins said the real woods would knock me on my butt, guess he was right."

"Redvere, give yourself more credit. You're a young man. Our commander has many tricks up his sleeve, we'll give the ogres a good battle yet."

* * * *

The sharp, hungry cry of a wolf howling in the forest carried a message that Ella understood clearly from the opened kitchen door.

"Men have been fighting and dying. It's a message to other wolves, but not for me," she said.

A chipmunk was keeping her company. Ella's red riding hood was hanging on its peg by the door. She clutched it in her hand.

"I wish there was news about Jack, wherever he might be, that he's safe. I miss our adventures, but no animal has seen him for months."

The autumn's chill carried a scent of smoke from the north. Ella let go of the cape and slipped off her shoes beside the fire.

"The hearth is warm," she said, as she rolled her stockings off, sitting in a chair by the fire.

The chipmunk gave a little squeak by the door, chomping an acorn.

"I'll keep the door open for you," said Ella. "I would offer you sunflower seeds but you seem to have brought your own dinner."

As all animals did at the sound of her voice, the critter stopped chewing and stared at her with all its attention.

Ella nibbled from a handful of the seeds and watched the smoldering embers, yearning for comfort from the ongoing sadness upstairs. A fortnight had passed since her mother could no longer rise from bed. The servants tiptoed up with washbasins, oils, and medicines, tending to her at all hours. Papa paced the hallway mumbling or shouting orders at them, only to apologize afterward, wringing his hands. Healers from different villages came and went without effect. Mama's condition only grew worse.

Hours earlier, Ella had brought a tea tray with Mama's favorite china cup to the bedroom but Papa took it away before she could enter. "This is not a good time, Ella," he had said. Before the door closed, she saw her mother drooped against Nessie, who was turning her over on the bed. Mama's face was chalk white and her body looked drawn. Her nightgown, which had fit only days before, was now much too big. Her eyes, rimmed with dark circles, twinkled at Ella for a moment before she winced and collapsed. Then the door was shut.

Mostly, Ella stayed downstairs by the fire.

"What I wouldn't give to have an adventure," she said, stoking the crumbled log with a poker and watching tiny sparks twirl up the chimney. "If only I knew where Jack was."

The chipmunk flitted off as Nessie bustled into the kitchen.

"Put your stockings on, child," she said, "And close the door or you'll catch yourself a cold. I can't abide with anymore sickness in this house."

Nessie grabbed a kettle off the grate and hurried upstairs. A raven landed by the kitchen door.

"Why hello, Sersi," said Ella, as the Crone's pet wobbled outside the threshold. "Any word of Jack?"

"Caw!" spoke the raven, and then it flew away.

"Thanks for trying," said Ella, shutting the kitchen door and curling back up in the chair.

She must have dozed because she awoke to the sound of the front door squeaking and voices in the hall. Her father was quietly conversing with a guest.

"Whatever you need. If it's a question of gold," he pleaded, "You can take all I have."

"I wish I could help but nothing more can be done."

Ella crept over beside the pantry and peeked through the doorjamb. Papa was speaking with Allwise of the Orchard.

"The roots will ease her pain," said the old sage.

"More of the same useless counsel we've already heard," said Papa, raising his voice. "Is this all the wisdom you bring here?"

"You sent for me and I came," said Allwise, gently. "Missus Vintner is a woman of rare quality. So is your daughter, Ella. Take comfort in her."

With a rush of cool air, the door was closed as Allwise left. Ella hurried back to the hearth and Papa entered the kitchen. His face was unshaven and his shirt untucked.

"You haven't changed your clothes, Papa," said Ella, caressing his hand. She offered him an apple from the sideboard. He just looked at it. "You should eat. It'd be good for you."

"Ella, I told you to stay in your room," said Papa.

"I can't rest," she said. "I like it better down here where it's warm. Is that alright?"

"It's probably quieter for you," said Papa, finally looking at her. He motioned, "Come closer." One of her ribbons had come undone and he fixed it. "Your curls. Just like hers used to be. You look so much alike."

"That's nice, Papa."

"It's late," he said. "If you can't rest, then see if you can be of help to Nessie." He put on his overcoat and left through the kitchen door.

Ella's scarlet cape still hung on its peg. She held it tightly, looking out the window. Her father galloped off on Chestnut, his favorite steed. "Why do I never make Papa smile?"

Nessie rushed into the kitchen, covering her face and choking back sobs. "Where's your father?" she said.

"He went out. I don't know where to."

"You can help me then, Ella," said Nessie. "Take some fresh cloths from the sideboard and follow me to your mother's room."

Nessie added warm water to a basin and went upstairs. A chill went from Ella's heart to her bones.

"I can't run now," she said, letting go of her cape. "It's Mama's time to journey. Not mine."

* * * *

The familiar beat of the raven's wings flapped outside the Crone's open window. Hepkatee patted her shoulder, "Sersi, my friend," she said, as the bird alighted there to perch.

"A grape leaf?" said Hepkatee, taking a sprig from the raven's beak. "I asked yeh to find the boy."

The raven cawed.

"As I suspected. He's not in these woods," said the crone, rubbing her chin. "I'll search for him myself."

She blindly fumbled to a work table, feeling with bent fingers for a stone mortar and pestle. "You flew a long way for this sprig. You wished to see Ella, didn't you?"

The raven warbled and hopped to the mantelpiece above the hearth.

Hepkatee crushed the grape leaf with bracken and added alder oil into the bowl, mixing it together. Piercing her thumb with a falcon's claw, she squeezed drops of blood into the mixture. "Green Mother, ichor, and oil," she said. "Be my eyes."

The old woman kicked aside the rocker and crouched low before the hearth fire. Ignoring the pain in her knees, she placed the red-hot poker into the mortar bowl, which flared with a burst of green and blue.

"It be I, your servant Hepkatee," she chanted, rubbing the warm paste from the bowl around her eye sockets and chucking the rest into the flames.

To open the doors of vision, the crone found her power always came by fire. For her witch-sister, Viviyann Greygeese, it came from the fragrance of flowers. For Ganzil it appeared in water and other reflections like glass.

"Sacred fire, be my eyes," said Hepkatee, withdrawing a falcon's feather from her apron pocket and flicking it into the blaze, which flashed with such intense green that she could make out its brightness.

A vision took over. What she saw next was her own decrepit body crouched before the hearth but no longer embodied by Hepkatee. Her untethered spirit was cast out of the cottage like a spark on the wind, beyond the trees and into the night sky. She became aware of a rapid motion in her shoulders as if she were beating wings in flight. All became clear. She was soaring over the Great Forest, seeing through the eyes of a falcon.

"To the war," said Hepkatee. Her voice issued forth as a screech.

Over a tree line she flew to a large field, where the grass was in flames. "This be the Swampland of the Crokees, my childhood home. The danger has drawn closer than I thought."

War engines hurtled fireballs. Hundreds of warriors clanged metal, cleaved, and slashed one another. The air was heavy with hatred and despair. Those who fell did not rise again. There were bare-armed warriors in bronze chest plates whose faces were tattooed with blue snakes. They swung curved blades and had an appetite for the killing.

"Ogres. The men of the deserts," said Hepkatee. "They seek to tear the forest down to the last sapling; claim it as theirs until it be barren like their own land."

The enemy was winning. Forestland men were outnumbered and mostly outmatched. Yet, a handful of rangers, far more skilled than the rest, stood their ground. Ardus Camlann, upon a white horse, swung his broadsword with such strength and command, he gave hope to the other men. Wherever the line held fast, it was he who they rallied to. Wherever he charged, the strength of a true champion went with him.

"Ardus Camlann," said Hepkatee, sweeping by him. "As he inspires, so will he rule."

One ranger fought at his side ran amok with mad eyes. Always first into the fray, the berserker swung his battle-ax with the fury of the Earth One.

"Gwachmai Camlann," said Hepkatee. "His name means 'hawk 'in the tongue of the Mist Hills. He be worthy of it."

An unusual foreign warrior – tall and black-skinned – fought alongside the rangers. He brandished a spear with skill, which prove to be formidable to his adversaries. "Ootan of Zan," said Hepkatee. "He bears a noble title, yet be exiled from his home."

Amid the battle, an ogre warlord charged through and knocked Ardus from his horse. The ogre raised his blade to strike the fallen leader but a quick arrow caught him in the throat, dropping him dead at Ardus's feet. Hepkatee tracked the shot to an archer, dressed in black, with a handsome, but sickened, face.

"Redvere, son of Bors Celot," she said. "He fights with a poet's heart and the battle has shaken his faith."

The falcon encircled the battlefield. "Where be the one who the spirits chose? The boy with the yellow eyes. Be he not here?"

In answer, the falcon winged far away from the smoke and flames. It landed on a fence post at Whispering Vine, where the Vintner family's chateau stood ivy-covered in the moonlight.

"What do the spirits guide me here to see?"

Prayers to the Green Mother issued from an upstairs bedroom, pleading mercy for Ella's earth mother, who lay dying. Through a window on the ground floor, Hepkatee saw the scarlet cape hanging on a peg near the kitchen door.

"Brave girl, she has found the courage to face this death. Never again will she run."

Hepkatee offered her own prayer, "Lell, Spirit of Darkness, carry the lady's soul to your sister of light."

For a while, time evaporated like vapors of morning dew. The sun broke above the horizon and sobs now came from the upstairs window.

"Her mother be gone," said Hepkatee, taking to the sky in falcon-flight and heading swiftly east to the rising sun. Above the peaks of the Broogs Range, higher and higher, she arced over the ice-tops, swooping into the valley where the giants lived.

"The boy be here."

The two cities of Giantdom, divided by a great river, tremored with unrest. "The flame of war stirs here too. The boy has played a part."

She found him, awkwardly manning a skiff on the misty river, heading alone to an ancient shrine. She flew to its ruins on the hillside. Chiseled above the colonnade of the crumbling roof, she saw a sacred symbol of the harp. "Ha, the old temple of the Wind One! Faithless giants, no wonder it be an empty ruin."

The boy berthed the skiff, overturning it upon the riverbank as he raced up the temple path. "He got a fever of greed for a stolen prize. His ways be not changed. From whom does he run?"

Three giants approached crossing a meadow.

"They do not expect the boy but will soon give him chase."

Jack disappeared into the ruins from which Hepkatee perceived heavenly thrums of harp music.

"Spirits light and dark," she pleaded. "Why be this troubled son your hero? The shadows have great interest in him. Better he dies in the giant's temple than he fails."

The vision weakened as the fire died. The crone drew a painful breath and pressed her hands into the floorboards of the cottage as she returned to the brittle body of an old woman, still crouched before the hearth.

"Ach!" she grimaced, her head reeling with pain and her miserable knees throbbing. "Forgive me, sacred mother. It be not I to question your wisdom but the boy be infected with greed. If he doesn't change, then nothing ever will."

Chapter 25

PLUNGE

Jack entered the hillside temple of the Wind One crawling on the ground and feeling for the Jadin flare he had left behind. He found the lamp and relit it with the flint chip from his coat pocket.

"Windy, ol' girl," he said to the sparsely lit statue. "Keep a lookout for me a bit longer."

The harp was still covered in the wheelbarrow inside the passageway. "Whew, sure glad to see yeh." The lantern flickered in the drafty, dark passageway. There were iron sconces along the wall and Jack set his lamp into one.

Deep voices and the scuff of sandals echoed from behind. Three giants entered the temple. Their voices were all too familiar.

"There's the statue, Barons," said Roidaroy.

"The passage runs beneath it," said Skootafrey. "Shine your torch over there."

A scornful gale blew through Jack's corridor. Lashing vines and cover-folds flapped against the harp. The strings, bound as they were, rattled loudly.

"Hush, Barons!" said Roidaroy to the others. "I hear something moving in the dark."

"It's the wind," said Krusedekulk.

"I smell something oddly familiar," said Skootafrey. "Why do I know that scent?"

The amber glare of their torches lit the mouth of the passage where Jack was hiding. He unraveled his vine coils and laid a snare on the ground." I gotta buy myself time to escape." He hitched it to a wall sconce and backed into the darkness.

"Somebody else's torch is lit," said Roidaroy. "Announce yourself, whoever is there!"

A wicked groan of wind blasted through the shaft and extinguished Roidaroy's torch. Jack was grateful for the timing.

"Suppose this place may be haunted?" said Skootafrey.

"Ooo-ooo-ee-ee," uttered Jack from the blackness like a ghost.

"I have a suspicious feeling here," said Krusedekulk.

"There's a large object down there near the light. Let's head to it, Barons." Roidaroy marched in and stopped beside the wheelbarrow. They joined him as he lifted the folds.

"Great goblets!" said Krusedekulk. "It's our missing harp."

"And this green torch," said Skootafrey, pointing at the sconce. "Most certainly belongs to a Jadin. Whatever did they intend bringing it here?"

"Ain't no Jadins torch!" hollered Jack. "It's mine."

"Who said that?" demanded Krusedekulk.

Jack gave the end of his snare line a good yank. The giants' feet were all lassoed and they fell to the floor. There was a heavy jangle of coins from their bags.

"Got yeh!" said Jack, who ran over and tied off the vine at the sconce. "I'm yer harp thief".

"Impossible," said Krusedekulk. "The Jadins stole it."

"Reckon not." Jack lifted the handles of the harp-cart and rolled it away through the tunnel.

"Yes! Yes! That's it," said Skootafrey, "I was sure I recognized his stench when we entered."

Roidaroy swiped at Jack but the snare held him back like a dog on leash. "Jack Spriggins has Faa-ther's harp! Help, Barons. Untie me and get after him."

Jack rolled the harp through the dark corridor. He struck a craggy sidewall at an abrupt turn, receiving a fresh welt on his thigh. "Ouch!" With a tug, he redirected the heavy wheelbarrow through the tunnel. It rolled downslope with uncontrollable speed.

"Whoa, easy." The path wove as the rolling cart went sallying against the sidewalls. "Oof! Ach!" cried Jack with each thud. "Slow down, yeh stupid harp!"

The handles jounced out of his grip and the harp rolled on ahead until it struck a wall with a noisy clamor.

Jack skidded on his rump into the midst of a round chamber. Daylight eked through cracks of broken rock, lighting the harp. The cover folds had ripped open so he used his bone knife to free it. Gold gleams shined forth and the bare strings thrummed as if it was concert time.

"I hear Faa-ther's harp," echoed Roidaroy's voice from within the tunnel. The flip-flap of their sandals neared.

Jack sheathed the knife. The cavern now forked with tunnels leading in different directions. "Which one do I follow?" He licked a finger and stuck it in the air. "There! That tunnel feels drafty, I'm taking it."

He tied a long, thin vine around his waist and fastened the other end to the harp's post.

"Wherever yeh go, Harpy, we go together."

Jack got the wheelbarrow rolling but was unable to keep the pace. It lurched forward, yanking him off his feet. He gripped the line and was dragged on his belly down the twisty corridor. "This plan ain't so smart!"

The cart knocked hard against the sidewalls, eventually spinning sideways to a stop. Jack slid right on by it, his eyes widening with terror. The cave floor ahead of him had collapsed, leaving a dark black pit that seemed to have no bottom. "Noo!"

He slid over the edge and dropped into blackness. Surely, this fall was the end. Then the line went tight. Caught by his waist, he dangled in midair. "Oof!" he grunted; his life nearly squeezed out at his cinched his gut.

The sweet sound of harp strings echoed into the chasm.

Jack looked up. Roidaroy was staring down from the mouth of the pit above, straining to keep the harp from falling. His huge arms shook as he tried to save it from falling over the edge. The barons arrived and together they heaved it back out.

"Those gold dumbbells you lift just saved the day," said Skootafrey.

Krusedekulk peered over the edge, chuckling. "How tragic, the Forestlander must surely be dead."

Jack realized they could not see him hanging in the darkness.

"Look, Barons!" said Roidaroy. "What's this green rope?"

The creaking vine drew their attention.

"How tragic. He may yet live," said Krusedekulk.

"Not for long," said Skootafrey, drawing his knife. "Hmm. My sharp blade does not cut his green rope. See here! It's unbreakable."

"Stop that, Baron," said Roidaroy. "We're taking Jack Spriggins and the harp back to Chelebraxia. Faa-ther will want to punish the traitor."

Jack felt a tug on his line, then was tugged up one giant arm's length at a time.

"Caught you, forest worm," said Roidaroy, as he pulled Jack out of the pit.

"Tell us the truth, Forestlander," said Skootafrey. "Did Vikuvis put you up to this? You spent a lot of time with that Jadin tutor. You're working for them, aren't you?"

"Naw, yeh big clod," said Jack, jutting out his chin. "It was the ogres. They wanted me to steal it. They hate yeh giants and are gonna pay me a load of coins if I bring em yer harp."

(For never being a great fibber, this lie of his was not half bad.)

The giants exchanged glances.

Krusedekulk lifted his bag of gold. "He's lying. The ogres would have nothing to do with a Forestlander. They would have scalped Jack Spriggins and left him for dead. That's their way."

"Throw him back in the pit," said Skootafrey. "I'll undo his green knot." The Cheleb attempted to do so but had no luck untying the harp.

"Ain't gonna work, giant," said Jack. "That's a stopper knot and yeh can't undo it."

"Untie Faa-ther's harp or I'll smash you!" said Roidaroy. He tried to grab Jack but got a stomp on the foot instead. "Yeow! You nasty bug!"

"I told yeh big lugs, the harp is mine!" said Jack.

He frantically searched for an escape. There was a thick wooden rail laying across the mouth of the pit. Still tied to the vine, Jack kicked the wheelbarrow and got it started rolling towards the pit. Then he ran and leapt over the chasm, landing on the wooden beam halfway across.

"Try if yeh like," said Jack, waving his arms for balance. "Yeh giants ain't ever gonna catch me."

Krusedekulk and Skootafrey reached for the handles as the wheelbarrow rolled over the edge. They were too late. The cart dropped into the pit carrying the harp. Jack watched it fall. The green vine unraveled and he gave the Chelebs his cheekiest wink.

"See yeh," he said, as he dove into the pit.

"Stop him!" said Roidaroy.

The free-fall seemed unending until the slack ran out. The
vine creaked as it squeezed Jack's gut again, bouncing him to a stop
by the weight of the harp tied on the other end. Strings jingled as the
instrument swung below. Jack lowered himself until he was standing
on top of its frame.

A gap in the mountain wall revealed a ledge outside. It was
wide enough to stand on if Jack could reach it. He rocked the harp
back and forth like a tree swing, wider with each pass.

"Just one more!" he said, leaning toward the window.

The ledge was just within reach when the beanstalk line gave
way.

"Huh?!" Jack and the harp flew sidelong through the gap and
toppled on to the rim.

"Did you see him fall?" said Roidaroy, his snide tone
vibrating through the chasm.

"Yes, I believe so," said Skootafrey. "I unloosed the beam and
down the pit went the whole works."

"How tragic. Jack Spriggins is dead," said Krusedekulk.

Roidaroy complained, "With Faa-ther's harp!"

"There is another route down," said Skootafrey. "Come, we'll
retrieve it yet."

"What good is it smashed to pieces?" said Roidaroy.

Many feet below, Jack stretched across the harp and reeled in
his green vine. For the first time in months, he could see the Great
Forest below. "The sweet smell of pines!"

He imagined the trickling water from Thin Creek and those
calming moments when the sunlight flickered through the boughs.
He could even hear Ma's squeaky singing voice and felt an ache of
regret for all the months that had gone by without sending any word

to her. Even worse was the guilt of how poorly he had treated
Beirboor.

"Reckon my plan was bad. Giants were never gonna help us
Foresters fight. Now, look what I done to Boor, after spending the
whole summer together. Ain't had a real friend like him before,
except maybe Ella."

The name" Rat Spriggins" burned in his head like a bad fever.

"Shake it off! Bum giants don't care about me. Why give a
hoot?"

He looked down and saw a group of iron wheels fastened to
the cliff side.

"Those're miner's pulleys."

Jack dug his fingers into a rock crease and shimmied down to
the nearest one, threading the beanstalk vine around its wheel.
Climbing back up to the harp, he shoved it off the ledge. With a
flurry of golden strings, it fell. The pulley wheel spun. Tension
tightened in his hands and he ground his boots into the cliff-side,
gaining control of the harp. Shimmying down, he planted his feet
triumphantly on top then let out the slack and descended the
mountain with the harp.

There were several windows cloven in the cliffside. The
openings were framed by colonnades that looked similar to those in
Chelebraxia. Jack passed beyond several of them before the slack ran
out. Finally, he settled the harp on a ledge and restrung the vine to
another pulley.

The forest still remained some thousands of feet below. His
hands felt sore and his climbing muscles ached after months of
lounging around the Gogmagogg manor.

"Can barely manage my weigh and the harp together but I think I lost the three giants."

He shook his hands and descended the next pitch when his line froze and would not move any further.

"Jack Spriggins!" called Roidaroy.

The heads of the three Chelebs were poking out of one of the cave windows above him. Roidaroy had hold of the beanstalk line.

"Stop, harp thief!" said Krusedekulk, pointing at him. "You have our property."

Roidaroy climbed out onto the window ledge.

"What in blazes are you doing, young Gogg?" said Skootafrey.

"We're climbing down there," said Roidaroy. "Jack Spriggins is not getting away with faa-ther's harp. Get him, Barons. I command you."

A chill went up Jack's spine as he watched Roidaroy scramble onto the line. The proud giant's weight caused the vine to start slipping through his grip. His arms shook as he clenched tighter.

"Roidaroy," shouted Jack. "Don't! It can't hold yeh. Yeh're gonna fall and break yer neck."

"I'm climbing down to break yours!" said Roidaroy.

Surprisingly, the only thing that mattered to Jack was the life of Beirboor's brother teetering above him. All plans about the war, rangers, and the Dark Lady's tune meant nothing.

"I'll give yeh back the harp," said Jack. "Just don't move."

"An obvious ruse," said Krusedekulk. "He's trying to trick us."

"Yes," said Skootafrey, "That line is unbreakable and he knows it. Let's go get the little rat."

It must have never entered their thick heads that Jack, who was far shorter and hundreds of pounds lighter, held the other end of the line. He could never support their combined weight. Nevertheless, the two barons climbed out of the gap toting their heavy sacks of gold and joined Roidaroy on the line.

"No!" cried Jack, his grip slipping. "Please don't!"

The next instant changed everything.

The vine flew fast out of Jack's hands, burning his fingers. He, the three giants, and the harp all plunged downwards.

Jack kicked the harp away and pitched himself towards a small ledge. He landed on his side with a devastating jolt, his body tingling as his ears rang. The world around him narrowed, blacking out.

The harp fell and struck the cliff with a tremendous clamor. Then came the bloodcurdling cries of the giants. Baron Skootafrey fell first, followed by Krusedekulk with a jangle of coins from their bags. Finally, Roidaroy fell, his terror-stricken eyes locked on Jack.

"Jaaaack Spriggins!" the giant cursed as he dropped by.

Their screams faded into the dark green forest below. The last thing Jack could hear as he passed out was the repeated clang of the harp as it struck the mountainside below again and again.

* * * *

"Ain't nothing more to tell," said Jack to the Silent One. "My story's over. I'm gonna die here now."

The smell of spice smoke was present but he got no reply from the spirit.

"Ain't this why yeh showed me all this again? So I'd see how bad and wrong I was all my life?"

"*You chose what to see, Jack,*" said the spirit. "*I just helped you look.*"

Jack let out a groan and curled up in a ball. "Roidaroy and the Barons. Look what I done to them." Tears streamed down his cheeks and he cried, looking upwards. "Beirboor, I'm sorry. Ma. Ella. Redvere. Yer all so brave but I ain't. I thought having friends and loved ones made me weak."

"*And now?*"

"Reckon I know different. But it's too late."

"*Then maybe this lonely ledge is more comfortable than you've been letting on?*"

"Aw bunk, we both know it ain't," said Jack. "Don't leave, Spirit. Please keep talking to me. I don't want to die. Not like this. I finally got thoughts in my head worth keeping."

"*That sounds hopeful.*"

It was a great surprise when Jack realized he was already standing, leaning out over the Great Forest tempting the sick knot in the pit of his stomach.

"What I done, I done," he said. "What I do from here on, I'll make right. I'll keep on learning."

"*I think you're ready,*" said the spirit. "*Go with courage.*"

"Yeh coming with me?"

"*You're never without me, Jack Spriggins. We may not talk to each other anymore but that's only because you know what I'll say now.*"

"Yeh want me to figure it out myself?"

"You always have."

The wind shifted. Jack staggered a bit, then realized the conversation was over.

"Spirit? Don't go!" he said, searching this way and that. "Spirit! How'll I be sure yeh ain't been some crazy dream?"

Lost in the solitude, Jack caught the lingering scent of spice smoke and broke into a grin.

"Reckon I'll trust yeh."

He took one last gander from the high rocky ledge. The beanstalk vines were gone so he climbed inside another window hewed in the cliff.

There was a sloping, downward path inside the mountain. Jack followed it while clutching one hand against his sore ribs. It took him hours to make his way down. His canteen had busted and his thirst grew. Eventually, the corridor grew noisy and damp, echoing with the roar of a waterfall.

Jack trotted out of the tunnel at the foot of the mountain directly behind the falls. He stood in the mist; his face blasted by the refreshing bursts.

"Thank yeh!" he said, and picked his way along the path.

Sore and woozy, Jack heard the crisp, tingling chimes of harp music. He turned to see what was making it and dropped on a bank of grass by the lagoon, unable to believe what he saw.

"The harp!"

The golden harp was not broken; it was not in a million pieces. It was whole and perfect; stuck on a mound of earth in the middle of the lagoon and covered with beanstalk vines. The spray from the falls struck its strings and gave voice to thousands of water drops. A breeze rippled across the lagoon spreading the trill of music like it would in a dream – but this beautiful vision was all too real.

Chapter **26**

REUNION

The broken forms of Roidaroy, Skootafrey, and Krusedekulk lay a thousand feet from the waterfall. Their gold coins had spilled from the bags and were scattered all around them. Jack kneeled amid the mess and sobbed.

"Yeh there, Spirit?" he said. "I can never make this right."

The only answer came from the falls and the pangs of the harp.

Jack removed his coat and shirt and began to dig graves in a spot between the pines using a sharp rock as a shovel. Each plow sent shooting pain to his ribs but he kept digging.

He was waist deep in earth when a familiar voice hollered through the trees. "Spit-o-the Wet Codger, it's Jack Spriggins!"

It was Gwachmai. The warrior's happy expression sobered the moment he saw what Jack was standing in.

"What's bin done here, laddie?"

"Reckon I done murder," said Jack.

A troop of men trod out of the woods behind Gwachmai. They were dozens of them in leather armor, looking haggard with splintered shields and swords.

"Dead giants," said the young officer called Leonel.

The spectacle of the corpses lying amidst the brightly shimmering gold sent ripples of surprise through their ranks.

"Cannot believe m'eyes," said Gwachmai.

"I tried to warn them," said Jack, fumbling for an explanation, "But they chased me out on the mountain and fell."

Leonel was examining Krusedekulk's body and picked a letter out of his robes and handed it to Gwachmai. "They were traitors to the Forestlands," he said. "This letter is addressed to the ogres."

Gwachmai would not take it; he only glared at the dead giant. "Spill it, Leonel, so we all know what it says."

"Sorry, sir, I forgot you can't re—" said Leonel, cutting himself off. He broke the seal and read the letter aloud:

"To the Commanding Chieftain of the Ogre forces in the Forestland:

Accept this tribute of gold coins as my word and bond that an alliance between us, Giants of Chelebraxia and you, Ogres of the Desertlands, now exists. I have sent my eldest son, Roidaroy, along with two of my most trusted counselors, Barons Skootafrey and Krusedekulk, to convey the sincerity of this proposal. If you agree and provide aid to our cause to defeat the Giants of Jadinobblis, then we shall support your dominion over the Great Forest. Most Sincerely, Lord Gogmagogg of Greater Chelebraxia."

Leonel glanced up. "Seems the whole world is mad with war," he said, chuckling, "Even the giants have one."

Gwachmai bent over and picked up one of the gold coins. "This be Dragonland gold," he said pitching it to the ground. "The giants turned me and Ardus out only to stab us in the back."

"Sir, the kid there probably knows what happened."

"Careful, Leonel," said Gwachmai. "Jack Spriggins don't take kindly to being *a kid.*"

"My apologies," said Leonel. "Why were the giants chasing you, Jack?"

"I was trying to bring em to the forest and help fight," said Jack, his voice hoarse, "I stole something and it all went wrong."

"Was it this money?"

Jack shook his head. "Naw, it was their harp. That's why they chased me."

Gwachmai burst into a rowdy laugh. "Jack the Giant Killer!" he said, lifting him out of the hole for a bear hug. "Look at yeh, little-chipper! Brought down three traitors who were out to cheat us all."

Cheers erupted from the men, who hoisted Jack upon their shoulders and paraded him around the glen, chanting: "Jack the Giant Killer! Jack the Giant Killer!"

"Set me down!" said Jack, his voice smothered in their cheers.

"What revelry is this?" said Ardus, who rode out of the grove with Ootan on their horses.

"Yeh cannot believe who's been busting up our enemies, Arto," said Gwachmai. "If dragon-slaying wasn't enough for Jack Spriggins, he's now been off fightin' giants."

Ardus's eyes fell upon the dead giants.

"I done no good," said Jack. "Y'all set me down."

The men lowered him as a flurry of notes issued from the harp across the glen, just beyond view.

"Sweet songs of Shaina," said Gwachmai, "There it is again. Have yeh ever heard such beautiful sounds? I been hunting for that music since we got in these woods."

"Over here!" shouted a soldier. "It's Jack's harp."

The company moved toward the music, stopping at the lagoon.

"A harp that plays by itself," said Ardus.

"It's a good sign," said Ootan.

"The very sight washes the doubt from m'eyes," said Gwachmai.

Leonel turned and looked at Jack with amazement. "*That's* the harp you stole?"

Jack could not fight back his tears.

"Make camp!" Ardus ordered the troops. "Get the fires going, our guest must be hungry." He dismounted and placed a hand on Jack's shoulder. "Jack, join me and share our fire. What we have is yours to share."

~ 291 ~

* * * *

The men looked small to Jack after his summer with the giants. They were loud, full of friendly jokes that made him glad to be one of them. "And they're *my* folk," he thought, with a pang of pride.

Ardus draped a wool blanket on him and offered cooked rabbit and venison to eat. The meat was warm, comforting and something Jack had missed terribly. While eating, he realized noticed someone was missing.

"Where's Redvere?"

"By Mad Mariah's harp, that wishy ward!" said Gwachmai, "One day it's his life mission to be a ranger and the next, he's run off scared."

"When he returns, as I'm sure he will" said Ardus, "We shall welcome him."

"A deserter?" said Gwachmai. "That by itself is a death sentence."

"Redvere's no coward, brother," said Ardus. "He proved that by how he fought in battle. Why are you always quick to ride him down?"

"Oh, forgive me, almighty general!" said Gwachmai. "And if a hundred more take to the trail like he did, what then?"

Ootan spoke up. "Redvere's arrow saved your brother's neck, as well as mine and yours."

"Officially, we've sent him on an errand," said Ardus to Jack. "Those were my orders and that's what we say to the men."

"Where is he for real?" said Jack.

Gwachmai grumbled. "Holed up in the Orchard trying to scratch the yellow off his belly."

"That's enough, Gwach," said Ardus. "Redvere just needs time to find his own answers."

"Let him," said Gwachmai. "We'll fare better with Giant Killer here anyway, young'un or no!" He slapped Jack on the back with a toothy smirk.

"You're a natural hero, Jack," said Ardus, indicating the campfires the soldiers had lit around the lagoon. "No doubt, the men have spun your adventures into great tales by now."

"I ain't no hero," said Jack.

The general stood. "Take a walk with me, son."

Jack followed him through the pines. They walked together for a long while without any talk. The stars were out and moonlight glistened on the harp by the waterfall.

Eventually, Ardus asked, "Are you ready to tell me what happened?"

"Like I said, I weren't no hero," said Jack. He told Ardus about the giants and how badly he wanted their magical harp, even though they had pampered, tutored, and overfed him.

"They taught me how to read and write," Jack explained. "But still, they called us 'tree choppers' and didn't give a hoot if the ogres wipe us out. It made me sick with hate."

By the time Jack finished his story, he and Ardus had circled the lagoon many times, finally resting at the gravesite of the three giants. A guard was posted by Roidaroy's Tree, as Jack now called it, but the grave was empty. The giants 'bodies were loaded in back of a wagon, covered by a grim canvas.

"Ain't we gonna bury them?" said Jack.

"Not here," said Ardus. "We'll send them up the mountain, back to their families."

"I should prob'ly go too," said Jack, resting his hands on the side rail. "Gotta right my wrongs."

Ardus shook his head. "What did you do wrong, exactly? They made their own choices, and they meant to harm you."

"Only 'cause I taunted them. Made them chase me."

"You owe no apologies by my account. These giants were consorting with our enemies, which makes them one and the same." Ardus leaned on the rail beside him." And all that time, you were there trying to help your own folk. If they had any sense at all, giants would have seen the value of our people by the one who was living among them. I'd say they were blind as fools."

The general channeled a warmth that made Jack feel for the first time in his life what it might have been like if his own pa had stuck around.

"Yeh wanna know something?" said Jack. "I done what I done cause yeh got me mad. I wanted to show y'all were wrong about me."

"No one can deny that you're determined."

"But I'm still a rat."

Ardus chuckled. "I thought that about myself too when I was young."

"Yeh did?"

"We're not so very different. I was like you, trying to survive, hanging onto Gwachmai's coat tails, scrounging for food, shelter, and sick with revenge. Yes, I was a regular rat."

"Ain't yeh got a pa?"

"My folks were killed by the ogres, right in front of me. The village was burned to the ground. Gwach grabbed me and we stayed hid in an empty grain pit for days until the ogres left. When we crawled out, we had no family, no home. Just each other. We stole what we had to wherever we could, barely surviving until Allwise came along."

"What did the coot do for yeh?" said Jack.

"Taught me to use my anger in a way that helped me never to live that way again."

"Yeh talking about yer sword?"

"It was more than that. *The schooling.* Allwise taught me how to learn."

"Great. More books," sighed Jack. "Gwachmai got learned too?"

"Not Gwach," chuckled Ardus. "He had joined the Hill Rangers and left the book-learning to me."

The captain straightened up. His eyes were fixed on the lagoon. "I never heard such music or felt peace on the wind, like I did when that harp rang out today. This harp is a great gift you have given the forest."

"It's stolen."

"Listen to the men, Jack," said Ardus. "They're laughing, singing bawdy songs, when we've had so little to cheer about. Yesterday, we felt broken. Then today, you came along. You put fire back into their hearts. *Hope.* That's the real gift. They're ready to fight again." The captain turned. "I kept you apart from the battle, but I never meant for you not to join us."

"I get it," said Jack. "But I got lots more to learn. And I want to."

"That's the ranger in you talking," said Ardus, ruffling Jack's hair.

A horse's whinny sounded in the woods accompanied by the rumble of galloping hooves.

"It's the Crokees!" called Leonel, who came running, out-of-breath. "Lothur leads them."

Ardus looked relieved. "The Swampland army is welcome. Ogres will get quite a surprise when they next meet all of us united on the battlefield." He then motioned towards the wagon with the giant corpses. "I have an errand for you, yeoman."

"Yessir?" said Leonel.

"Drive this wagon to the mountain border of Giantdom. I have a message for the giants." Ardus handed the officer a sealed letter, "It is addressed to Lord Gogmagogg of Greater Chelebraxia informing him of the accidental death of his son and friends. Make sure they understand it was an accident. It also states that if the giants are in need of assistance, they should ask it of *us* and make no further entreaties to the ogres. Their gold is also to be returned."

"The Dragonland gold?" said Leonel.

"That's right."

"Sir, if I may?"

"Go on."

"With all respect, the men might be better served if we kept the gold for this war campaign."

"No, we must not. If we stand to reunite the Forestland, we cannot take the giants 'money," explained Ardus. "That's my direct order. Understand?"

"Yessir," saluted Leonel, as he returned to his duty.

"Now, Jack," said Ardus, "Would you be willing to do something for me as well?"

"Ain't gonna make me Champ, are yeh?"

"I want you to return to the Orchard and learn from Allwise, as I did."

"Yeh think he can teach a no-good like me?"

"I was a Mist Hills roughneck who didn't know a spoon from a fork when he took me on," said Ardus. "I managed well enough. You've already dined in the Giant's halls and have been tutored by their wisest teacher. You'll do just fine."

Chapter 27

FAME

It was astonishing to find a crowd waiting at Bend's Ferry. Many folks had followed the cavalcade south ahead of the invasion and were a nuisance with their belongings stacked all over the landing.

Jack winced. His ribs were hurting something fierce as he leaned on a hickory branch. It had taken him three days to hobble here. For once, he did not mind taking his time for the welcomed rest. The ferry came and went twice before he could nudge his way aboard.

~ 298 ~

Neither the ferryman nor his son recognized Jack, who paid for his passage this time (a few Dragonland gold coins having somehow found their way into his pocket). Odd habits were hard to break.

As the vessel moved downriver, it seemed everybody had a sob story to tell. Jack was grateful when the ferryman changed the subject to news about the war. It seemed that General Ardus Camlann had rallied his troops in a successful battle against the ogres forcing them to retreat north along the Timberok Road.

"He's turned a bad hand into good luck," said the ferryman. "Tricked them ogres into fighting at Codger's Bog. When the desert chieftains saw how small and worn out his company looked across the battlefield, they all charged out. A big mistake! That wily Camlann had a battalion of Crokee soldiers waiting in the tall grass. It was too late for the ogre scalawags to change their minds."

The passengers cheered.

"Yeh betcha!" said the ferryman. "Camlann boxed em in and they was routed."

One passenger, a fisherman who kept his family huddled close, spoke. "Them ogre got weapons that sling fireballs. How do you figure the general beat that?"

"The bog," said the ferryman. "Ogres can't move em fire-slings in that mush."

"Reckon not," grinned the man.

"Praise Green Ma," said an old lady.

"Praise Green Ma," echoed the rest.

"All yeh good folks observe!" said a lumberjack, passing round a jug to the other passengers. "General Ardus hails from the

Mist Hills. It's fitting he'd make good and bring pride to these parts."

"Now. hold up a darn second, mister," spat a farmer, wearing overalls. "We got folk born and bred here local too who make us right proud."

"The kid!" said his wife. "The hero from Rivercross, whatshisname?"

"Jack the Giant Killer," said the man.

"Darn toot," agreed the lumberjack. "He's a regular Rivercrosser."

"Jack Spriggins is his rightful name," said the ferryman.

Jack's ears near fell off when he heard this. "They're saying my name," he muttered, keeping his head down.

When the ferry arrived at Rivercross, he was among the first to disembark, flabbergasted to hear his name shouted again by a complete stranger.

"Jack Spriggins, the hero of Rivercross!" said a vendor, waving copies of the *River Reader*. "If y'all ain't read about Jack the Giant Killer, outsmarting traitorous giants, then read it here!"

"High times, we should have something to cheer for," said a paying customer.

A drunkard stumbled over and thrust the periodical in Jack's face. "The boy must've growed near the size of a giant."

"Naw," said the vendor. "Jack the Giant Killer's not even a man – just a boy. He's the same kid who rescued Red Riding Hood last spring."

"*He's* the boy who killed that big, bad wolf?" said the farmer's wife.

"The Green Ma hath blessed him," said the old lady, beckoning with a coin to the vendor. "And us. I'll take one. We need heroes in times like these."

Jack hobbled toward home, shaking his head. "A lot of ballyhoo that don't come near the truth," he muttered. "If they knew what a scrawny rat the 'Giant Killer' was, they'd prob'ly chuck stones at me."

"Jack the Giant Killer!" shouted the peddler behind him. "Read it here, he's a living legend!"

* * * *

When Jack returned to Thin Creek, Ma was nowhere to be found. The hut was clean and tidy, the water barrel filled, the garden was well-tended, and beanstalks had grown as high as the trees. Yet, no Ludi Spriggins.

Jack shouted toward the outhouse. "Hey Ma!" Then again down by the creek. "Ma?"

There was no answer.

"Chee, ain't like her to go anyplace," he said, returning to the hut.

Antsy, Jack decided he to hike to the Orchard.

When he arrived, the school gates were open. Autumn smells of hickory and cinnamon made the air downright homey. Students still trained in the yard. Ladders leaned against the trees for the apple harvest as first years hauled fresh picked bushels off with shoulder sacks.

"Sperg-sperg-spergins," said an unforgettable voice, calling from a plum grove. The shiny bald head and wide smile of Humfrey teetered atop a big ladder, waving excitedly.

~ 301 ~

"Yeh keep steady, Humf," said Jack.

The jolly little guy waddled among the branches of the tree and disappeared.

"He's been asking about you," said another familiar voice.

It was Redvere, leading a black stallion from the stable.

"I thought yeh was finished with school," said Jack.

"Funny, I thought the same about you," said Redvere, absently rubbing the horse's nose. "Allwise needs a combat and riding instructor. One who's seen battle."

"That yer horse?" said Jack.

"Isn't he a beaut? His name is Blackberry."

Jack was awed by the steed. "I'd like to stick round, learn to ride him."

The young ranger smiled. "Somebody here might be able to teach you how."

"I saw them riders go out," said Jack. "They looked older than y'all."

"Allwise has a great mind for military schemes," said Redvere. "This is more than a school now, you know."

"Where they headed?"

"Back to the army. Ardus is going to be appointed to Chief General."

A group of boys were wrestling on the lawn instructed by Perdur.

"Master Cai used to be their trainer," said Redvere.

"What happened?"

Redvere was downcast. "He was killed in the front lines. I'll tell you something, Jack."

"What?"

"Killing. I'm no good at it."

"And I'm too good," said Jack. "But I heard yeh done right when the fight came. That counts. The Champs ain't mad at yeh for leaving. The school needs a good riding teacher *and* yer a good shot. Yeh got lots to share."

"So do you," said Redvere, brightening. "Climbing mountains with bean vines and spying on the giants. You're already the most famous hero of the war."

"Naw," said Jack. "Y'all just forget that. "

"Nobody ever will."

Jack reached up and petted Blackberry. "What folks say and what really happened ain't the same thing."

Blackberry snorted and pawed the cobblestone.

"He likes you," said Redvere.

Humfrey waddled over from the garden with a basket of plums and beets. "Bunk-bunk-bunk," he said, handing Jack a beet then going inside the main house.

"Humfrey's moved on to purple," said Redvere.

Jack hesitated a beat. "Sooo, is ol' Goatbeard around?"

"Allwise is in his study." Redvere took hold of Blackberry's bridle and mounted the horse. "Word to the wise, I wouldn't call him *Goatbeard.*"

"Already did."

* * * *

"Good afternoon, Thief," greeted Allwise.

The study was dimly lit and smelled of turpentine and lamp oil. The crafty geezer was writing at his desk, hidden behind a pile of books that did not fit on the packed shelves. The plume of his grey-feathered quill flicked as he scrawled beside a desktop lamp. More books lay on the floor around his desk.

"Your smell has improved," said Allwise, not looking up. "I hardly detected you. You've taken to bathing since living with giants?"

A frustrated twinge crept up Jack's neck. "Starting a clean streak, I reckon."

The old man set down his quill. "I see you've had a decent meal or two and you've grown." His tone was unwelcoming. "Well, what can I do for you?"

Jack felt sweat trickle down his sides and he pried at the floor with his hickory crutch. "I come for schooling."

Allwise indicated Jack's walking stick. "Your ribs?"

Jack nodded. "I took a little tumble."

"Well, thief," said Allwise. "What's changed your mind?"

"*Thief* ain't my name," said Jack.

The old man stared at him but said nothing.

Jack added, "I done a bit-o-book-learning up there with the giants. I wanna learn more."

"You *have* changed," said Allwise. "Good start." He rose and walked to a table, filling two cups with a wood pitcher. "Lemonade?"

Jack took a gulp. The lemon drink was deliciously tangy and very sweet. "How'd yeh make it taste that way?"

"Sugar," said the old gardener. "A cane plant we grow here in the greenhouse. It comes from an island habitation I once visited. Good, isn't it?"

Jack nodded.

"So, you came to study," said Allwise. "You would be required to live here, work in the gardens, and follow my rules. And that temper of yours will have no place among us, is that understood?"

"Yeh mean I can stay?"

"I should apologize to my other students in advance, but yes," said Allwise, who drank from his own cup and smacked his lips together. "So, tell me about Giantdom."

Jack glanced at a map that was hung on a wall. "They know about more places than y'all."

Allwise lit an oil lamp on his desk. "What places?"

"Well," said Jack, pointing," Yeh got the Dragonlands in the wrong place. It's bigger with more sea in between. And the Thunder Territory ain't even on yer map." He tapped an island in the lower quadrant with a cocky nod. "Vikuvis said Shirwood here has got more trees than the Great Forest."

"You met the Jadin senator?" said Allwise, narrowing his eyes as if to detect a lie.

"Yep," said Jack. "Don't think he likes yeh too much but he's the one taught me. Got more books on his shelves then yeh too."

Allwise grinned, "Within these walls, we will all learn about the real Jack Spriggins. Reading, writing, and arithmetic will be part of your curriculum, of course, but together we will chart a map of yourself; emphasize your talents; utilize your skills; and challenge your will. Are you prepared for that?"

"I'm here ain't I?"

Allwise rolled his eyes. "Fearless as ever. Boldness runs in your family."

Jack wondered what he meant. "Well, I heard my pa was a hunter."

"I was speaking of your mother."

"Ma?"

"Yes. Since moving to the village she's unabashedly taken to coming here. She has many suggestions for how I should use my beans. It's quite annoying, really."

"She moved?"

"To Rivercross," said Allwise. "You haven't seen her yet?"

"I went home to Thin Creek but she weren't there."

"Ah-ha. Much has changed while you were gone. Pay her a visit in the square. Return here and we will begin your education."

Rivercross was booming. New inns and eateries had sprung up and the square was bustling with an inrush of hapless folks fleeing the war. "*Ludi's Bean Tea Inn*," said Jack, slowly reading from a sign above the door of a three-story public house in a busy corner of the square. A large, stained glass window on the eaves depicted a beanstalk vine against a blue sky.

Jack spotted Ma on the outdoor patio, rushing from one table to another filling teacups, laughing, and carrying on with the guests. She wore too many colors – a bright green blouse, yellow bodice, blue skirt, and an orange apron.

"Ma," said Jack, hailing her from the patio gate, "Did a rainbow done explode on yeh?"

~ 306 ~

"Swee Sleeping Beauty!" she said, tossing her hands up, which sent iced tea in a glistening arc across the tables. "Tis me boy, Jacky the Giant Killer!" She charged through the gate and squeezed him with her motherly might.

"Good enough," said Jack, still feeling pain from his bandaged ribs. "Glad to see yeh."

Folks stamped their mugs on the tables and cheered, "Hurrah for Jack the Giant Killer!"

"Ain't seen yeh in ages, son, but I heard yeh gone and made yerself a hero," said Ma. "So much to tell! Look at all I done while yeh was gone. The money yeh brought me helped set up a booth. I brewed the beans here in the square. Next thing y'know, I got this place. Our own inn."

"Real nice," said Jack.

"Are yeh home to stay, son?"

"Gonna be schooling at the Orchard, Ma."

She slapped her hands to her cheeks and nearly sat on one of the guests. "Why, yeh'll be the first Spriggins to read and write. I'm busting with pride."

Ma hooked his arm and led him indoors. The inn was full of talkers who made the place obnoxiously loud. Ma's customers were seated around oak tables. Underneath the staircase, a piano man played *The River Green Reel*, a rinky-dink tune Jack had always liked.

He tried to take the rollicking place in when he bumped into a serving girl.

"Not much of a dancer, are you?" she said, turning playfully. She appeared to be a year or two older than Jack with long blonde braids and sea-blue eyes. "Pardon me, unless you'd like to serve these," she added, holding up the pitchers.

Jack stumbled aside.

"Ganzil, dearie," said Ma. "This be my boy."

"Yes, I gathered," said Ganzil. "Jack the Giant Killer."

"Oh, my jumping beans!" said Ma, giddily. "I can't get over yeh being home, Jacky. Let me show yeh the boarding rooms."

"I can handle things down here, Missus Spriggins," said Ganzil, waving them on.

"Ganzil's such a help," said Ma to Jack. "She was at the orphanage in Arborvale, just like me when I was a girl. Viviyann Greygeese herself sent her here for work."

Jack watched the blonde beauty as he followed his ma up the stairs. There was something was oddly familiar about her, like he had once seen her in a dream. "I can't quite place where," he shrugged. "Maybe it'll come to me later."

Ma showed Jack the inn's second and third stories. The narrow hallways had six bedrooms. "Travelers fill 'em every night. Even got some regulars cause of the war and all, but I always keep an empty room fer yeh, Jack." Ma pushed open the last door on the top floor. "It's got a real feather mattress and big pillow. It's yours."

"Real homey, Ma, but what about our place by Thin Creek?"

"It's ours too," she said. "Yeh can stay there or have a real cozy bed right here. Only, listen to yer ma, yeh never cut them stalks down, son. I collect the beans twice a week."

"I'll gather those for yeh, Ma," said Jack. "I reckon I'll be around here a lot but I'm gotta bunk at the Orchard. School rules, I guess."

"Oh, what a good boy yeh are," said Ma, steering him back down to the tea room.

Jack snatched a biscuit off a plate on the sideboard and took a bite. It was rock hard made even worse by Ma's sour gooseberry jam. He grimaced, wishing he could spit it out.

"Most people just wash it down with the tea, dearie," said Ma, offering a cup.

"Naw," said Jack, shaking his head. "Don't think I'd take to the brew."

"Ganzil is taking over cooking duties. She bakes wonderful gingerbread," said Ma, nudging his side. "Yeh think she's pretty?"

Across the room, Ganzil stopped by a wall mirror to run a hand through her hair.

"Too pretty, I reckon," said Jack, still trying to remember. "Did yeh say 'gingerbread'?"

At this moment, a pair of regular Rivercross customers entered.

"Missus Spriggins," said Scratch, the shoemaker with the odd twinkle in his eyes. "Isn't this your famous boy?"

"Why, Mister Scratch, tis indeed my Jacky," blushed Ma. "Won't yeh have some tea?"

To Jack's disgust, Tinner the grubby tinker was the other patron.

"Yer taller," he said with a large amount of spittle.

"What a model young man," said Scratch, tapping the steel tip of his cane on the floor. "Oh, how the good folks of Rivercross appreciate you now. Isn't that so, Tinner?"

~ 309 ~

The tinker shrugged. "Guess so."

"Jack Spriggins, not your average boy, no, no, no!" said the shoemaker. "So maligned and misunderstood in the past. You've gone and proved them all wrong, didn't you? How satisfying that must feel."

Ma carried on."Makes me proud to be his ma. And that ain't all. Jacky's gonna study at the Orchard. Get hisself edjacated."

"Say," said Scratch. "That *is* something. Allow me to shake your hand, young man."

The shoemaker's grasp was as firm as iron, with long thin fingers. A terrible sense of doubt overcame Jack as he considered whether he was truly cut out for book learning.

"Allwise is certainly a learned man," continued Scratch. "Tell me, Jack – I feel free to call you *Jack*. Don't you think you're ready to claim your fortunes? Why, I don't know a single merchant, trader, or craftsman who wouldn't take you on as an apprentice. Wouldn't you agree, Mister Tinner?"

"Mebbe," said Tinner.

The shoemaker laughed and twirled the ends of his beard, which was trimmed to two points. "I'll wager someone like you might look on school as a step down after all you've accomplished. A fine trade perhaps, making shoes, might better suit a young man with your bright future. Have you ever considered that, Master Spriggins?"

"Jack ain't never had proper schooling," said Ma. "He's gonna finally git some."

"Can't say that Allwise knows what's best," said Scratch, shaking his head. "Can't say, can't say."

"I think he do," insisted Ma.

"Of course, dear madam," said Scratch, tipping his hat. "Well, I've soles to sell and few heels to buy."

With a sly wink, the shoemaker rose to leave. In ways, he seemed as crafty as Allwise. In others, he came off like a grinning lunatic. He went out the door with a half-skip. Tinner skulked behind him, slow like a slug, spitting on the porch as he left.

"They're good customers," said Ma. "Two mugs-o-bean tea a day."

"Hey, Ma," said Jack. "Suppose I ain't cut out for school like he said?"

Ma leaned in close." Don't take Mister Scratch's words to heart. He's fast talker but listen to him and yeh'll never make up yer mind about anything. Yeh go study with Allwise. He's got what yeh need. No *maybe* about it."

"Glad the beans been good for yeh, Ma," said Jack.

"Yeh was right to bring em when yeh did."

A surge of laughter erupted in front of the inn as a troupe of elf minstrels took to entertaining a crowd in the square. Jack went out and watched from the porch.

Four red-haired imps danced and sang for the market goers with ridiculous antics. Three of them acted out the part of a snorting giant, standing upon each other's shoulders. A fourth, the puniest, playfully ducked and danced around the foe, pretending to attack. "I'm Jack the Giant Killer," he mimicked. The elf on top playing the giant's head, narrated in a silly, high-pitched voice:

"Fe, fi, fo, fum!

Up a beanstalk Jack does run

Beats the Giants like a drum,

Down they fall, one-by-one!"

The play giant fell to pieces as the three minstrels tumbled to the ground causing great laughs from the crowd. Jack's puny mimicker began to pelt them with rotten pears and beat his little chest:

"Fe, fi, fo, fum!
Stole the harp from Giantdom,
Made the Giants, run, run, run,
Never catch this forest son!"

The elves continued hurling fruit at each other amidst the cheering throng.

"Red-headed nits!" said Jack, who would have thrown rocks if he had any handy.

"Why, son, they do honor yeh," said Ma.

"I hate elves," said Jack. "That ain't like what happened."

The crowd cheered, nevertheless. The tiny elf then donned a scarlet cape and hood and started skipping around.

"Hello, Little Red Riding Hood," said another elf holding up a wolf-mask made of tree bark." Come closer and give Old Gran a kiss."

"What big teeth you have, Grandmama," uttered 'Red', "And what big ears."

Jack sneered and went back inside.

"Stupid show. Now they're making fun of Ella."

"Aw," said Ma. "It's just fun and games."

"Has the real Ella been around?" said Jack.

"Oh, yer little friend's facing sad days, son," said Ma. "I've been meaning to tell yeh. Her ma passed on. I hear they lay the poor lady to rest today."

Jack recalled the vision shown him by the Silent One. "Ma, I gotta go see Ella. Right now."

Chapter 28

FALLS

The mourners were gathered in a secluded meadow at Whispering Vine beneath the boughs of an enormous blue fir tree. It was a lovely resting place for a kind lady like Ella's mother.

Jack kept his distance and watched from the woods. It would have been easy for him to pick out Ella's red cape but, at the funeral, she wore a simple black dress and shawl and blended in beside her father, holding a white rose.

Pallbearers lowered the coffin into the grave with ropes as folks sobbed. Nessie, the cook, sang a plaintive spiritual. Her rich voice expressed their love and loss better than any sermon.

"Guide me with your grace,
Through the trees, through the trees,
Guide me, Gentle Lady, through the trees.

"Let me bow my head,
Beneath the breeze, 'neath the breeze,
Bow and rest beside you 'neath the breeze.

"All time will last forever. All thought will turn to
Dreams.
My ties I'll gladly sever and leave on pillow seams.

"Then I'll row a boat,
Across the sea, 'cross the sea,
Ferry weary travelers 'cross the sea.

"Til I hear your voice,
Through the trees, through the trees,
Telling me to waken, through the trees."

Mister Vintner stepped forward and tossed his white rose into the grave. Ella also dropped in her flower then left the gathering to sit alone by the large tree.

Jack noticed a wagon loaded with a wardrobe, chest, furniture, and paintings. He scrambled along the tree line and then snuck through the tall grass to get in closer.

One by one, the other mourners stepped forward and tossed their roses. Seeing Ella so glum just did not sit well with Jack. He decided to take his chances and moved in close to get her attention. "Hey," he whispered, brushing her on the hand.

" Jack," she said quietly, with a sniffle. "Look what's happened. "

"Yer ma was a real special lady."

"Papa's taken all Mama's things; her dresses and dishes and favorite chair." Ella indicated the loaded wagon. "He's going to bury them with her as if she never lived at all."

"Reckon that hurts awful," said Jack.

Ella pulled her knees up close, wrapping them with her arms. "He won't even look at me anymore." Tears welled in her big gray eyes. "I think he'd bury me too, if he could."

"Cut it out," said Jack, grabbing her hand. "Words like that should never come out of yer mouth."

Ella's eyes returned to her father. "He even took my red cape and hood," she added, "The one Mama sewed for me."

"Here's yer red riding hood," said Jack, presenting the scarlet cape to her. "I yanked it out of a chest in that wagon."

"How?"

"It's something I'm just darn good at."

Ella's smile was like a parting of the clouds.

Parson Barns stepped forward and read long verses from the Book of the Spirits.

"How I wish I was somewhere far away," said Ella with a sigh.

"When yeh feel better, I'm gonna take yeh somewhere."

"Take me there," said Ella. She got up and side-stepped around the tree.

"Right now?" said Jack.

The mourners hung their heads, listening to the solemn verse. Mister Vintner stared like a lost man into the pit. No one was going to notice Ella's absence.

"C'mon then," said Jack.

He and Ella ducked behind the wagon and scurried away through the maples.

"Put this on," he said, handing her the cape. "Frost's coming."

She pulled the scarlet hood up. "Where are we off to?"

"Someplace magic."

The sound of Nessie's voice sang out again from the burial, which they could hear as they went their way:

> *"Bless the life, She's ever-giving,*
> *And this soil that we sow,*
> *Keep our bonds forever living,*
> *Father, Mother, let us grow."*

* * * *

The spot Jack had in mind was reached by a long ride on the Green River ferry, which seemed to do Ella some good. She started chitchatting with the ferryman, who became an eager friend once she

~ 317 ~

mentioned that Jack the Giant Killer was her companion. The boatman chose to skip his usual stops along the river and delivered them to Bend's Ferry landing without delay, not accepting a single coin for his trouble. From there, he hailed a friendly wagoner and his wife, whose cart had room to spare for a lift to the forest edge.

By afternoon, Jack and Ella were hiking over woodland trail to the foot of a certain waterfall at the base of the Giant Mountains. The sight of the golden harp, glistening amid tumbling drapes of water, caused Ella's face to light up with joy.

"Jack!" she exclaimed. "This is Harp Falls." The trill of harp strings swept over the lagoon. Ella twirled with her arms opened wide. "I heard the stories but didn't know it really existed."

"Knew it'd do yeh good to see it."

"Oh, how Mama would love it here. It really is magical."

She dropped onto the grass beside him. Together listening, nothing else in the world mattered beyond the harp and the peace of the falls. Clouds scudded over the lagoon.

"Caw!" A black raven swooped and landed in the grass a few feet away.

"Why, it's Sersi!" said Ella. "Granny's raven."

"Stupid bird's spying on us," said Jack.

The bird let out another sharp"Caw, caw."

"Sersi, that's not a polite thing to say," giggled Ella. "Remember, Jack's my friend too."

"What did it say?"

"She's just keeping an eye on me, Jack."

The raven hopped into the air and flew around the falls before it soared west.

"What's it like?" said Jack.

"What's what like?"

"Talking to birds and critters. Y'know, having that Spirit-gift?"

"When I was a baby, Mama said I'd coo, but she could always understand me." Ella smiled. *"She just knew what my cooing meant.* I guess it's the same for me when birds twitter and critters bray."

"Just like the Green Ma's supposed to do."

"But you know, Jack, everybody's born with a spirit gift."

"Chee, not me."

"The spirits certainly came to your naming. You're the bravest boy alive. That has to be a gift from them. Nobody knows the woods better than you. Some of the animals even say so. You always spot danger when it gets too close and you always help me."

"Cause yer always getting into trouble."

"And they blessed you with those sharp, bright eyes. "

"Is there a spirit for ugly yellow ones?"

"Your eyes are lovely hazel, Jack Spriggins." Ella splashed him with a handful of water from the pool. "The Light Spirit must have chosen the color herself."

Jack knitted his brow, listening to the notes of the harp, which called out with a familiar tune. "That's my song," he realized.

Glancing up, he caught sight of Lell, the lady in black, amidst the streaming falls. Her veiled face was turned away and she was running her long thin fingers over the strings. She vanished amid the light of the falling plumes of spray but would reappear in its shadows.

"Yeh see her?"

"I don't see anybody, Jack, but I hear her music," said Ella. "Who is she?"

"The dark lady. The bad spirit. If anyone came to my naming, she did."

"Lady Lell? She's not bad. Never think that. Remember the story of the baby princess? The old king, her father, refused to allow Darkness to bless her."

"Yeah. She grew up not knowing a thorn from a rose and became the Sleeping Beauty."

"And she sleeps still, so that we can all learn the difference." Ella bowed her head, with the same gloomy expression Jack had seen on her at the morning's funeral.

"Yeh alright?"

"Mama said I needed to learn that lesson," she said. "She told me there will always be shadows but I think accepting Darkness as part of life is what guides us past them."

"So, the Dark Lady don't want to hurt us?"

"She gives us strength to handle the bad things, like losing Mama. I imagine it's the greatest gift of all. I hope Lell hears my prayers."

"Yer the bravest girl I know."

"Thank you, Jack. Really."

"For what?"

"For always looking out for me."

It was a perfect day. The best Jack had ever known, sitting there with Ella by the lagoon, enjoying the harp together. Of course, it could not last.

"Sun's getting low," he said, pulling her to her feet. "Last ferry leaves at sunset. We gotta make tracks or we ain't getting home before nightfall."

"It's so wonderful here, Jack," said Ella. "Even with the whole world breaking up around us. Can't we stay a bit longer?"

"Naw, I don't want yer pa frowning at me any more than he already does. Besides, ain't we done running away?"

"We certainly are. But if you find another adventure, you won't leave me behind, will you?"

"Aw chee. Who else but Red Riding Hood can help Jack the Giant Killer?"

Ella raised her eyebrows. "Why, Jack. You really have changed."

Jack felt a smile grow on his face. "I'm learning," he said.

* * * *

The Forest watches children grow,

By inches and by leaps,

Its paths once feared, they come to know,

And still the Beauty sleeps.

ABOUT THE AUTHORS

James Kelton was born and raised in Minneapolis, educated in London, and currently lives in southern California. His professional career has hit the highs and not-so-highs of acting, swimming, illustration, work in comic books, and animation - always coming back to the love of telling a story.

Dennis Harold lives in Calabasas, CA with his wife and two kids. His mantra is to "create." He is a storyteller, editor and marketing professional who can craft compelling narrative. Through imagination and collaboration, he seeks to produce a world that is beautiful, hopeful and even tolerable.

Made in the USA
Middletown, DE
20 November 2020

24642805R00186